SL

Ashok K. Banker is the author of the internationally -
acclaimed Ramayana Series® and other books. He
lives in Mumbai with his family. Visit him online at
www.ashokbanker.com.

BOOKS BY ASHOK K. BANKER

Slayer of Kamsa

KRISHNA CORIOLIS – BOOK I

ASHOK K. BANKER

HARPER

First published in India in 2010 by Harper
An imprint of HarperCollins *Publishers*
a joint venture with
The India Today Group

ISBN: 978-93-5029-000-2

2 4 6 8 10 9 7 5 3 1

Ashok K. Banker asserts the moral right
to be identified as the author of this work.

HarperCollins *Publishers*
A-53, Sector 57, Noida 201301, India
77-85 Fulham Palace Road, London W6 8JB, United Kingdom
Hazelton Lanes, 55 Avenue Road, Suite 2900, Toronto, Ontario M5R 3L2
and 1995 Markham Road, Scarborough, Ontario M1B 5M8, Canada
25 Ryde Road, Pymble, Sydney, NSW 2073, Australia
31 View Road, Glenfield, Auckland 10, New Zealand
10 East 53rd Street, New York NY 10022, USA

Typeset in 11/ 12.7 Adobe Jenson Pro
InoSoft Systems

Printed and bound at
Thomson Press (India) Ltd.

For Biki and Bithika:
My Radha and my Rukmini.

For Yashka and Ayush Yoda:
My Yashoda.

All you faithful readers
who understand
that these tales
are not about being Hindu
or even about being Indian.
They're simply about being.

In that spirit,
I dedicate this gita-govinda
to the krishnachild in all of us.
For, under these countless
separate skins, there beats
a single eternal heart.

preface

If it takes a community to raise a child, then it surely takes a nation to build an epic.

The itihasa of the subcontinent belongs to no single person. The great epics of our culture – of any culture – may be told and retold infinite times by innumerable poets and writers; yet, no single version is the final one.

The wonderful adventures of the great Lord Krishna are greater than what any story, edition or retelling can possibly encompass. The lila of God Incarnate is beyond the complete comprehension of any one person. We may each perceive some aspects of His greatness, but, like the blind men and the elephant, none of us can ever see everything at once.

It matters not whether you are Hindu or non-Hindu, whether you believe Krishna to be God or just a great historical personage, whether you are Indian or not. The richness and wonder of these tales have outlived countless generations and will outlast many more to come.

My humble attempt here – within these pages and in the volumes to follow – is neither the best nor the last retelling of this great story. I have no extraordinary talent or ability, no special skill or knowledge, no inner sight or visionary gift. What I *do* have is a lifelong exposure to an itihasa so vast, a culture so rich, a nation so great, wise and ancient, that its influence – permeating into one like water through peat over millennia, filtering through from mind to mind, memory to memory, mother to child and to mother again – has suffused every cell of my being, every unit of my consciousness.

And when I use the word 'I', it is meant in the universal. You are 'I'. As I am she. And she is all of us. Krishna's tale lives through each and every one of us. It is yours to tell. His to tell. Hers to tell. Mine as well. For as long as this tale is told, and retold, it lives on.

I have devoted years to the telling, to the crafting of words, sentences, paragraphs, pages, chapters, kaands and volumes. I shall devote more years to come, decades even. Yet, all my effort is not mine alone. It is the fruition of a billion Indians, and the billions who have lived before us. For each person who has known this tale and kept it alive in his heart has been a teller, a reteller, a poet, and an author. I am merely the newest name in a long, endless line of names that has had the honour and distinction of being associated with this great story.

It is my good fortune to be the newest reteller of this ancient saga. It is a distinction I share with all who tell and retell this story: from the grandmother who whispers it as a lullaby to the drowsy child, to the scholar who pores over each syllable of every shloka in an attempt to find an insight that has eluded countless scholars before him.

It is a tale told by me in this version; yet, it is not my tale alone to tell. It is your story. Our story. Her story. His story.

Accept it in this spirit and with all humility and hope. Also know that I did not create this flame, nor did I light the torch that blazes. I merely bore the torch this far. Now I give it to you. Take it from my hand. Pass it on. As it has passed from hand to hand, mind to mind, voice to voice, for unknown millennia.

Turn the page. See the spark catch flame.

Watch Krishna come alive.

	yadrcchaya copapannah	
	svarga-dvaram apavrtam	
	sukhinah ksatriya partha	
	labhante yuddham idrsam	

> Blessed are the warriors
> Who are chosen to fight justly;
> For the doors to heaven
> Shall be opened unto them.

Kaand I

King Vasudeva raised aloft the ceremonial sceptre of the Sura nation. The rod, shaped to resemble a cowherd's crook, was impressively cast in solid gold and studded with precious gems at the curve of the handle. It caught a bar of morning sunlight streaming in from a slatted window high upon the soaring walls of the Andhaka palace and gleamed. Beside him, King Ugrasena of Andhaka raised his rajtaru too. The Andhaka sceptre was no less impressive than that of the Suras.

Both rajtarus – the Sanskrit word literally meant *kingsrods* – reflected the sunlight, sending shards and slivers flashing to the farthest corners of the great hall. A calico tomcat, lying curled in the south corner, closed his eyes to slits and bared his teeth, peering against the blinding gleam of the rajtarus. The well-fed palace cat's expression resembled nothing so much as a satiated grin.

The watching assemblage crowding the sabha hall to the limit of its capacity, and the lords and ladies resplendent in their finery, blinked, then caught their breaths. The sight of the two lieges standing on the throne dais, their traditional rajtarus raised and glittering in the sunlight, presented a startling tableau. To some of the older clanschiefs in the great hall, it was a sight they had never thought they would witness as long as they lived: two ancient enemies – sovereigns of two of the wealthiest herding nations in the great land of Aryavarta – standing together with sceptres, not swords, aloft! Could it be true? Surely it was just maya? That sight – nay, that vision – could not be real, could it? After generations of cross-border blood feuds, broken only by intermittent outbreaks of war; after so much bloodshed and bitter enmity; after so many failed peace summits and parleys; after a long and bloody history had stained the pure soil of both nations, polluting the sacred Yamuna with the offal of vengeful violence, could peace finally be at hand?

Most of the assemblage, as well as the enormous throng crowding the palace grounds without, doubted it severely. Suspicious frowns creased the faces of many clanschiefs, ministers and merchant lords. Only a few hopeful souls smiled beatifically and fingered their rudraksh-bead rosaries, silently chanting shlokas to ensure the fruition of this historic pact.

There were few such personages; the golden age of Brahminism had long since ebbed, and the long-dreaded Kali Yuga was imminent – the prophesied dark age of Iron and Death. Most doubted that this historic pact, wrought after months of anxiety and expectation, would last, or that it would be honoured at all. Yet, even the most sceptical of ministers, the most cynical of generals, even the hardened veterans who had somehow survived the first violent decades of this dark age, prayed as fervently as their Brahmin brethren. For a while, few believed, all hoped, all desired. If it could somehow be brought to pass, if the devas truly saw fit to grant them this reprieve, they would accept peace, nay, embrace it, with all the warmth they had in them.

So, when both kings brought their rajtarus together in an inverted V, touching the gem-studded crooks lightly together, every citizen, high and low, watched with bated breath. Even the calico tomcat, stretching himself in preparation for a foray into the royal bhojanalya – he had sniffed the unmistakable, delectable fragrance of sweetwater fish being grilled there – paused and turned his head, smelling the sour sweat of hesitant hopes and anxious prayers in the air. The rhythmic, martial count of the dhol playing in the background underscored the whole scene like a giant unified heartbeat, marking the four-by-four count to which all Arya ceremonies were performed.

King Vasudeva's soft tenor blended with King Ugrasena's ageing gruffness as both kings recited the ceremonial shlokas aloud, each line cued to them by whispering pundits seated behind the dais. The sacred flame, symbol of Agni, the god of fire, flared up brightly as a purohit, one of the many priests who oversaw the arcana of traditional rites and customs, tossed a ladle of ghee onto the chaukhat. The flames shot up almost to the raised sceptres, licking briefly at the point of their unity. Sunlight above, fire below. It was an impressive and auspicious moment, brilliantly and meticulously conceived and staged by the purohits of the two kingdoms. To the dwindling Brahmins of Aryavarta, such occasions grew more precious with each passing decade since the world was turning away from old ways and traditions.

For the duration of this ceremony, the pomp and grandeur of Aryavarta – literally, the noble and proud – would shine as brightly as a beacon fed by the light of Brahman shakti. The chanting of the kings rose to a peak, ending with a final shloka that seemed to sing out from the very walls of the sabha hall. This last bit of theatrical magic was, again, wrought by the Brahmins, who, strategically positioned at the far walls of the hall, joined in with the kings' chanting at the penultimate quartet and raised their voices – to match the well-rehearsed baritones of the kings – until it seemed that the entire world was chanting the verses.

|| *yadrcchya copapannah svarga-dvaram apavrtam* ||
|| *sukhinah ksatriya partha labhante yuddham idrsam* ||

The chanting died, the doleful drumbeats fading away at precisely that instant. In the silence that ensued, the gathered assemblage could hear the crackling and snapping of the sacred flame as the purohit continued to feed ladlefuls of sanctified ghee to insatiable Agni. The faces of the kings had grown warm from the heat of the flames, a few beads of sweat standing out on the clean-shaven good looks of the young King Vasudeva and the tips of King Ugrasena's grey-shot beard.

Moving in perfect unison, they lowered their rajtarus to form an inverted V. The crooks of the sceptres dipped directly into the flames and the purohit ceased his ghee-tossing to allow the sacred fire to quell itself somewhat, lest the kings lose the skin of their arms. Beads of perspiration swelled and rolled down their faces as both monarchs held the crooks of their rajtarus in the fire just long enough to let the heat travel up to their bare hands.

Finally, the royal purohit uttered the words quietly enough so that only the kings could catch it, and both lieges broke their stance, stepping away from the fire. They exchanged their sceptres, each handing over his proof of kingship at the exact same time as he accepted the other's royal seal. This was executed with surprising ease, considering that both rajtarus were close to blistering hot by now. The watching assemblage could hardly know that both kings had had their hands anointed with a special herbal paste prior to the ceremony, or that the near-invisible paste prevented the transmission of heat quite effectively.

The sight of the red-hot rajtarus being exchanged and then held aloft to allow every individual in the hall a chance to witness this momentous event, seared itself into the minds of all present. The painstakingly staged ceremony had served its purpose. Then, with obvious relief, and great smiles creasing their tense faces, the two kings embraced.

The crowd released its breath. Upon the fortified palace battlements, waiting courtiers blew long and hard on their conch-shell trumpets. The low, deep calling of the conches filled the air for hundreds of yojanas, echoed from end to end of both kingdoms, announcing the most welcome news in over two centuries. Peace. Shanti.

Outside the Andhaka palace, the waiting crowd, which had now swollen to tens of thousands, broke into a ragged roar that almost drowned out the conches. Royal criers rode through the avenues and streets, pausing at corners to shout out the news – in Sanskrit, and then in commonspeak – confirming the details of the peace pact. Stone pillars, carved and ready for weeks, were hastily but ceremoniously erected at strategic spots in the capital city and at junctions along the national kingsroad, setting down the same details for posterity – or at least as long as stone and wind and rain would allow, which would probably be a millennium or two.

Sadly, the peace pact itself was not to last even a fraction of that time.

two

The massive teak doors of the banquet hall flew open as if struck by a battering ram. They swivelled inwards on smoothly oiled tracks and crashed against the stone walls, swatting aside the guards milling about the entrance. Vasudeva glanced up from his meal just in time to see a young soldier's foot caught by the lower bolt of a door, dragged to the wall, and crushed against the relentless stone with a bone-crunching impact that left the poor fellow's face white.

The other guards, drunk on the festive atmosphere and milling about jovially, responded belatedly, joining their lances and challenging the rude entrants. The armoured bull elephant that trundled into the banquet hall paid no heed to their shouted challenges. It was armoured in the fashion of Andhaka hathi-yodhhas – the dreaded war elephants of the Andhaka clan – its head couched in a formidable headpiece bristling with spikes that made it resemble some demon out of a myth, its tusks capped with brass horns tapering to resemble spears, and rows of ugly spikes protruding out of its sides.

Vasudeva had seen the destruction that these hathi-yodhhas left in their wake during close combat. His heart lurched at the thought of the havoc even a *single* such monster could wreak in a confined, crowded space like this hall. The dried, brownish smears on the elephant's armour left no doubt that the shield was not merely for decoration. This particular hathi-yodhha had seen active combat this very day and had taken lives in that action. Vasudeva prayed silently that they were not Sura lives, then felt mean and small for having thought so. All life was precious, all humanity united in brotherhood. No matter whose blood lay dried upon the armourplate of this hathi-yodhha, it was a death he would not have wished for anyone.

Supremely confident of its strength and tonnage, the elephant trundled forward without heed for the puny sipahis pointing their spears at it. Its flailing trunk, pierced with studs, knocked three sipahis carelessly to the floor; then it proceeded to pound their prostrate forms with its leaden feet. The sipahis convulsed and screamed, the screams cut abruptly short as the massive grey feet smashed their heads with practised ease, spilling their lives onto the polished marble floor. Gasps and exclamations of protest met this callous life-taking.

The hathi-yodhha swung its massive head from side to side, checking for more challengers before covering the last few yards into the centre of the banquet hall. The surviving gate guards, brave though they were, shuffled aside hastily, their faces blanching at the fate of their companions. Even the lot of them combined could hardly expect to face a battle-ready war elephant, and this, as they well knew, was no ordinary war elephant. This was the feared and hated Haddi-Hathi himself, named for the pleasure he was rumoured to take in crushing human bone, haddi. It only made things worse that the elephant, like its rider, was on their side. Theoretically speaking, at least.

In fact, Vasudeva thought grimly, they had more to fear from their kinsman mounted on the elephant's back than from the hathi.

That heavily muscled figure, clad in a blood-spattered brass armour to make himself resemble an outgrowth of the elephant rather than a separate being, was none other than the universally feared and hated master of Haddi-Hathi, Prince Kamsa himself, who had evidently returned from a new campaign of reaving and ravaging. Vasudeva glanced around to see his aides-de-camp, indeed his entire entourage of clansmen, reaching instinctively for their swords and maces. They found no weapons: the party had divested itself of its metal implements at the gates before entering at dawn in accordance with the terms of the treaty. But even so, their faces and clenched fists betrayed their rage at the sight of the man mounted atop the elephant. That man – nay, that *beast,* for he was more truly an animal than the creature astride which he sat – had left his bloody handprint upon the spotless reputation of every last one of the Sura houses represented here.

Over the last few years, none of these proud families had escaped the rapacious raids and ruthless violence of Prince Kamsa and his marauders. Vasudeva raised his hands to quell the muttered noises of provocation rising from his party, sensing the desire for just revenge that swelled in their proud warrior hearts. He himself, as king and chief justice of the Suras, had grown heartsick at hearing the innumerable atrocities committed by the prince of the Andhakas and his white-clad mercenaries. Their exploits far exceeded any conceivable desire for revenge or simple war lust; theirs was a campaign of brute destruction.

The list of war crimes, in utter violation of all Arya warrior codes, streamed past his memory's eye like a herd of sheep impatient to return to the stockade before dusk: women violated, homes and herds put to the torch, entire families wiped out overnight ... yes, the White Prince had much to answer for. But that reckoning would not be here, or now. King Vasudeva kept his hands raised to either side, and his clansmen subsided reluctantly, their faces still dark with angry blood.

Atop the blood-tainted elephant, Prince Kamsa's proud, handsome face turned from side to side, his piercing grey-blue eyes sweeping the length of the banquet hall, briefly and contemptuously scanning the faces of his many enemies assembled here. He lingered briefly on the women, dressed in colourful and enticing festive garb. The leering grin that twisted his face betrayed his utter lack of respect for any regal protocol.

Even Vasudeva felt his jaw clench as the prince stared with rude intensity at an attractive woman amidst the throng of richly clad nobility only two tables down. That was Pritha, Vasudeva's sister, who had travelled here from her home in Hastinapura. Her husband Pandu had been unable to attend the function due to ill health, but Pritha's presence was meant as an official seal to show the great Kuru nation's solidarity with and approval for the peace pact.

Vasudeva's hands clenched into fists as he struggled to restrain his warring emotions. What manner of beast was a man who would storm thus into a feast hosted by his father in bloody armour, dash down his loyal kin-soldiers and insult a noblewoman who was under the protection of his father's hospitality? Often had he heard the tales whispered along the length of the Yamuna, among the many clans and sub-clans of the Yadava nation. It was said that Kamsa was a rakshasa begot upon his mother Padmavati by a demon who assumed the form of his father Ugrasena. Vasudeva was a rational man, and not given to superstition. Yet, looking at those almost-translucent, greyish-blue eyes that glared at the gathered nobles and chieftains with such unbridled hostility, he could almost believe the gossip. Violence exuded from Kamsa like waves of heat from a boiling kettle.

Then Kamsa's gaze sought out and settled upon Vasudeva. And his entire aspect changed so suddenly, it was almost as if he had seen something quite different from merely the king of the Suras.

As if he's seeing some terrible foe rather than just me standing here, overdressed in my ceremonial robes, Vasudeva thought. Kamsa took a step back, then another, and Vasudeva thought he saw something akin to ... *fear?* ... cross the prince's otherwise handsome face. Kamsa's magnificently wrought arms rippled with muscle beneath the chainmail armour he wore.

Vasudeva was caught off-guard by the look on Kamsa's face. What had the feared reaver of the great and powerful Andhaka clan to fear from a simple, peace-loving man like him?

The stunned silence in the hall gave way to surprised whispering as the assemblage took note of Kamsa's strange reaction to seeing Vasudeva. At the same moment, the Haddi-Hathi raised his trunk and issued a bleating call that oddly echoed Kamsa's own mixture of awe and terror. The sound served to snap the Andhaka prince out of his daze.

The look on his face changed at once. The fearful, awestruck expression dissipated and was replaced instantly by a mask which was blank and inscrutable but to those who had already seen or worn it themselves – it was the mask a warrior wore when he prepared to launch an attack on the battlefield, severing his normal human self from the battle machine he was about to become.

But it was the glimpse into Kamsa's naked inner self that caught Vasudeva's attention. Yes, *that* look had been unmistakably an expression of fear. He was still pondering the meaning of that expression when Kamsa issued a loud curse, raised a barbed spear, and flung it with a roar of fury – directly at Vasudeva's breast.

Devaki shrieked as her brother threw the spear at her betrothed. Her planned union with Vasudeva was yet to be formally solemnized; but she already thought of him as her husband-in-waiting. There was no man she would be happier to unite with in matrimony than the chief-king of the Sura Yadavas. That their joining would help further the cause of peace between the neighbouring nations was incidental to her. She had always been a woman led by her instinct and spirit, and she knew that she would love Vasudeva deeply, indeed had come to feel great affection and admiration for him already, after only a few meetings; and *that* mattered more to her than politics and statecraft.

She had watched with rising horror as her brother stormed into the sabha hall, then proceeded to slight, dishonour, and variously embarrass her royal dynasty as well as their entire clan by his behaviour. To come thus armed and armoured was bad enough, but to bring a war elephant – especially that brutalized and perverted beast for whom she simultaneously felt pity and disgust – was a terrible act, a flagrant slap on the face of their royal guests. When Kamsa had stared at Vasudeva with that peculiar expression, she had thought that perhaps, for once, sanity and sense had percolated into that dense brain.

When Kamsa had turned, plucked out a barbed spear from the side-saddle of Haddi-Hathi and flung it with vehement force at her husband-to-be, it shocked the life out of her and she could hardly help shrieking her dismay.

To her further amazement, Vasudeva made no move to twist, turn, dodge, or otherwise avoid the trajectory of the missile.

The spears Kamsa favoured were brutal things. Metal heads barbed in an asymmetrical pattern of recurved points, any one of which was sufficient to rip to shreds a person's flesh and organs, and impossible to remove without further damaging the wounded individual. His aim with these inhumane missiles was renowned. She had once seen him fling a spear at a grama chieftain in a dense milling crowd and strike him in the throat without touching anyone else on either side.

This time too, his aim seemed perfect. The spear was flying towards Vasudeva's chest, poised to shatter the Sura chief-king's unprotected breastbone and destroy his heart, and to kill him instantly. Her shriek was echoed by an outburst of screams and shouts of dismay, male as well as female, from across the crowded sabha hall. The distance from Kamsa's hand to Vasudeva's chest was barely twenty yards, and the spear bridged that distance in a fraction of a second; yet in later years, as the legend grew, it would be said by some that the spear had slowed in mid-air as if travelling through water or against a powerful headwind, rather than simply across empty stillness.

If such a phenomenon truly occurred or if it was merely a product of the active imagination of those watching, she would never know for certain. For no sooner had the spear started on its trajectory than a man rushed forward, blocking Devaki's view. It was Akrur, a close friend and ally of Vasudeva and a chief mediator in the peace alliance between the Sura and Andhaka nations.

She would later learn that he had attempted to fling himself into the path of the onrushing spear, to take the death that was meant for Vasudeva, but at that instant, all she knew was that his body had blocked her view. As if galvanized by Akrur's action and the violence that had abruptly exploded into a peaceful event, everybody else began moving as well, further obstructing her view.

All she saw was bodies and moving heads, none belonging to Vasudeva. But even above the cacophony of shouts and exclamations that had erupted, she heard one sound clearly. The sound of spear striking flesh and bone came to her like a half-remembered nightmare that would plague the deep watches of restless sleep for many moon-months to come. This sound she would remember because, with her vision obscured, she sincerely believed that it was the sound of her brother's ill-intentioned spear shattering the bone and flesh of her beloved betrothed: the sound of widowhood even before her nuptials could be solemnized. It would haunt her until another, far more terrible sound replaced it for sheer nightmarish horror. But that other sound still lay in the future.

For now, the sound of metal flung at great velocity, shattering bone and splintering it like matchwood – flesh and fluid resounding wetly from the impact – was a horror beyond imagining. She shrieked again, and if she could, she would have flung herself directly at her brother. She could see him clearly as he stood in the centre of the hall, like one of the many stone pillars arranged in even rows to either side.

In that instant of panic and terror, she saw him turn his head at the sound of her voice. For it was his name she was shrieking. '*Kamsa!*'

His eyes found her in the melee and locked on her briefly. The malice and glee she saw therein, the sheer lascivious delight at what he had just done, was in such stark contrast to the awestruck expression he had exhibited only moments earlier that she could not help thinking, as she had a thousand times over the years, *My brother is no mortal man, he is a rakshasa born in mortal form.* For even if a mortal man had done such an act, whatever the reason, surely he could not have such an expression on his face: a look more demoniac than anything the most imaginative artists and sculptors could conjure up when recreating scenes from the legendary wars against the rakshasas in the Last Asura Wars or from that even more legendary battle of Lanka waged by the great king Rama Chandra of Ayodhya. Kamsa could have modelled for those artists and sculptors, yet none would have possessed sufficient skill or art to capture the sheer malevolence of the look his face bore at this moment.

Then the moment passed, and he turned back to look in Vasudeva's direction, no doubt to gloat over the new murder he had just added to his epic tally. Devaki wished at that moment that she had a spear of her own within reach, for she would surely have flung it at this instant. To hell with filial loyalty and feminine propriety. The fact that Andhaka women were no longer permitted to go to battle did not mean they were good only for the bhojanalya and bedchamber. A daughter of Raj-Kshatriyas, she had been trained and schooled in the arts of war as thoroughly as her brother. Better, probably, for she had not been banished from her guru's ashram as a child as Kamsa had been for incorrigible behaviour. But, of course, there were no weapons here and even at the peak of her rage, Devaki could not simply murder her own brother, however just her motive under dharma.

But in her mind, she flung a barb of retaliation no less deadly and far more portentous: *Some day, my brother, your reign of brutality will end. And mine shall be the hand that flings the spear that ends it. This I swear here and now, by Kali-Maa, avenger of the oppressed.*

Then she pushed her way through the crowd, desperate to reach Vasudeva's side, if only to offer her lap for his head in his last moments. The crowd did not resist her passage, for everyone there knew what she was to the Sura chief-king; and they stepped aside to let her through. She reached the circle that surrounded Vasudeva and looked upon a heart-stopping sight.

four

Blood pounded in Kamsa's head with the ferocity of a kettledrum. His vision blurred for a moment and, once again, he saw the horrendous vision that had met him moments ago – the sabha hall was filled with fierce Kshatriyas and mighty yoddhas, all determined to destroy him and his kin. To wipe out his entire race from the face of the earth. He recognized many of the faces as new aspects of old foes, reborn in this age for the express purpose of decimating and committing genocide upon his blood-kin. He had met them before, in another city, another age. A place named Ayodhya where, twice before, he had bravely attempted to strike a blow for his people's cause, and had tasted the bitter fruit of their deceitful thwarting of his noble efforts. He had been in possession of a different form in that age and place, and been known by another name. It eluded him now, but he knew that his name in this life simply meant 'amsa' of 'Ka', 'Ka' being the first syllable of that ancient name and 'amsa' meaning his partial rebirth, similar to an avatar. This was but the newest round of battle in an age-old conflict with the greatest enemy of his kind.

He glanced in the direction of their leader, the one who sat on the Andhaka throne bearing the raj-mukut, the crown of beaten gold that was placed upon the head of the people's chosen leader, for the Andhaka Yadava nation was a republic in the truest sense of the word.

The being seated there glared down at him with a look of pure fury. He bore the familiar aspect and human garb of Chief-King Ugrasena. He was shouting stern commands that he foolishly expected Kamsa to obey. That old man seated upon the Andhaka throne was not his true sire; that honour fell to a noble being named Drumila, a powerful daitya from the netherworld. Unable to take birth in this age in his true form, he had disguised himself as the chief-king of the Andhakas, Ugrasena, and in this guise, he had deceived Ugrasena's wife Padmavati in younger days, siring a male child upon her. Kamsa was that child, and he felt the rich, noble blood of his true father raging in his veins now, as he did at such times, and ignored the blathering objections and orders of Ugrasena, a feeble old man who possessed neither the will nor the strength to do what had to be done: *Exterminate all enemies. Kill them where you find them, by any means possible.* Yet, somewhere within Ugrasena's incompetent form, there remained a vestige of Drumila and it was to this truth that Kamsa bowed and conceded lordship.

'Fear not, Father!' Kamsa said aloud, as the stunned gathering still reeling from the shock of his bold intrusion and even bolder act of recklessness turned to stare at him. 'I have slain the enemy in our midst. No more will his deception veil our senses from the true nature of his evil mission!'

He saw Ugrasena blink several times as he absorbed this shouted message. Beside him, Kamsa's mother Padmavati, once known for her beauty, now a wasted shadow of her former self, covered her face and seemed to weep. *Tears of joy, surely*, Kamsa told himself. *She must be overjoyed at my speed and boldness.* His true father Drumila did not respond as Kamsa had expected either: he did not loudly hail his son's achievement to the assembly or come to Kamsa and press him to his breast in that fierce embrace that Kamsa had craved for so often during his growing years and received so rarely. But that was only to be expected; in his human disguise as Ugrasena, Drumila must needs conceal his true feelings for his son. No matter. Kamsa knew his parents were proud of him, and that was enough.

He executed a deep bow in the direction of the throne, and raised his head, smiling. The smile faded as he saw the crowd that stood encircling the spot where Vasudeva – that wretched spy and eternal enemy of his clan – had stood only moments ago, part to reveal something quite extraordinary.

Vasudeva stood as he had before, facing him. The stupid cowherd that he was, he had neither flinched nor taken evasive or defensive action when Kamsa had flung the spear. Not that anyone could deflect or dodge a throw by Kamsa easily; but the man might at least have made an attempt. To simply stand there facing death was an act so contemptible, it made Kamsa want to spit his mouthful of tobacco on the polished floor in disgust. Of course, such steadfastness might be misconstrued as heroism – a yoddha facing certain death without so much as flinching. But Kamsa knew better. The man was a coward and so unexpected and stunning was Kamsa's action that he had no time to react. He simply stood there as Kamsa's spear sped towards him to end his life. Kamsa had flung it with force enough to punch through armour, bone, flesh, gristle, sinew and spine, and emerge out a man's back – he had done precisely that to other men a hundred times before and knew exactly the force, trajectory and impact of his throw.

The spear still stood there.

In mid-air.

Before Vasudeva.

Kamsa stared, blinking several times to make sure his eyes were not still obscured by the blood from his last skirmish with some cowherds who had strayed across the demarcated border into Andhaka territory. Well, technically, they hadn't strayed, but the heads of their cattle were pointed towards Andhaka territory, so it was obvious they intended to cross over. He had slaughtered the cowherds and their cows, down to the last suckling calf and mother of both species. Their blood had spattered on his face, obscuring his vision, and it had taken considerable scrubbing to remove the stubborn spatters. Damned enemy blood. Burnt like acid too.

But no amount of blinking and rubbing his eyes made this particular sight vanish or change.

His spear stayed there, hanging inches from Vasudeva's chest, its deadly barbed tip pointed precisely at the point where the breastbone met the ribcage, that soft yielding spot in the centre where the spear would have punched through with minimal resistance, bursting through the heart and emerging out of the rear of the Sura's body.

It had stalled midway, suspended by no visible means. It wasn't floating exactly, for it did not so much as move an inch, merely hung as if embedded in some solid object.

But I heard it strike! It hit bone and flesh and cartilage with that typical wet crunching sound they always make at this distance and force.

Then again, he was so accustomed to hearing that sound that it was possible that he had simply remembered it from previous occasions. The outburst that exploded from the onlookers the instant he flung the spear had drowned out everything else, after all.

He strode towards the Sura chief-king, people stepping back or moving away, wide-eyed, to give him a wide berth.

He saw a man beside Vasudeva stand his ground staunchly, along with several others he recognized as the Suras' clan-brothers and allied chieftains. They stared fiercely at Kamsa with the look he had seen so often before. He saw fists clench empty air, muscles tighten, jaws lock, and knew that they were prepared to take him on with their bare hands if need be. They did not worry him; he could take them on single-handedly even if Haddi-Hathi was not there to back him up, which he was.

Kamsa stared at the spear. He walked around it; examined it from all angles. He could not fathom how the trick had been pulled off. The spear simply stood there, embedded solidly in … in thin air!

He grasped the spear to dislodge it from its position. He felt a shock as it refused to budge.

He yanked down upon it, hard.

Nothing.

He pulled it to the left, then to the right, then pushed it upwards. His biceps and powerful shoulder muscles bulged, and he knew that were this a lever he was exerting all this force upon, he could have moved a boulder weighing a ton with this much effort.

Yet the spear just stayed there, as immobile as an iron rod welded into solid rock.

This was impossible!

He looked at Vasudeva. The Sura chief-king's face was hard, ready for anything, yet not cruel and mocking as Kamsa had expected. Not the gloating glee that a triumphant enemy ought to have displayed at such a moment.

'HOW!' Kamsa screamed. 'BY WHAT SORCERY DID YOU DO THIS?'

Vasudeva looked at him for a moment with eyes that seemed almost cow-like to Kamsa's raging senses. The kettledrums played out their mad rhythm, pounding his brain with unending waves of agony.

Then, to the sound of a shocked *Aaah* from the watching assemblage, Vasudeva reached out and took hold of the spear, which came free of its invisible hold as easily as if he had picked it up from a wall-stand. Several spectators clasped their palms together and cried out *Sadhu! Sadhu!* in reverential tones – for what had happened was no less than a miracle.

And to Kamsa's continued disbelief and amazement, the Sura chief-king held out the spear upon raised palms, the action of a man surrendering rather than opposing.

'It was not I,' Vasudeva said quietly, 'but the great Lord Vishnu who did this. For it is clear that he desires our people to be at peace. Accept this as proof of his grace and a sign of his protection over all those who work to achieve shanti upon prithviloka.'

five

'**F**ather?'

Devaki had scoured the palace for Ugrasena. When a sipahi informed her that her father was still in the sabha hall, she was surprised. It was the last place she had expected to find him, so long after the ruckus caused that afternoon by her brother. But when she entered the darkened hall, lit only by the light of a few flickering torches that created as many ominous shadows as they threw light, her heart sank.

Ugrasena sat on his throne in exactly the same position in which he had been seated when she had left the hall hours earlier, after the fracas over Kamsa and his boorishly violent actions had disrupted the celebration. As she walked the several dozen yards to the throne dais, the crackling mashaals sent the shadows of the endless rows of carved pillars fleeing and skittering in every direction. The echoes of her footfalls whispered from the far corners of the large chamber which was acoustically designed to carry the words of every speaker at the public sabha sessions to even the farthest reaches of the great hall.

She shivered, feeling the cold damp stone of the chamber pressing down upon her. Through her childhood and brief youth thus far, she had come to associate this hall with war: war councils, preparations, emergencies, talks, negotiations, breakdowns in talks … Until today, her strongest memory was of angry voices raised in heated discussion over some seemingly insignificant matter of territorial water rights or foraging boundaries – those twin bugbears that had plagued the Sura and Andhaka clans since the time of their mutual forebear Yadu himself.

She reached the foot of the dais and instinctively bowed formally, awaiting the liege's permission before approaching closer.

Ugrasena sat like a statue wrought of old wax, his lined and worry-worn features as deeply etched as with a sculptor's chisel. His posture, leaning back and resting sideways, with the side of his head resting on one palm, suggested anxiety too. She waited patiently for him to respond. Finally, he broke out of his reverie and registered her presence. He sighed and frowned down at her, eyes watering either from strain or age.

'My good daughter, why do you stand there? Come, come to me. Why do you stand on ceremony so? You need no permission to approach.'

'Father,' she said, climbing the stone-cut steps to the raised platform that served to elevate the Andhaka seat of governance above the sabha hall's floor. She knelt on one knee, taking her father's hands in her own. She was shocked to feel how cold and withered they were. Had they been so weathered this morning when he clasped her hands and uttered the traditional blessings? She didn't think so. He seemed to have aged years in a single day. Her heart went out to him and she leaned forward and kissed him quickly on the brow. His eyebrows rose in surprise at the unexpected affection, but she knew he was pleased. Her mother was not given to demonstrations of affection, and she had often felt that her father must suffer from its lack.

'What occasions this generosity?' he asked, a faint trace of a smile on his puckered mouth. It pleased her to know that she was the one responsible for it.

'I am rich today,' she said brightly, determined to elevate his mood. 'I am rich in family and friends and allies. And soon I shall be rich in matrimony too. This is the happiest day of my life, Father. And I owe it all to you. You promised that I would wed Vasudeva and you kept your promise. You are truly a king among men!'

He laughed. A brief chuckle, gruff and involuntary. But still a laugh. It gladdened her heart to hear the sound of his amusement as she now felt confident that he could overcome the day's setbacks and Kamsa's awful transgression. He was her father: King Ugrasena, lord of the Andhaka Suras, the greatest nation in all Aryavarta – in all prithviloka – and nothing was impossible for him!

But the chuckle turned to a choked cough, then into a bout of violent chest-racking bursts that bent him over double and turned his face red. Alarmed, she patted him on the back and poured him water from the decanter beside his throne. Why had he sent away even his serving boys and girls? When the coughing fit finally ceased, it left him looking stricken, like the time he had taken to his bed with the purging sickness. It pained her to see him so weakened.

Then he did something that alarmed her even more.

He bent over, pressed his palms to his face, and wept.

'Father,' she said urgently, concerned, 'why do you weep so? You are lord of the Andhakas. The world lies awaiting your command. Nothing can resist y our power.'

His greying head shook with the force of his weeping. She felt her heart sink, all her bonhomie and optimism waning like water dripping out of a leaking pot. She felt the fear that had clutched her mind that morning return, strengthened by the ugly rumours and gossip that was circulating around the palace like a fetid odour carried in the wind.

When he raised his head at last, she was dismayed to see his eyes red-veined and rheumy, streaming tears. 'I fear ...' he said in a choked voice, faltered, then continued, 'I fear that your brother may go out of hand this time.'

A chill swept down her back. 'Control him, Father. He respects you greatly. He will abide by your commands.'

He shook his head, still coughing into his fist. His beard was flecked with saliva and shiny with caught tears. She was frightened and made nervous by his seeming collapse of nerve. 'He has no respect for me or anyone else,' he said gruffly, almost scornfully – though the scorn was not directed at her but at the subject of their discussion. 'Not even his own mother! Nay. He only fears me ...' He paused, musing sadly. '*Feared* me. Now, even that may not be enough to keep him in check.'

She clasped his hands. 'You underestimate your powers, Father. I am sure you can control him even now. He is nothing more than a spoilt child running amok. Too long has he lived as he pleased, done as he willed, without care for dharma or karma. It is time he was checked. And you alone can do it.'

His eyes, gazing out with a lost expression into the dark flickering shadows of the sabha hall, turned back down towards her, finding her face. They softened and a semblance of a smile twitched his careworn features. 'My child. My jewel. You would believe your father capable of crossing swords with almighty Indra himself! And perhaps once, yes, I would have dared to attempt even such a feat. But not now. Not in my current state and age. More importantly ...' and here his face darkened by degrees, as if the mashaals had begun to snuff out one by one, 'you do not know your brother's present strength. He has the shakti of a danav, a daitya, a rakshasa, and every other breed of asura all rolled into one now. He is far, far more than just a spoilt boy run amok. He is a force of destruction.' His head dipped in evident shame. 'Perhaps once he could still have been tamed and checked, put on a leash or trained and commandeered. But now ... now it is past sunset in the deep recesses of his soul. Now he has descended into the pit of madness. And he is well on his way to destroying us all.'

Devaki's heart was chilled by her father's lack of hope. What had made him so pessimistic? Where was the proud, bombastic Raja Ugrasena she had grown up watching round-eyed from behind pillars as he held entire sabhas and congregations in the spell of his oratory? How had this ageing, ailing, white-bearded, weak-kneed old man taken his place?

'Do not speak so, Father. We have signed a historic treaty. The kingdom is finally at peace. The Sura nations are once again neighbours and equal sharers of the land and the water. You are a great and powerful ruler. I am about to be married to the wise, wonderful and widely loved leader of the Yadavas. Our union will herald a new age. All will be well. I *know* it will,' she persisted adamantly, displaying the same stubbornness that she had seen *him* display on numerous occasions – after all, she was *his* daughter.

But he only looked away, unable to meet her eyes. 'I pray it may be so,' he mumbled half-heartedly.

six

Vasudeva raised a hand, quelling the clamouring voices that filled the large cattle shed. As he waited for his agitated countrymen to quiet down, his gaze swept across the gathering, noting that his clansmen had travelled from as far away as the southern-most nations to be present. Representatives of all the major tribes and clans of the Yadava nation – the gyati sanghas as they were called – were present, although, of course, the Sura sangha dominated, this being Sura territory. There was an air of tense anticipation for the meeting, and he had seen people talking in groups in every street he passed through the previous day. From the anxious way their eyes darted to him and their voices lowered as he approached, he knew that the one concern they all shared was the same as his own: Would the peace hold?

Now, every pair of eyes settled on him with the same anxious gaze, asking the same implicit question. He knew how hard it had been to hold these disparate sanghas together in order to form a united front for the long, painstaking negotiations. Water rights and access to the river were only one of many pressing concerns that divided even longtime neighbours and turned old allies into bitter foes; he had had to contend with a host of other issues, foremost of which had been the deep rancour over the terrible war crimes committed by the Andhakas.

The Yadavas were an honourable race, ruled by dharma, and that precept extended to their wartime actions as well. However, some of the things the Andhaka Yadavas had done in the past few years did not deserve to even be judged under dharma. And at the forefront of those war crimes was always the same name, the same bloodstained face, the same sigil and banner: Kamsa and the White Marauders.

Much more terrible than Kamsa's adharmic misdeeds were the growing reports – increasing in number with each passing day – of similar atrocities and abuses being perpetrated by other kings in surrounding nations. Vasudeva himself had heard bloodcurdling accounts of eerily similar, Kamsa-like outrages perpetrated by kings such as Pralamba, Baka, Canura, Trnavarta, Agha, Mustika, Arista, Dvivida, Putana, Kesi, Dhenuka, Bana, Bhauma, and above all, Jarasandha, the demoniac king of Magadha.

What was peculiar in the extreme – disturbing, to say the least – was the almost identical nature of these outrages. It was as if all these several monarchs and tribal chieftains – many of whom had aggressively wrested power, rather than rightfully earning or inheriting it – were giving in to the same animalistic impulses. It had provoked nervous babble which consisted of ancient myths and creatures from the annals of the puranas, a compendium of legends and histories of ages past. This only worsened matters. Vasudeva wondered if these rumours of asuras and rakshasas rising and walking the earth were the product of overactive imaginations or propaganda spread by the perpetrators themselves. It certainly suited the purposes of those bloodthirsty despots and usurpers to be regarded as hell-beings and demons rather than as the opportunistic war criminals that they actually were. Only moments before this very meeting, he had received word of an entire village gathering up its younguns and cattle and fleeing on word of the imminent approach of the terrible Agha, rumoured to be a vetala, a mythic being who sucked the life energy from his victims simply by laying his lips or fingers upon them. How convenient for Agha, who had been able to seize the entire village without losing a single arrow.

'Bhraatr,' he said now in a measured, level voice, 'I urge you all to calm yourselves and cast aside your agitation. Rising tempers and turbulent emotions will only worsen this crisis, rather than resolve it.'

Several murmured their approval of his words, but many more simply glowered and brooded. Vasudeva sensed their hostility and singled out one who had been receptive to dialogue in the past.

'Bhraatr Satvata, you, above all, know that anger will not resolve our problems.'

Satvata, a man in his middle years, with a darker complexion than even the usually dark Yadavas and a drooping moustache, shook his head sadly as if answering Vasudeva's unspoken request for support in the negative. 'Then what will?'

'Well said, Satvata! What do you expect of us, Vasu?' said Uddhava from the eastern tribes, an old friend who was accustomed to addressing his king informally, even irreverently at times. 'We have already tried ahimsa, talks, appeals to mercy ... even signed a peace treaty.'

'A peace treaty with asuras!' exclaimed Chitraketu of the borderland clan, one of those responsible for perpetuating the rumour of ancient demons reborn in human form.

'... and despite all our efforts, the Andhakas continue to ravage our lands, slaughter our people and our kine without cause, violate and carry away our women ...' Satvata's voice caught and he buried his face in his hands briefly, overcome by emotion. 'They even butcher our children ... my little Nala—'

'Satvata speaks the truth! We have played the hand of peace, met our foes with palms joined in respectful namaskar – and each time they respond with drawn swords and stretched bow-strings!' Uddhava cried in support as he clasped a burly arm around his northern clansbrother.

'Yes, why should we be the ones to be humble and merciful, at all times?' cried another chieftain whom Vasudeva didn't recognize for a moment. He then realized that it was the fourth brother of a southern clan, the fourth to attend Council in as many sessions, his three brothers all having been killed in succession in marauding raids. 'I am the last of my father's sons to survive the bloodlust of the Andhakas. If I too am killed, the Kannars will come no more to Council!'

Several voices spoke together in angry incoherence. Vasudeva raised his hand for silence but this time the tide was too fierce to brook. He lowered his hand and let them speak out their anger for a while longer. Finally, they subsided of their own accord, glaring in his direction. He was saddened by the disappointment in the eyes that met his own.

'Bhraatr, we have all suffered. But we at least have a treaty in place.'

'What good is a treaty that is honoured only by one side?' Chitraketu demanded. 'When Ugrasena's son shattered the door of Brihadbala's house and entered with his cohorts to rape and loot at will, Brihadbala reminded him of the treaty. Do you know what Kamsa said to our bhraatr?'

Vasudeva lowered his eyes: he had heard the story from Brihadbala's son, who was weeping and nursing a broken arm and crushed ribs as he recalled the last moments of his father, followed by the hours-long brutal assault on his mother and sisters by Kamsa and his men.

Chitraketu went on, red-rimmed eyes flashing, 'He said, "*This is the only treaty I uphold!*" and showed Brihadbala his raised sword before hacking him down. In his own house!'

This time, the cries of outrage were sadder, mourning Brihadbala as well as the other recent victims of Kamsa's brutality. Even Vasudeva had to take a moment to gather his wits and emotions. Being clan-chief did not free him from feeling the anger, despair and frustration they felt; it merely obliged him to refrain from succumbing to it.

'I know this,' he said softly, earnestly. 'We all mourn the dear ones we have lost. But what choice do we have? If we overturn the treaty, it will just lead to a sure end. Outright war. Is that what you all desire?' He held up his hand even as several moustached and bearded mouths opened to answer him. 'I can assure you, it is what Kamsa desires! We will be playing into his very hands if we take up arms against our Andhaka brothers. That is exactly what he wishes to provoke us into doing.'

'What choice do we have?' demanded Satvata in as earnest and soft a voice. Heads turned to look at him. His eyes were red from crying. Yadava men were passionate and generous with their emotions, and unafraid to cry openly. What good was a man's freedom if he could not show the world how strongly he felt about something or someone?

'How do we go on enduring this abuse? It is beyond endurance now.'

'Yes!' cried many other voices, all with genuine grievances and causes. 'Beyond endurance!'

Kratha – a slender, ageing man who leaned on a shepherd's crook – spoke up; having lost all his sons, he had been forced to come out of retirement to attend Council once more, almost two decades after retiring to a pastoral life. He said in a halting voice that shook with age as well as emotion: 'What of the Andhaka king? Is Ugrasena blind and deaf to the atrocities of his son? Why does he not leash his mad dog?'

'Or put him down as a mad dog deserves!' cried another voice.

Vasudeva sighed. 'He knows all. And he has tried his utmost to leash him. But it seems that Kamsa is out of *his* control as well. I just returned after a meeting with Ugrasena this morning. He wept as he heard of the fresh blood shed by his son and his fellow rioters.'

At this, the Council fell silent for a moment. In the distance, Vasudeva heard the lowing of the cows asking to be milked again. All the gothans were short-handed, with most of the able-bodied men patrolling the borders to warn of any impending raids; the womenfolk could not keep up with the extra chores they had to do now that all the men were away. There were cows lowing all across Mathura and the Yadava nation today because the gentle cowherds were forced to look to their borders with fear rather than to their herds with care.

'If even Ugrasena cannot leash his son,' said old Kratha, 'then who will stop Kamsa?'

seven

'I must do it,' Vasudeva said at last. 'I must be the one to stop Kamsa.'

Devaki stopped and turned to look at him, aghast.

They were walking in Vrindavan, the idyllic tulsi grove at the heart of the Vraj nation. The cookfires of Gokuldham, the nearest village, were visible in the distance, curling lazily above the treetops. Vrindavan was a place of great importance to the Yadavas, a veritable botanical garden jointly maintained by a concatenation of clans. Apart from providing the Yadava nations with the countless herbal flowers, roots, seeds, fruits, leaves, stems, and the like which were needed for the making of medicinal preparations and unguents, the vast grove also contained fruit groves, vineyards, honey hives and a variety of similar resources. It was long believed by the Yadavas that anything that took root in Vrindavan grew under the protective gaze of Vishnu himself, the great protector.

Vasudeva and Devaki had taken to meeting here, away from prying eyes and wagging tongues. Sad that it should be so; after all, they were legitimately betrothed. But the rising tensions between their nations and Kamsa's ever-watchful spies had led them to a mutual agreement that it was best to meet in private. These evening walks, once or twice each week, had become the highlight of Devaki's days. She looked forward to them from the moment they parted; and, of late, they were also the setting for her nocturnal dreams in which Vasudeva and she indulged in more sensual activities than merely walking and talking.

Now, she clutched his arm tightly, alarmed by his decision. 'You must not! There is no talking to Kamsa. Not any more.'

He sighed, his forehead creasing in three vertical lines like a ripple as it always did when he was fretful. 'Everyone can be talked to. Besides, if I don't, who will? Your father has thrown up his hands in despair.'

'Yes,' she said, then more urgently, '*Yes!* Exactly. Don't you see? If even Father dares not talk to Kamsa, you certainly must not even attempt it.'

Vasudeva put his hand over hers, moving it from his arm to his mouth. He kissed her fingertips. She felt a tingle of sensation ripple down from her fingertips down to her toes, a delicious shudder thrilling the centre of her being. 'Beloved one. He is my brother-in-law-to-be. He shall be present at the wedding. Once we are wed, he shall be free to come and go as he pleases. Whatever his crimes, hideous and heinous as they are, he is still connected to us by family and law. I can hardly ignore him. Besides,' he pressed her hand to his chest where she could feel his heart beating with surprising quietude, 'if I do not speak with him, who will? Someone must, and soon.'

She shook her head insistently. 'It will do no good.'

He shrugged. 'Well, then it can do no harm either.'

'You do not comprehend, Vasu, my deva. My brother is not …' She stopped short, as if reluctant to utter the words.

He frowned, curious. 'Not …? What? In his senses? I know that already. He is power maddened, power hungry, and a warrior to whom violence and the suffering of other human beings has become a kind of soma, an intoxicating addiction.'

She looked up at him quietly, then said in barely a whisper: 'I was about to say … he is not human.'

He stared at her. 'Come now, my love. You cannot have meant that, surely. He is a terrible man, it is true. But merely a misguided and ill-intentioned one. Not some manner of—'

'Rakshasa,' she said flatly. 'A demon. A monster reborn in human form.'

He sighed and looked away. 'There are no such things as rakshasas.' He shrugged, spreading his hands to gesture at the setting sun above the fragrant groves. 'Perhaps there were such things once, in the days of Rama and Sita. Perhaps not. We shall never know for sure, although I believe even those so-called rakshasas and asuras were merely mortals too. If not, we should surely have found skeletons or carcasses of such extraordinary beings by now! None have ever been found or heard of till now.'

'That's because all the rakshasas were destroyed in the age of Rama. That was why Vishnu took an avatar in human form, to cleanse the earth of rakshasas forever, and to end Ravana's evil reign.'

He put his hands on the tips of her shoulders, turning her towards himself. 'Maybe it was so. I do not wish to debate itihasa and matters of science with you. But Kamsa is no rakshasa.'

'He is evil,' she said without a trace of doubt, 'the most evil being in the Yadava nation.'

'No, my love. There is no such thing as Evil. Or Absolute Good either. These are oversimplified concepts used by rabble-rousers to goad warriors into fighting the enemy. If you tell every foot-soldier that his counterpart in the opposite rank is as human as he is, earns the same pittance, eats the same bad food, and takes almost nothing home to his long-suffering wife and children, he will rebel and walk away, rather than fight. By telling him that he is fighting for the forces of Good and that the other man is Evil Personified, you motivate him to fight to the death – the other man's death. It's the manipulation tactic used by leaders … as old as troop warfare itself.'

She did not debate, simply said with utter conviction, 'You do not know my brother. He is Evil Incarnate.'

He looked at her, about to argue further, then sighed and looked away. Devaki saw her own thoughts reflected in that action: What were they debating? Kamsa's malevolence? Rakshasa or human, evil or merely badly flawed, he was no paragon of dharma. That was certain; the rest was semantics. Although, of course, she knew. She *knew.*

'I believe he can still be reasoned with, talked to, his better instincts appealed to.' Vasudeva spread his hands. 'There must be a way to get through to him. This madness has to stop.'

She clutched his arm again, feeling herself shivering as if with a sudden chill, despite the balmy weather. He looked at her, concerned.

'You must not,' she said, beseeching him now. 'He is a killing device. Like a sword with a dark hunger that must be fed all the time. Can you reason with a sword? Talk to it? Appeal to it? I beg you, my love, do not risk your life and limb.'

He sighed, putting his arm around her. Vasudeva listened to her, unlike so many men; he actually listened and could be persuaded with reason and good sense. That was one of the many things she loved about him.

'What would you have me do, then?' he asked. 'I am king. I must do something. The barbarism must be stopped. It cannot go on. Just this day, I received word of …' He trailed off, then looked down, and she saw the dark grooves beneath his eyes, sensed the deep sadness in his soul. 'My people are being brutalized. I cannot simply stand by and let it happen.'

'No, you cannot,' she agreed. 'You must not. You must act now. Before it is too late. Before Kamsa's power and bloodlust grow too great for even him to control.'

He gazed at her, puzzled. 'So you agree I should speak with him?'

'Not *speak*! Words are no good. You must *act*! *Stop* him!'

'How?'

She laid a hand upon his chest, staring straight into his eyes.

She said quietly: 'Kill him.'

He balked. 'He is your brother.'

She shook her head. 'Not any more. If he ever was my brother, that man has long been consumed by the rakshasa that now governs his body and mind. He is not human. Not any longer. And if he is not stopped, he will grow more powerful, more terrible.'

'You cannot truly believe that, my love.'

'I do not *wish* to believe it. But I *know* it to be true, nevertheless.' She covered her face, realizing how terrible she must sound. 'I am ashamed to be his sister.' She gathered herself together. 'I mean what I say, Vasu, my most beloved of all devas. He is a rakshasa and the only way to stop a rakshasa gone berserk is to kill him.'

Vasudeva stood silent for a long time. The sun descended below the treetops. Birds sang louder in the grove, filling the air with their music. A pack of monkeys chattered and raced through the trees on some mischievous errand. The sweet aroma of honey wine wafted to them from nearby.

At last, he said sadly, almost regretfully: 'I cannot. It would be against dharma to kill my brother-in-law. In fact, if I were to break the peace treaty by such an act, it would certainly lead to decades-long warring between our nations. An assassination of a royal heir will render all my peace-making efforts useless.'

'The people will understand, Vasu. They know Kamsa is not fit to be king. His own citizens would not shed a single tear once he is gone.'

But Vasudeva's mind was made up. He shook his head firmly. 'It is out of the question. Violence is never a means to lasting peace.'

She looked up at him. She was on the verge of bursting into tears, yet fought them back. She did not want him to see how hopeless she thought his cause was. She tried to make herself feel hopeful, even confident, about his ability. Words had deserted her.

Ever sensitive to her feelings, he put his arm around her and comforted her. 'We are people of dharma, Devaki. Taking up arms to defend ourselves is something we do only as a last resort. Violence only begets more violence. Ahimsa is the only way to peaceful coexistence.'

She wanted to say, *Kamsa will not let us coexist, he is a monster. He seeks only violence and nothing but violence. Ahimsa is a word unknown to him.* Instead, she looked at him, wiping an errant tear from her cheek. 'You are truly a deva, my Vasu. I pray that you do not underestimate my brother's capacity for evil.'

eight

Kamsa rode grinning through the smoke and chaos of a burning village.

His henchmen were busy ransacking the remaining houses for anything of value before setting them ablaze. He would give them time to enjoy themselves and relish the spoils of war. Stopping on a high verge, he watched with satisfaction as the settlement was razed to the ground. It amused him that the Yadavas could be so easy to kill, their villages so vulnerable, their women and children so unprotected ...

A high-pitched scream ripped the air. He turned to see a young boy in a coloured dhoti tied in the Vrajvasi style charging at him with a shepherd's crook, of all things!

Kamsa laughed and deflected the point of the crook with his sword. A twist of the reins drew the bit tightly enough into his horse's mouth to make the beast sidestep, causing the boy to overshoot his aim and fall sprawling to the ground. His turban, the same bright saffron colour as his dhoti, fell into a muddy puddle and was sullied.

Kamsa sheathed his sword and pulled the reins up short, making the horse rear. There were specks of blood on its mouth as he had a habit of whipping his mounts on their mouths if they failed to respond quickly, but he hardly noticed it.

The boy was moaning and struggling to his elbows. As he turned and looked up, he froze at the sight of the massive Bhoja mare rearing up before him. Kamsa brought the forehooves of the horse down with a loud thud. The boy cried aloud and moved his legs out of the way, just in time to avoid them being smashed.

A gust of breeze from the village carried the voice of a woman screaming pitifully for her children to be spared, followed by three short, sharp cries that cut off abruptly as each of her wretched offspring were despatched by Kamsa's efficient soldiers. The boy turned his head to listen; his pain and empathy marking him out as either the woman's son or a close relative. In a moment, the desperate woman's voice rose again, now launching into wailing cries of grief and pity for her own plight as the soldiers turned their attention to her.

The boy glared up at Kamsa with hot brown eyes filled with hatred. 'Rakshasa!' he cried. 'Only a rakshasa would attack unarmed gokulas protected under a peace treaty!'

Kamsa grinned. 'Then why don't you call upon your devas to protect you? What good are they if they can't defend their own bhaktas?'

The boy shook his fist. 'They will come. Our devas always hear the prayers of the righteous. Lord Vishnu himself will come down to earth and make you pay for your crimes!'

Kamsa roared with laughter. 'Lord Vishnu himself? I must be *very* important to attract *his* attention!'

While talking, the boy had managed to get hold of a fist-sized rock. Now, he flung it hard at his aggressor, his aim good enough to hit Kamsa a glancing blow on the temple. Kamsa's right ear rang and warm wetness instantly poured down the side of his head. He stopped laughing and grinned down at the boy who was scrabbling around in search of more missiles to throw.

'It's a helpless deva who arms his devotees with just stones to defend themselves,' he said, blood trickling down his neck.

The grin stayed on his face as he yanked back on the reins and forced the horse to rear, bringing down both forehooves on his intended target with a bone-crunching impact – again, and again, and yet again – until what remained on the ground was no more than a crumpled bundle of shattered bones and leaking flesh.

'Lord Vishnu can't be here today to help you,' he said to the remains of the child. 'He has more important things to attend to than saving weak, pathetic cowherds in remote Vraj villages.'

A contingent of riders approached at a brisk canter, slowing as they neared him.

Bana was leading the group, Canura beside him. Both exclaimed as they saw Kamsa's head streaming with blood.

'Lord Kamsa, you are injured,' said Bana, dismounting and jogging to Kamsa's side to examine the injury more closely. 'Canura, call for our lord's vaids at once.'

Canura barked an order, sending two riders back to the Andhaka camp a mile or two upstream. Kamsa and his ravagers tended to ride much ahead of the main force, leaving the sluggish supply caravans trailing in their wake.

'It's just a scratch,' Kamsa said absently, gazing out across the village. The woman's screams had stopped, although other equally terrible cries could be heard across the ruined settlement as other women and victims suffered at the hands of the Andhakas. To Kamsa, the screams were like sweet music, acknowledging his superiority as a military commander and soldier.

'Tell me,' he said to Bana, who knew at once what he wished to know.

Bana began recounting the tally of the dead. The ratio of 'enemy' dead to their own dead was ludicrous. They had killed or left for dead some two hundred and lost only three men.

'Because we take them by surprise and after the treaty many have returned to herding and farming, they rarely have weapons close at hand,' smirked Bana, licking his lips. 'And the women and children are almost always alone and defenceless in their homes.'

Bana then proceeded to recount the spoils of private treasures they had appropriated as tax -- Kamsa had forbidden the use of the term 'looted' – measuring up to a substantial amount.

Bana chuckled as he finished the tally. 'A good day's work, My Lord. These herders and farmers make for easy prey. Almost too easy. We roll across the landscape like chariots across millet, crushing them underfoot like crisp grain.'

'Yes, well, that won't continue much longer,' Kamsa said. 'Word must be spreading already about our campaign. We should expect to meet some resistance soon.' He raised a clenched fist, adding, 'I pray we do. I am tired of hacking down feeble herders caught unawares and boys with sheep crooks!'

Canura grinned slyly. 'It has its advantages.' He jerked his head in the direction of the village where the screams of dying women rent the air and the crackling of burning straw-and-mud huts filled it with smoke. 'The men enjoy it too.'

Kamsa didn't respond. He stared into the distance. Bana and Canura exchanged a glance. Kamsa often had these phases when he would just stare into the horizon, brooding. Such periods almost always preceded some new plan or strategy.

Finally, he said, 'We shall swing north and east. Towards Vrindavan.'

'Vrindavan?' Bana repeated. Even Canura gaped. 'But My Lord, that is the heart of Sura territory. King Vasudeva will not brook an assault on his heartland silently.'

'Bhraatr Bana speaks the truth,' Canura added cautiously. Kamsa did not always appreciate being corrected or having his plans questioned. A scar on Canura's cheek testified to that fact, as did the rotting corpses of two of Kamsa's previous advisors. 'Until now, we have only, uh, *taxed* outlying villages and border territories of the three nations. Our actions could be defended as legitimate policy against border crossings and water or cattle thefts. But if we ride that far into Vraj heartland, it would be a total violation of the peace treaty and a declaration of open war against Vasudeva himself. The Sura nation might respond with an all-out war. And the Bhoja Yadavas might feel outraged enough to get involved as well.'

Bana cleared his throat, also careful to couch his suggestions in cautious terms. 'Besides which, Vasudeva does happen to be the betrothed of your sister Lady Devaki, My Lord. The wedding is set to take place in—'

Kamsa gestured them both to be silent. They subsided at once. The wind changed, bringing a heavy odour of smoke and the stench of burning corpses along with the fading screams of the last suffering victims.

'I am sick of this peace treaty,' Kamsa said. 'My father did not consult me, the crown prince, before signing it. Why should I be compelled to uphold it?' At the mention of his father, Kamsa's eyes glinted – both Bana and Canura noted this with growing nervousness – and a gleam of naked rebellion shone there. 'It is time to put it to the test. Let us see how long Vasudeva upholds his end of the treaty when I come galloping into his lands and lay waste his townships.'

Being Kamsa's friends and advisors, the pair glanced at each other, increasingly uneasy. Yet none dared speak a word. It was one thing to offer a suggestion or two, but quite another to defy his gesture ordering them to be silent; if either one spoke now, he would find his own corpse piled upon one of the several dozen burning heaps that were all that remained of the village they had just pillaged.

'They call me a rakshasa,' Kamsa said, unmindful of the blood still streaming down the side of his head. 'They call upon Lord Vishnu to protect them from me. Let me see if Vishnu has the courage to descend to prithviloka in yet another avatar, this time to confront Kamsa. It will be good to have a worthy opponent to sink my sword into for a change. I am tired of stabbing cowherd flesh and slaughtering hairless boys.'

He raised his head towards the smoke-filled sky and bellowed: 'YOU TOOK AN AVATAR ON EARTH TO BATTLE RAVANA. THEY SAY WHENEVER YOUR PEOPLE ARE UNABLE TO DEFEND THEMSELVES, YOU DESCEND TO PROTECT THEM. NOW DESCEND TO FACE ME, KAMSA OF MATHURA! I CHALLENGE YOU!'

Bana and Canura exchanged startled glances. Even the soldiers accompanying them looked shocked at Kamsa's bold, blasphemous challenge.

As if in response, a deep rumbling roar came from the smoke-stained sky, followed by an angry crash of thunder. Canura winced, his horse neighing. The smell of imminent rain filled the air, along with a damp coldness. Thunder crashed again, far away in the distant horizon.

Kamsa listened, head cocked to one side like a curious hound, then threw his head back and laughed long and hard. The laughter echoed across the razed settlement, silencing the last desperate cries of the hopeless and the dying.

nine

Queen Padmavati listened with mounting horror as her spasa, a personal guard specially deputed to collect intelligence discreetly, recounted the many atrocities and war crimes perpetrated by her son. At last, she shuddered and interrupted him mid-sentence.

'Enough! *Enough!* I can hear no more.'

She rose from her lavender seat and went to the casement, fanning herself. Summer had come down upon Mathura like a hot brand and even the coolest chambers in the palace were barely endurable. The whiff of wind from the window felt like steam off a boiling kettle.

She turned around to see maids watering down the flagstone floors to cool them. Her spasa waited, head bowed. The sight of him made her stomach churn. If she had not already heard rumours and other snatches of news corroborating parts of his report, she might have ordered her guard to drag him away to be executed instantly. As it was, she was tempted to give the command, if only to prevent him from recounting the same horrific tales to others in the palace. But, she reasoned with herself, what good would that do if these things were already known! In fact, it appeared that she was the last to learn of her son's misdeeds – at least the extent and severity and sheer volume of those misdeeds. No, it was no fault of the spasa; the poor man had only done his job as she had commanded.

Even the fragrance of the water being sprinkled on the floors, drawn from the deepest well and made fragrant with the scent of roses from the royal gardens, could not calm her nerves. Her son? Doing such terrible things? How had things come to such a pass? Oh, that she should have lived to see such a day!

Suddenly, she lost her patience. Trembling, she shouted at the maids, the spasa, even at her personal guards standing at the doorway.

'Out! Everyone out! I wish to be alone.'

A moment later, sitting in the privacy of her chamber, she broke down, sobbing her heart out. She thought of little Kamsa, a pudgy, fair boy with curly hair and a fondness for young animals of any breed. He had always had a kitten, a pup, a fawn, a cub, or some other youngling in his chubby arms, cradled close to his chest.

She remembered calling out to him on numerous occasions: 'Kaamu, my son, give the poor thing room to breathe. You'll smother it with your love!' And both Ugrasena and she laughing as Kamsa blushed, his milky-fair face turning red in the same splotched pattern every time as he ran away in that shambling hip-swinging toddler's gait, his latest acquisition clutched close to his little chest.

She smiled, wet-eyed, remembering how adorable he had been, how proud Ugrasena and she had been of their son, their heir. What dreams they had spun, what plans, what ambitions ...

But then she recalled something she had almost forgotten, a seemingly insignificant fact suddenly made significant by the spasa's report.

All those tiny kittens, puppies, fawns, squirrels, calves and other younglings ... where had they gone?

Kamsa had always had a different pet every few days or weeks. At first, they had stayed for longer periods, she thought, with one or two even growing noticeably larger and older. But over time, they seemed to change with increasing rapidity. Until finally, by the time he was old enough to play boys' games and outgrew the toddler phase, he seemed to have a different pet every time she turned around, at least one every day, until it had become a matter of great amusement to his parents. She even recalled Ugrasena's joke about Kamsa being an avatar of Pashupati, the amsa of Shiva who ruled over the animal kingdom.

What had happened to the earlier pets? Where did they go once Kamsa finished playing with them? Where did the new ones go each day?

A cold sword probed her heart, piercing painfully deep, her feverish blood steaming as it washed upon the icy tip.

Where indeed!

And there, with a lurch and a start, her memory
threw up the recollection of a day when she had found
Kamsa crouching in that peculiar toddlers' way at
something in a corner, something wet and furry and
broken that had once been a kitten, or perhaps a whelp.
Kamsa standing over a pile of burning rags and a tiny,
charred carcass in the back corridor, eyes shining in the
reflected light of the flames ... Kamsa carrying a stick
with a sharpened tip sticky with fresh blood.

There were more memories. Many, many more.

She had dismissed all those incidents as accidents
or merely the passing phase of a young boy's normal
growth pangs. But now, they sent the tip of that icy
sword deep into her bowels, raking up terrible guilt
and regret.

There *had* been signs. Kamsa had never been quite
like other boys, other princes. Even when older, he had
not made friends easily, had gotten into fights that
ended with terrible consequences for at least some
of the participants – almost always those who defied
or refused to side with him – and there had been
incidents with servants, serving girls, maids, a cook's
daughter ... A minor scandal over a young girl found
dead and horribly mutilated in the royal gardens, last
seen walking hand in hand with Kamsa the day before,
which was his twelfth naming day.

Yes, signs.

Many signs.

But nothing that had prepared her for *this*.

A mass murderer? A leader of marauders,

ravagers, rapists, slaughterers of innocent women and children?

Her Kamsa?

Her little boy with the fair, pudgy face and curls grown up to be the Rakshasa of Mathura, as they were calling him now?

It wasn't possible! There had to be some mistake.

She stormed out of the chamber and went striding through the palace, her guards and serving ladies in tow. Curious courtiers and ministers' aides watched her sweep imperiously through the wide corridors with the marbled statuary, brocaded walls and art-adorned walls.

She stopped outside the sabha hall only long enough to ask the startled guards if the king was alone or in session.

A dhoot had just arrived bearing news and the king was in private session, they replied with bowed heads, not daring to meet her agitated eyes.

She cut them off abruptly, ordering the sabha hall doors to be opened to let her in. They obeyed at once, without protest. Like most traditional Arya societies, the Yadava nations had long had a matriarchal culture. Women owned all property, from land to livestock, right down to even the garments on everyone's back. Inheritance was by the matriarchal line, as was lineage. Every stone, brick and beam in Mathura was quite literally the property of Queen Padmavati.

She strode into the sabha hall, past the startled guards and surprised courtiers. There were not very many. Inside, Ugrasena and a few of his closest advisors and ministers sat listening keenly to a road-dusty courier – a dhoot – who broke off and peered fearfully over his shoulder at her unexpected entrance, as if afraid it might be someone else.

Padmavati strode up to the royal dais. Ugrasena frowned down at her, openly surprised.

'Padma?' he said, lapsing into informality.

'My Lord,' she said, 'I have urgent *private* business to discuss with thee. Kindly send away these honourable gentlepersons of the court.'

Ugrasena looked at her for a long moment. In the flickering light of the mashaals, she saw how he had appeared to age in the past few weeks. The peace treaty had taken a greater toll on him than the troubles of the preceding years, was what the wags were saying around court.

No, not the peace treaty. Our son's devilry.

'It is about Kamsa, then,' he said, without a trace of uncertainty in his words.

She did not answer, not wishing to say anything impolitic in front of the others.

He nodded as if he understood.

'Come, my queen,' he said kindly, in a weary voice. 'Seat thyself and listen to the latest tales of derring-do of our beloved son.'

Ugrasena and Padmavati sat on the royal dais. Except for the mandatory royal guards at the far end of the hall, by the doors, they were alone. The dhoot had finished his report in Padmavati's presence, recounting further episodes of Kamsa's vileness. From the sighs, head-shakes, shrugs and other gestures and reactions of the others, she had understood that these reports were now commonplace. She shuddered at the realization: innocent lives snuffed out, butchered by her own son, and even Mathura's wisest heads accepted it as commonplace. She did not know which was worse: the fact that he had committed and was still committing such terrible acts, or the fact that they were tacitly accepted and tolerated by those governing the kingdom.

She turned to Ugrasena now, her mind raging.

'We must curb him,' she said. 'This cannot be allowed to go on.'

He sighed, rubbing his hand across his face, looking terribly weary and old, a pale shadow of the man she had wedded, loved, and shared her life with for over two decades.

She now understood why he had taken ill these past several weeks, why he had not come to her bed at nights, why an endless procession of royal vaids seemed to always be coming from or going into his chambers, why the annual festival had been cancelled, why no entertainers or artists had been invited to the palace of late ...

Her father had once told her that no matter how comfortable and luxurious it may appear, a royal throne was the hardest seat to sit on. And to remain seated on it meant foregoing all comfort forever. 'All these things,' he had said, gesturing expansively at the rich brocades, luxurious adornments and gem-studded furniture, 'exist to pay homage to the seat itself, to the role of king or queen. For the man or woman who sits on that hard spot, there is no luxury, no comfort, no rest.'

She saw now the truth of those words. Truly, Ugrasena, at the peak of his reign, at the helm of the greatest Yadava nation that had ever existed, had no comfort.

'Yes,' he agreed at last. 'This ought not to be permitted to continue.'

She waited, knowing that he was not merely echoing her words but qualifying them.

'Ought not,' he repeated, still rubbing his forehead. 'Yet, what can we do to stop him?'

She felt her throat catch as if she had swallowed a dry, prickly thing and it had stuck in her gullet. 'We can speak to him.'

He laughed softly. There was no humour in the laughter; it was merely an acknowledgement of the inherent humour in her suggestion. 'Yes, of course we can. And he will talk back. And then go out and continue doing what he is doing now. And then what shall we do?'

She moistened her lips. 'We will have him confined to the palace. To his chambers. Prohibit him from leaving Mathura. Strip him of his privileges.'

He shifted in his seat and looked at her. There was no anger or irritation on his face, merely sadness, perhaps even sympathy. 'And how will we do that? Kamsa is the commander of all our armed forces. It is he who is in charge of even the city's security, the royal guard. You must recall that I had vested him with those powers when I crowned him heir and king-in-waiting.'

Yes, of course he had. And he had done so precisely because they had felt at that time that once he was given power and responsibility, and began handling all the administrative and other burdens of state, he would cease his adolescent antics and be compelled to settle into a more serious state of mind. Instead, he had simply used the power and leapfrogged to a whole new level of adolescent rebellion.

'There must be somebody you can depute with the task.' She glanced around, looking at the empty seats, trying to remember the various courtiers. 'What about—?' She named a senior minister, formerly a general in the King's Akshohini, the most prestigious regiment of all. 'Or …' She named several others.

Ugrasena shook his head. 'He has grown too strong. He commands the loyalty of the troops now. They would mutiny to support him if we act overtly.'

She was shocked. 'But surely they know of his brutalities?'

Ugrasena looked away. 'He gives them freedom to enjoy the spoils of war as they please. He plays cleverly upon the natural rivalries between the Andhaka and the Sura clans. He uses past enmities, petty feuds, tribe conflicts, anything that serves his purpose. Recruitment is at its highest mark ever. Every eligible young boy old enough to hold a weapon is lining up to join Kamsa's army. That is what they call it now, by the way, *Kamsa's* army. Not Mathura's. Or Ugrasena's. Or even just the army. Kamsa's Army.'

She looked around for water, wishing they had not sent away the serving staff. There was wine everywhere, as always, but no water to be seen. Water was too precious to be kept lying around. It was always brought fresh, untainted, and closely checked on command. And only royals and the wealthiest courtiers could afford to have potable water served at will. The vast majority of their people still had to draw it from wells or drink it from rivers or ponds when they desired to slake their thirst. Water, after all, was the main bone of contention and the reason for most of the troubles of the past decades. Like all causes of war and violence, it was merely the most visible evidence of a deeper social dissatisfaction. If she understood Ugrasena right, it appeared that Kamsa had cleverly tapped into that deep groundwater source of discontent, using it for his own devious purposes.

'When did he become so savvy?' she wondered aloud. 'Where did he learn to manipulate so?'

Despite her horror and disgust at his misdeeds, she was impressed by his ability to command such loyalty and adulation. Kamsa's army? And for years, Ugrasena had always grumbled to her that Yadavas were only fit for fighting in brawls over stolen cows, and utterly useless when it came to disciplined armed combat. Apparently, all that was required to goad them on to ruthless, single-minded pursuit of blood was someone like Kamsa to come along and promise them the pleasures of unlawful spoils and the setting aside of the laws of Kshatriya dharma that forbade a soldier from doing anything other than defending his nation under duress.

'That is what troubles me most, my queen,' Ugrasena said, leaning on the armrest of his throne. 'He must have advisors and they must be very wily to enable him to gain so much power and loyalty so swiftly.'

She frowned. A part of her was loath to accept this view, for it undercut the last vestige of motherly pride she could hope to take in her son's dubious achievements. But she knew at once that Ugrasena was right in his assessment. However brilliant Kamsa's political skills might be – and she had seen no great evidence of any such skills during his growing years – this achievement was too great for him to have accomplished entirely on his own. Surely, there was another hand at work.

'Whom do you suspect?' she asked with growing dismay, now trying to remember the faces and names of all those who might qualify as opponents of Ugrasena's rule and who might harbour sufficient ill will to plot against him. She felt so parched that she could almost feel desert sand grating against her throat.

'Jarasandha, Bhauma, Trnavarta, Baka, Arista, Pralamba, Putana, Agha, Mustika, Dhenuka, Bana, Canura, Dvivida, Kesi,' he said, reeling off the names as if by rote. 'But most of all, Jarasandha. There have been reports from all these places about developments that are curiously similar to those in Mathura …' he paused thoughtfully. 'Almost as if some great plan was being executed and Kamsa is only playing out his part in the scheme.'

Padmavati's mind had frozen cold when Ugrasena had uttered the first name. 'Jarasandha,' she repeated fearfully. 'The king of Magadha.'

'Yes, and a demon in mortal form, if the tales of his misdeeds are to be believed.'

Suddenly, she felt choked, as if her throat was filled with sand. 'But he is extremely powerful.'

Ugrasena nodded. 'Powerful enough to crush us in open war. But also shrewd enough to know that if he declares war against the Andhaka nation, the Suras and Bhojas will set aside all their differences and stand by us. And that would outmatch even Magadha's considerable resources by two to one.'

'And if all these kings you just named were to align with him?' she asked, agitated.

'That is not what worries me.'

She stared at him intently. 'You mean …' She swallowed hard, putting into words the thought she could barely bear to think. '*Kamsa* might be deluded into allying with him? Our greatest enemy? Surely not!'

Even the thought made her feel sick. But Ugrasena's response made her feel sicker still.

'I fear that he might already have allied with him.'

eleven

Akrur put a hand on Vasudeva's shoulder as they approached the Andhaka camp.

'Bhaiya,' he said, for, to him, Vasudeva was no less than an elder brother. 'I beg you. Reconsider your decision. I fear nothing good will come of this.'

Vasudeva patted his friend's hand affectionately. 'When the mission is for good, the outcome is always good.'

Akrur dropped his hand back to the reins. The track was heavily pitted and full of holes from the passing of large numbers of troops and wagons, and it required close attention to avoid cracking a wheel or breaking an uks' foot. But that was not the main reason why Akrur stayed silent the rest of the way. He was dead set against Vasudeva's visit to the Andhaka camp and had not hesitated to show his disagreement with his elder's plan. For all their formality and love for ritual and tradition – 'parampara' was the correct term – the Yadavas were fiercely independent people, quick to express their individual opinions, no matter how contrary, unproductive or impractical. That was the reason why the Yadava nations functioned as true republics; no other system would suffice to encompass such an independent-minded individualistic people. And of all the Yadava clans, even among the three largest nations of clans, the Vrishnis were the most independent, idealistic and individualistic. As the old saying went: Easier to draw milk from a bull daily than to convince a Vrishni Yadav.

Vasudeva was as much a Vrishni as Akrur. None of his friends or allies had been able to talk him out of this impossible mission. He was determined to take his petition to Kamsa in the sanctity of the latter's camp and risk his neck.

And he was adamant that he would do it alone and unarmed, with just Akrur to drive the cart. 'One cannot petition for peace with a sword in hand,' he had said, and had then joined both palms together to demonstrate, 'when you join your hands in namaskar, you would cut your own hands with the blade!'

Nobody had smiled at his wit. They were all too anxious that he would lose his life.

'You are putting your head in the lion's jaws,' they said.

And Vasudeva had smiled his good-natured smile and said, 'I shall check for rotten teeth while I am in there!'

Now, the uks-drawn cart trundled around the long, curving marg that led through the thickly wooded area towards the Andhaka camp. After running amok across several border villages and towns, Kamsa and his marauders had set up camp here. Nobody was quite sure why, but the theory was that the Andhakas had ruffled too many local feathers and realized that were they to continue further into Sura territory, they might have to bear the consequences.

Kamsa was notorious for his lightning raids, often undertaken under the cover of foul weather, at night or during festivals. He preferred these to risking full-frontal confrontations and, in the past, when things got too hot for him to handle, he went scampering back across the river. Vasudeva prayed that this camp was only a temporary show of bravado before Kamsa retired from the current campaign of 'patrolling the borders' – which was the official excuse, even though this spot was yojanas within Sura Yadava territory. It was on the verge of Vrishni territory, in fact, and the Council believed that Kamsa lacked the guts to risk facing the wrath of the heartland farmers who were now forewarned and enraged by the reports of his atrocities on their countrymen further south and west.

He frowned as the cart turned around the final curve and the road dipped sharply. As Akrur handled the uksan, Vasudeva stared with consternation at the field ahead. This was not merely a clearing housing Kamsa's hundred-odd marauders. The Andhakas had obviously cleared a much larger space in the centre of this thickly wooded region, creating a clearing large enough to house a small army.

Indeed, from the rows upon rows of horses, tents, and even large makeshift shacks, and the hustle and bustle everywhere, it was quite apparent that there *was* a small army residing here!

From the far end of the egg-shaped clearing,

sounds of timber being felled and axes chopping away furiously meant that they were widening the field even further. Already, the length of it was at least three hundred yards, and almost every inch of it was bustling with Andhakas.

Vasudeva glanced sideways to see Akrur gaping open mouthed at the same sight.

His friend's eyes met Vasudeva's with an expression of horror. 'They're mobilizing an army! They mean to invade us, Vasu!'

Vasudeva struggled to find an alternative explanation. 'Perhaps they're setting up a cantonment to house a border brigade.'

Akrur made a sound of disgust. 'Look at them! They're clearing more area. And there, at the south end, that's a marg they're making, broad enough to carry a dozen horses abreast. That way lies the pass across the ranges into Vrishni territory. They're planning to invade the heartland, Vasu.'

Akrur clicked his tongue furiously at the uksan, working the reins frantically. The cart began to turn slowly back to the direction which it had come from.

'What are you doing?' Vasudeva asked.

'What does it look like? I'm getting us out of here so that we can go back and warn the Council. We have to prepare for war.'

Vasudeva stopped him. 'Akrur, I still mean to speak with Prince Kamsa.'

Akrur stared at him, white faced with shock. Vasudeva recalled that Akrur had family in the hilly tribes on the far side of the ranges, only a few dozen yojanas from here. They would be the first Vrishnis Kamsa's army would encounter if it indeed meant to invade. *If*, Vasudeva reminded himself, *is a very big word.*

'But, Bhaiya, see for yourself. What good will talking do? These rakshasas mean to attack us!'

Vasudeva held his gaze firmly. 'If they do, and mind you, that's still a big *if*, all the more reason why I should be attempting to talk.'

Akrur stared at Vasudeva as if he were insane.

Vasudeva turned his face towards the camp again, saying calmly: 'Ride on into the camp. Let's do what we came here to do.'

Akrur started to say something again, but Vasudeva refused to look at him and showed him only his profile, which was hard and determined. After a moment of silence during which Vasudeva thought he heard the faint tones of several curse words spoken under Akrur's breath, mostly directed at himself for having thrown in his lot with a pacifist, the uksan were turned straight ahead once more and they resumed their trundling progress.

As they reached the main camp and rolled past men at work, sharpening weapons, eating, drinking, chopping wood, and doing various other chores, Vasudeva noted with surprise that nobody seemed to give a damn about them. They may as well have not existed!

The same thought occurred to Akrur as well. The younger man said in a strangled tone that failed to disguise his anger: 'The devils don't even know that two of the enemy are right in their midst. We could run amok here before they realize it.'

Vasudeva replied quietly: 'Oh, they know all right. They just don't care. Even if we run amok, what would we achieve except get ourselves killed in a hurry? The lion doesn't tremble when a rabbit enters its den.'

'Speaking of which, how are we supposed to find this lion? Do you want me to ask somebody where their commander is billeted?'

'Not just yet.' Vasudeva thought that while his mission was most certainly one of peace, there was no harm in learning as much as they could about the Andhaka camp.

As the cart rolled on, Vasudeva's heart sank. Any doubt he might have had about the camp's purpose was made abundantly clear as they took in more and more of the sights. There were people putting up solid wooden cabins and raising thatched mud huts. There were cooks and cleaning people and all manner of craftsmen, all hard at work. This was no temporary camp or even a token 'border' brigade. This was indeed an army being mobilized. He heard the sounds of elephants lowing not far away and realized that there were soldiers in the woods as well, probably clearing more areas to either side of the main clearing. He realized that it was impossible to tell the full extent of this operation; but one thing was certain – this was a cantonment for thousands, perhaps even tens of thousands of soldiers.

They had barely reached halfway across the length of the field when the rumbling thunder of hooves announced the arrival of more cavalry and Vasudeva saw a sizeable contingent come down the new road that had been cleared through the south end. Cheers and whistles went up all over the camp as a band of some two hundred riders rolled in with obvious jubilation.

'I think our lion has just returned home,' Akrur said with a telltale flash in his eyes.

Vasudeva was glad that he had insisted they bring no weapons along, to demonstrate how serious they were about peace.

'His jaws still red with the blood of our people.' Akrur's tone was steely.

He was right. At the head of the riders came a familiar, arrogant, straight-backed man in full armour.

Kamsa was here.

twelve

Kamsa could scarcely believe his eyes as he approached the uks cart. He slowed down before it, feeling his mouth twist in a leery grin.

'Vasudeva? Clan-chief of the Vrishnis, lord of the Sura Yadava nation? Riding only an uks cart?' He laughed, and his men, tired and satiated from another successful and richly rewarding raid, laughed as well. 'Does your nation have no chariots for a king? No entourage, royal guard, nothing?'

He turned to his men, grinning and winking. 'At least they could have sent a few of those Gokuldham milkmaids along to protect you!'

A loud round of guffaws greeted that comment. The camp's attention was centred on their leader now, and word spread quickly up and down the cantonment of Vasudeva's presence. Many off-duty soldiers and other workers crowded around to catch a glimpse of the great Sura king whose prowess as a general as well as a ruler was legendary. Kamsa saw their surprised reaction as they took in the rusticity of Vasudeva's transport and his simple gowala apparel.

He also noted the absence of any visible weaponry.

Vasudeva replied in a disarmingly good-natured tone, 'We are like this only, Prince Kamsa. Simple cowherds and dairy farmers, we are not sophisticated castle dwellers like you Andhakas. We live close to the soil and love the smell of the earth and cattle around us.'

There was a buzz of amusement at these words. Some of Kamsa's men even clapped and cheered at the response. Kamsa glared around in sudden fury, losing his good humour instantly.

Conscripted soldiers though they were, even the most hardened Andhaka veteran was at heart a gowala. Cowherds with swords, Kamsa called them contemptuously during drill rehearsal, working his whip arduously 'to beat out the traces of milk from your bloodstream'. Never having worked a field or milked a cow, growing up in the lap of luxury in his father's palace, Kamsa had a deep, enduring resentment against rustic men. The resentment came from envy, from hearing other boys and men talk of crop cycles, soil types, the effect of climate on harvests, bird migrations, cow feed, cattle ailments and such matters. These were things from which he had always been excluded, and his lack of knowledge had often been greeted with laughter and derision in the early years, giving him a powerful sense of inferiority. His first fights had been over this very difference between him and other Yadavas, and he had never truly gotten over being an outsider to such things.

Now, he sneered at Vasudeva: 'Yes, well, we seem to be stamping your countrymen back into very the soil they love so much, mingling their blood and brains with cow shit. I'm sure they're very content now.'

At once, the gathering grew grim. His men, knowing Kamsa's peculiarities and nature, immediately lost whatever good humour they had, and began to drift away to their respective tasks. Curious to a fault though the Yadavas were, they knew better than to incur the wrath of their lord. Kamsa was given to flinging maces randomly at his own men, killing anyone who happened to be unlucky enough to be standing nearby. His sensitivity at being reminded of his lack of rustic skills and knowledge was equally well known.

The sight of Vasudeva's face – and that of his companion – helped restore much of Kamsa's good cheer.

'Then you admit to killing innocent Suras,' Vasudeva said in a level voice.

'Suras, certainly. Innocent, no.' Kamsa made his horse trot a few steps closer to the cart, placing the head of his Kambhoja stallion almost nose-to-nose with the uksan which made unhappy sounds and tried to retreat. Kamsa's horse snickered and snorted hot breath down on them contemptuously, showing its superiority. 'They were about to transgress into our territory, some even in the act of crossing the river, others illegally diverting channels from the river for irrigation. My soldiers and I were merely upholding the terms of the treaty.'

Vasudeva's companion glared at Kamsa with a cold rage that promised blood and mayhem if only he had a sword in his hand. He was clearly controlling himself only under duress. Kamsa tilted his head and smiled cattily at the man, tempted to toss him a sword just to see how well his self-control held.

'And you can prove these transgressions?' Vasudeva asked.

Kamsa shrugged. 'There were several witnesses. Hundreds. Take your pick.'

He gestured vaguely at the mounted contingent behind him, still seated astride their horses until their leader dismounted.

Vasudeva kept his eyes on Kamsa. 'And if I question your word and produce witnesses of my own?' He added sharply: 'Survivors of your "treaty" raids who will counter your claims and give witness that you were the transgressors, entering unlawfully into our lands, giving no notice of your approach, grossly violating all rules of Kshatriya dharma, slaughtering unarmed innocents, including children and the old and infirm, and abusing our women … If I provide this countermanding evidence, what would you say then?'

Kamsa shrugged, looking away from Vasudeva. For a milk-sodden cowherd, the man had a manner that was unquestionably king-like and commanding. He could see how the Vrishni had developed a reputation for leadership. Vasudeva reminded Kamsa of his father when Kamsa was young and soft and Ugrasena was one of the toughest military commanders in all Aryavarta, notorious for his campaigns of conquest.

'You can drag out anyone you want, claim anything,' Kamsa said. 'As crown prince and heir of Mathura and military commander of her armies, I am answerable to no one. I pass my judgements based on my observations and conclusions. No so-called witness or survivor can question my actions.'

'But I can.'

The statement was simply spoken, with no trace of challenge or defiance. Yet, the steel in that statement was undoubted. Vasudeva's face was like a granite carving, his eyes shining like beacons. 'I am the king of the Sura Yadava nation, lord of the Vrishnis. It was I who signed the peace treaty with your father, King Ugrasena. I stamped my seal on the terms and conditions of the treaty. I have every right to question your actions and intentions.'

Kamsa raised his eyes to meet Vasudeva's. The atmosphere on the grounds had suddenly changed. Not a sound could be heard anywhere along the length and breadth of the clearing: every single man was watching and listening.

'Are you calling me a liar, Lord Vasudeva?' Kamsa asked softly.

Vasudeva looked at him with an unblinking gaze. He seemed to be considering, weighing, debating. Though his face remained calm and composed, it was evident that a great battle was raging within his soul. Even his companion turned to glance quickly,

searchingly at his lord, as if wondering what his next
words might be. Finally, truce was declared as the
prudent side won out over the other.

'I am asking you to uphold the peace,' Vasudeva
said. 'To return to Mathura at once, with all your
forces, and leave the policing of this side of the river
to me. This is my territory to control, not yours. You
are here without my authorization or permission. I
request you kindly …' he raised his hands and joined
them together in a sincere namaskar, '… I beseech
you, as one king to another, to let me control and
police my people myself. Go now, at once, and kindly
give my eternal love and best wishes to your father and
mother as well. The Sura nation and Andhaka nation
are now allies and neighbours at peace. I beg you, let
us stay in peace.'

There was a long, deafening silence after this
pronouncement. Vasudeva remained standing on the
cart with his hands joined in namaskar, head bowed.

Kamsa heard the distant calling of birds across the
clearing and, out of the corner of his eyes, glimpsed a
flight of kraunchyas rising from the forest and taking
to the skies in a long-wheeling half circle.

Every man on the field had heard – or been
informed about through word of mouth – Vasudeva's
unequivocal command couched in humility, and
was now waiting with bated breath for Kamsa's
response.

thirteen

Kamsa's first instinct was to draw his sword and lunge at Vasudeva. A natural-born warrior with an athletic disposition and the easy, instinctive familiarity with the physics of combat, he knew that by spurring his horse with a quick jab of his bladed heels, he could leap forward, slash at a diagonal upward angle, and cut off Vasudeva's head with one powerful stroke. It would require control of his shoulder to avoid straining the muscle and he would have to stand on the stirrups to extend his reach and force, but it could be done. He had done it before – often. The companion would be no trouble at all. The moment Kamsa acted, the instinct for self-preservation would force his men to follow suit. The man's torso would bristle with arrows in an instant.

But something stayed his hand. Something he had never encountered before in his young experience. For, despite his long history of cruelties, Kamsa was barely more than a boy, hardly eighteen summers of age. Apart from magnificent physical strength and robustness, he was also gifted with an exceptional ability to perceive what others around him were feeling at any given moment.

He had never known such ambivalence in his soldiers.

He could feel, to his astonishment, that the vast majority of them actually desired that he concede to Vasudeva's request. He sensed also their respect and admiration for this simple cowherd who, even though the ruler of a nation no less rich and powerful than his own, could dress and travel and speak with simplicity and utter fearlessness. Had Vasudeva come here with a contingent of heavily armed warriors and all pomp and ceremony, he would not have commanded such respect. But by riding in on a simple uks cart with a solitary companion, unarmed and unshielded, and by daring to address Kamsa and asking him to go back in no uncertain terms, he had won their respect and love. This was courage, Kamsa realized with seething resentment. True courage. To go unarmed before an army and still make one's demands without fear of consequences. In that instant, he hated Vasudeva bitterly enough to want to see him trampled under his horse's hooves until no bone in his body was anything more than gristle in the dirt.

He knew that were he to attack Vasudeva, the hatred his men felt for him, for his ways and actions, would only increase. Yet he felt he had no choice. He could not back down from such a clear pronouncement. Either he did as Vasudeva said and lost face, or they argued and debated like old men at Council until Vasudeva reeled out more arguments and witness accounts and facts and figures to prove him a liar, or he did what he always did: Prevail. By any means necessary.

He unsheathed his sword and pointed it at Vasudeva. A held breath greeted his action as every man watching and listening prepared for the inevitable violence that must ensue.

But, instead of attacking as he usually did – always did, in fact – he only said, in a tone that was deceptively calm and masked the rage and resentment simmering inside: 'By threatening me and casting aspersions on my righteous actions, you violate the terms of the treaty, Vasudeva. As of this moment, I declare the peace treaty to be broken by you! The Andhaka nation is now at war once again with the Sura nation! All cooperation extended to you thus far is taken back. You are enemies of our state and your presence here is an affront to our nation's self-respect. I command you to surrender yourselves as prisoners of war or face the consequences!'

For the first time, Vasudeva seemed to lose his composure. 'This is preposterous,' he said, frowning. 'You do not have authority to cancel the treaty, nor can it be cancelled thus, summarily. It took years to broker this peace accord and no amount of bluster or threats will affect its sanctity. The peace accord stands. If you wish to move against me, then that is your choice. But note first that I carry no weapons, nor come with armed companions. I mean you no harm. I come in peace only to speak with you and request you to leave in peace. Once again, I beg you, do not misinterpret my words. Just leave us in peace and let us live together as neighbours, as allies, as brothers.'

At that moment, something strange happened. As Kamsa stared at Vasudeva, feeling pure hatred surge through him for his glib talk and smooth speeches, he saw a peculiar phenomenon. A circle of white light appeared around Vasudeva's face, glowing like a garland of white blossoms. The light was tinged with blue at the corona, and he could not discern its origins or nature. He rubbed his eyes, frowning and grimacing as he tried to clear his vision. But the ring of light stayed.

He was about to speak, to demand of Vasudeva whether he was attempting to use sorcery against him, and to remind him that the use of maya was forbidden in Aryavarta, as it had been since the reign of Rama Chandra of Ayodhya, when suddenly the world around him went black as night, and a deafening silence descended on the world.

His horse whinnied, reacting to the phenomenon, and he realized with a shock that whatever it was, could be seen by the steed as well. It was not just *his* imagination.

He looked around.

The night-black darkness that had descended was not an absence of light. It was the presence of some dark force. He could feel its power, singing and thrumming as he looked around, reverberating at the edge of hearing, flickering at the periphery of vision. He could still sense his soldiers on the field around him, or their presence at least. But the blackness hummed and buzzed like a dense swarm of bees, blocking clear sight.

The only thing he could see was Vasudeva's face, ringed by that bluish-white light, as if disembodied and detached from everything else. It floated before Kamsa, looking down at him, and in Vasudeva's eyes he beheld the same bluish tint, as if the same eerie light glowed *within* Vasudeva!

It took all his effort and skill to hold his horse steady, patting its neck, keeping the reins – pressed low against its mane – in check. Months of harsh treatment and regular whippings had taught the stallion not to risk angering its master, and it subsided reluctantly, still snickering nervously and rolling its eyes as it tried to make sense of the unnatural change that had come across its vision.

Then a voice spoke. Deep, vibrant, booming. It echoed inside Kamsa's head, the sonorous richness of its bass quality hurting his auditory nerves. He could feel it reverberate inside his chest. It spoke a single word that filled his entire being.

Kamsa.

'Kamsa looked around fearfully. There was nothing to be seen. The voice was coming from everywhere, from nowhere, from beyond the world, from within himself.

Kill him. Kill thine enemy or he will destroy you over time.

The thrumming of the darkness enveloping Kamsa and his horse suddenly grew more frenzied, like a wind whipping itself up to gale proportions.

He? This cowherd? Kamsa thought scornfully. *He couldn't destroy a calf born with three legs.*

Do not underestimate him. He is no simple cowherd.

Kamsa stared at Vasudeva's floating face, ringed by blue light.

He is the means by which Vishnu incarnate will enter this world to destroy you.

Kamsa swallowed. *Me? Why would the Great Preserver bother with a mere prince of Mathura?*

Because you are no mere prince, either. You have a great destiny. Yours will be the hand that will lead Mathura to supremacy over the whole of Aryavarta.

Kamsa liked the sound of that. *If so, what do I have to fear from a mere cow—?*

Even before he finished, the gale around him increased to the intensity of a storm. The horse began to buck, terrified now. Kamsa held it firmly, forcing it to remain in place with an effort.

Destroy him. Or be destroyed! The choice is yours.

And as suddenly as it had appeared, the phenomenon vanished. One moment, a black wind raged around him like a storm on a monsoon night. The next, he was sitting on his startled horse in the midst of the clearing, surrounded by a thousand of his best soldiers, facing Vasudeva on his uks cart. He glanced around. Nobody else seemed to have witnessed the extraordinary event, although he saw Vasudeva's companion staring at him curiously, as if wondering if he was mad.

Kamsa's mind felt as clear as a fresh pool in sunlight. He knew now that no amount of talk or wrangling would suffice. All came down to a simple choice: he either gave in to Vasudeva or opposed him.

Since when had he given in to anyone, let alone a mere cowherd?

He grinned, and at the sight of those brilliant white teeth flashing in the afternoon sunshine, his men stirred uneasily, already knowing his mind.

Kamsa unsheathed and raised his sword in one swift action, the steel ringing loud in the silent afternoon. He roared loudly enough to be heard from one end of the clearing to the other, before spurring his horse the few yards to Vasudeva's cart.

'KILL THEM BOTH!'

fourteen

Initially, Vasudeva saw *something* occur to Kamsa, though he was not sure what it was. For an instant or two, it was as if the world went dark and a black storm surrounded him and the Andhaka prince. He saw Kamsa staring as if in a daze: wild-eyed, struggling to control his panicking horse.

So the horse can sense what Kamsa is sensing as well ... But nobody else can ... not even Akrur, Vasudeva thought. *What does it mean?*

When the booming voice began to speak, even Vasudeva was startled. It was clearly directed at Kamsa, yet he heard it too, quite distinctly. He had never encountered something of this sort before ... or perhaps he had.

He recalled the sensation that had struck him when Kamsa had flung the barbed spear at him in Mathura. The way the world had seemed to reduce to only a few yards: only he and Kamsa contained within a shell, surrounded by roaring, rushing wind. Beyond the roaring wind, he knew that the world still existed, but within that space, there was only Kamsa, he and the flying spear. And then a white streak had flashed before his eyes, tinged with blue at the centre, and the spear had embedded itself into the light!

It struck home as hard as if it had struck flesh and bone and, for a moment, Vasudeva had thought it had hit *his* flesh and bone. He had looked down at his chest, certain he would see the spear protruding, his life-blood spilling out onto the marbled floor of the Andhaka palace. Instead, he saw the tip of the spear in the distance, captured by the white-and-blue light, as securely as a dragonfly in amber.

Then the roaring wind had receded, bringing back the sounds and cacophony of the mortal world, and Kamsa had attempted to dislodge the spear, to twist and pull and turn it – without success. And Vasudeva had known instinctively that were he to reach down and grasp the pole of the weapon, it would come free of the insubstantial light easily.

He had done so, and been rewarded with success. As he took hold of the spear, the white-and-blue light had dissipated. He saw motes of blue drifting away, sparkling like starlight on a moonless night; then they were gone.

Something similar had occurred now. Kamsa and he had once more been detached from the mortal world by some supernatural force, and he had seen that blue light glow around himself again. He had also seen fear flash in Kamsa's hot-red eyes as Ugrasena's son also recognized what was happening. Then the voice had spoken, urging, commanding, demanding … and Kamsa's fear was replaced by malevolence.

The world cracked back to life, like a tree split by lightning.

The sound of a thousand soldiers roaring with shocked emotion struck him like a wave. They were roaring, not out of battle rage, for this was no army they were facing on a field of war. They were roaring with outrage at their own prince's actions.

Mingled with their outrage and shock was the warrior's throaty rasp of blind rage. Theirs not to question why; theirs but to kill or die. Their *prince*, their *commander*, had spoken his orders, and with Kamsa, it was either follow and obey without question or be killed without question.

And so they all leaped forward, encircling the two unarmed and defenceless men on the uks cart.

A thousand against two.

Had slaughter ever been this simple?

Vasudeva heard Akrur's cry of outrage and frustration. His friend had warned him against precisely this event. He had expected no less of Kamsa. Vasudeva felt sad that Akrur had been proven right and he, Vasudeva, so disastrously wrong. Yet he took consolation from the fact that he was not the one who was wrong. It was Kamsa who had chosen to act against dharma. Kamsa's actions here would be condemned by Kshatriyas everywhere; and after Vasudeva's and Akrur's death under such grossly unfair and unacceptable conditions – two unarmed men cut down by a thousand belligerent soldiers –the Suras and Bhojas would unite against the Andhakas.

The war that would follow would be to the bitter end, for no Yadava, let alone a Vrishni, could stomach such adharma. Kamsa would be destroyed in time by his own precipitous folly. And Vasudeva and Akrur would be held up as martyrs.

But I do not wish to be martyred, Vasudeva thought sadly. *I came not to die but to win peace for my people using non-violence. Is this your justice, Lord? Is this how you treat your children who desire peace? Then why should not every Arya raise a sword and let a steel edge speak instead of his tongue?*

And then Kamsa came at him, standing on the stirrups of his horse, sword raised at a diagonal, the slashing blade aimed at Vasudeva's neck.

Vasudeva raised his hand instinctively. He was unaware that he held his crook in his hand, the cowherd's crook he carried everywhere when travelling. It had been lying across his lap on the journey here and he had used it to swish away flies from the haunches of the uks a couple of times on the way to the camp. Other than that, it merely lay there, virtually forgotten.

Now, he raised his hand and the crook rose with it.

The blade of Kamsa's descending sword met the length of the crook. Two broad inches of finely honed Mithila steel, sharpened well enough to split the sturdiest body armour, struck an inch-thick yew stick, veined and cracked with age, for it had been Vasudeva's father's crook before him, and who knew when *he* had picked up the frail branch of a tree fallen to the ground while tending to his cattle and cut and shaped it, and how many decades it had served both father and son.

The warrior's sword met the cowherd's stick.

And the sword shattered.

For a moment, the world stood still. The roaring of the thousand soldiers died away to silence. Each pair of eyes was transfixed. Every face turned. Every voice stilled.

As if time itself had stopped, the earth paused in its turning, the sun and wind and heavens stood transfixed as well; the sword struck the crook and dissolved. It didn't break into pieces or shards or even splinters ...

Dust.

One moment, a beautifully lethal Mithila sword, capable of hacking easily through Vasudeva's neck, or halfway through the trunk of a yard-thick sala trunk in a single stroke, was descending to accomplish its butcher's work. The next instant, it had shattered to powder.

Only the hilt remained in Kamsa's hand; and the battle cry in his throat.

The cry dried up as well.

As he swung the sword, the dissipation of the blade, the lack of impact and his own considerable strength almost toppled him off the horse. He held his seat, then stared at Vasudeva as his horse, spurred on, trotted past the uks cart a yard or three, turned abruptly and finished a complete circle before coming to a halt beside the cart. Kamsa stared at Vasudeva's neck in stunned incomprehension.

Then he turned his eyes to the hilt of the sword in his fist. Bejewelled, intricately carved with the sigil of the Andhakas, finely worked by the most illustrious craftsmen of the kingdom.

Now merely an objet d'art, to be mounted on a marble cup and displayed in a museum, utterly useless as a weapon.

He stared at the hilt in disbelief, blinking.

All around him, his soldiers stared as well.

Then he looked at Vasudeva again, who was lowering the crook to his lap.

A few specks of silvery dust were still swirling in the air, and as Kamsa gazed at Vasudeva – along with a thousand Andhaka soldiers – the flecks swirled round, rose up and were carried away by the wind. They were tinted with blue, and sparkled as they dissipated.

fifteen

Fury rose in Kamsa like bile in a drunkard's gorge.

He reached down and yanked out a javelin from its sheath. It too was finely wrought and bejewelled at the hilt, his sigil carved into the base. He always left one such javelin at the site of any place he attacked – standing on the chest of the chief or leader of the enemy as a symbol of his conquest.

He raised the javelin, hooked it in his armpit, like a lance, and kicked his horse forward. He charged at the uks cart, aiming the javelin at Vasudeva's chest, screaming as loudly as he could.

This time, there was no answering roar from his soldiers. They were still too stunned by the shattering of the sword.

But as the point of the javelin plunged directly at Vasudeva's chest, the cowherd chieftain raised his crook again, barely a few inches, and countered the powerful lunging weapon with barely enough force to push back a gnat.

It was force enough.

The point of the javelin shattered, the pole itself splintering into a dozen shards. The pieces fell to the ground, some knocking woodenly against the forward right wheel of the uks cart before tumbling to the ground. Only the base remained in Kamsa's armpit – a jagged edge poking out – and a small piece in his fist. He stared at it in disgust as he rode past the cart, turning his mount around again, then tossed it aside. It was good for no more than starting a fire now. He had brought down elephants with that javelin, men by the dozen.

And yet his arm and body thrummed as if he had struck against a stone wall. His fingers were numb from the impact, his armpit and shoulder sore from the force of the strike. He had struck armoured shields with lances at top riding speed and experienced less pain than with this impact.

He stared at Vasudeva in fury. The Vrishni had an expression of frank wonder on his face, as if he too could not understand how what was happening was happening. Kamsa desired nothing more than to smash that face, demolish that expression.

Kamsa turned to look around. He saw a mace in the hands of one of his soldiers, a burly, muscled fellow who had been exercising with the weapon as his men often did, swinging it round over their head to build upper-body bulk and strength.

Kamsa rode over and, without a word, snatched the mace from the man's hands. The soldier stepped back to avoid being knocked down by Kamsa's horse, lost his balance and fell into the mud. Kamsa turned back, the soldier already forgotten, and hefted the

mace in his left hand – the right was still numb and
senseless from the impact of the javelin.

He roared with rage, and rode straight at the uks
cart. He saw the whites of the eyes of Vasudeva's
friend, who was as shocked as Kamsa's soldiers, but
with a notable difference: the soldiers were merely
watching as spectators; Vasudeva's companion was
in the firing line of Kamsa's assaults. Kamsa saw the
man flinch as he rode straight at the cart, swinging the
mace overhead in a classic mace attack approach, then
flung and released it.

The mace flew through the air barely three yards
or so.

It ought to have caught Vasudeva in the chest,
neck and jaw, shattering bone, smashing flesh and
battering the heart to pulp. It was meant to be a death
blow. The mace weighed no less than half a hundred
kilos. Flung with that force from a galloping horse,
it would have struck Vasudeva with ten times that
weight on impact.

Vasudeva raised his crook just in time to meet the
oncoming mace.

It turned to pulp.

Kamsa saw the solid metal crumple as if striking
against a house-sized boulder, heard the sound of
the metal being crushed, and saw the mace wilt like a
flower sprayed with poison. It thumped to the ground,
no more than a piece of twisted metal.

Kamsa roared his fury.

Then he turned and pointed at the company

of archers who stood staring in disbelief at the extraordinary proceedings.

'ARCHERS! RAISE YOUR BOWS!'

He had to repeat the order twice more before they obeyed; even so, they moved sluggishly, like men under water. One of them remained gaping open-mouthed and Kamsa vented his fury by pulling out another javelin from its sheath on his saddle and flinging it at the man. The javelin punched through the archer's neck and came out the other side in an explosion of blood and gristle, almost decapitating the man. His body fell, shuddering and spitting blood from the horrific wound for several moments, accompanied by a wet gurgling sound as the air in his lungs was expelled out of the severed throat. After that, the archers moved more efficiently, their years of training and relentless discipline taking over their numbed minds.

'AIM!' Kamsa shouted. The target was obvious.

The officer commanding the company of archers called out in alarm. 'Sire, if we miss our mark, we shall hit our own!' The danger was obvious: in a field crowded with their compatriots, the arrows were bound to overshoot their mark and strike friendly bodies.

Kamsa didn't care. 'LOOSE!' he cried.

White-faced and blinking, the archers let loose their arrows.

Over three dozen longbow arrows flew through the air at Vasudeva and his companion. This time,

Vasudeva did not even bother to raise the crook. There was no way he could block forty arrows with a single stick.

But he faced the barrage calmly. His face had progressed from the expression of wonderment that Kamsa had seen earlier to a look of acceptance. It was almost beatific in its calmness.

The arrows shattered in mid-air as if striking an invisible wall.

Blue light sparked where their points struck nothingness.

Vasudeva's companion flinched, then stared around in amazement as splinters fell around them in a harmless shower.

Kamsa screamed with frustration.

'AGAIN!' he cried. 'LOOSE AGAIN!'

Another barrage. The same result.

Kamsa lost his senses completely.

He pointed at the cart, yelling, 'ATTACK! KILL THEM BOTH!'

But not a soldier moved on the field. The archers lowered their bows, ashen-faced. Those nearest to the cart gazed up in amazement. Several joined their palms together in namaskar, as if paying darshan to a deity in a temple.

Kamsa rode forward, striking these men down, crushing them under his horse's hooves.

He whipped others, roared again and again. 'ATTACK! I COMMAND IT. ATTACK!'

But not one man of the thousand moved to obey.

Kamsa rode around in a red rage, killing and maiming his own men. Unable to get them to respond to his commands, he took a fresh sword and hacked them down where they stood. He killed at random, not bothering to check if the man was dead, leaving many mortally wounded. None cried out, none protested. All gazed at Vasudeva and joined their palms in awe, dying without argument.

sixteen

Finally, with dozens of his own soldiers lying in bloody splotches on the field, Kamsa's anger dissipated.

He leaned over the mane of his horse, pressing his hand down on its neck, the blade of his sword dripping blood. He was more exhausted than after a battle.

He looked up at Vasudeva at last.

'I accept,' he said in a voice unlike himself. 'I will respect the terms of the treaty.'

He gave the command to break camp and return to Mathura. His soldiers obeyed with evident relief, glancing back with fearful respect at the uks cart as they gathered their implements and weapons, and prepared for the journey home. The men spoke in hushed voices of the miracle they had witnessed, of the will of the devas, of the great hand of Vishnu that had protected Vasudeva from Kamsa's adharmic attack. For Vasudeva's devotion to dharma was legendary, and while Yama was Lord of Death and Dharma, it was Vishnu, in his many avatars, who was the ultimate upholder of dharma. The Sword of Dharma, as some called him. There were many who whispered that Vasudeva was no less than Vishnu's amsa on prithviloka, descended to restore dharma on the earth.

A little later, Kamsa's battalion was riding homewards.

Vasudeva and Akrur sat in the centre of the empty field, scarcely able to believe what they had accomplished.

The last stragglers disappeared from sight, their passing lit by the fading saffron glow of the setting sun.

Vasudeva turned to Akrur. 'When we set out this morning ...' he began. Then stopped.

Akrur was looking at Vasudeva with brimming eyes. They shone in the sunset like golden orbs. He joined his palms in namaskar and bowed his head. He touched Vasudeva's feet.

'My Lord,' he said, 'forgive me for having doubted you. I did not recognize you in this mortal guise.'

Vasudeva clicked his tongue impatiently. 'Come now, Akrur. You have known me since we were both boys with snotty noses. I am no amsa of Vishnu. I am merely a mortal man, like you.'

Akrur shook his head. 'No mortal man could accomplish what I witnessed today.'

Vasudeva nodded. 'I confess I cannot explain how or why this happened. But even so, I would credit this miracle to my conviction in the power of dharma and my belief in ahimsa. I came here determined to convince Kamsa without resorting to violence, and

I succeeded. Today's victory is a triumph of dharma and pacifism.'

'Whatever name you give to it, Bhaiya, it was a miracle. Call it a miracle of dharma or Vishnu's hand intervening. Either way, you are a deva among men. Of that, there is no doubt at all.'

Vasudeva smiled ruefully. 'I am a deva only by name. But if my sense of dharma pleases the gods and helps me serve my people, so be it.' He looked around at the empty field. 'At least, I think Kamsa will not come again to *these* parts to do his wicked work.'

Akrur made a sound of disgust. 'Rakshasa. The way he butchered his own men! I wish you had killed him.'

Vasudeva had taken the reins from Akrur. He clucked his tongue, driving the uksan forward, starting the journey back home. 'Had I done so, I would have been no better than he. Nay, Akrur. I think what transpired today was a shining example of the power of peace over the path of violence. Violence only begets more violence. Peace ends violence. Had I slain Kamsa today, his people would still have had just cause in attacking my people again, and yet again, the cycle continuing endlessly. By not raising a weapon or causing anyone harm, I proved my point more effectively than a dozen battles could ever have done.'

'This is true,' Akrur acknowledged. 'I do not think we shall see Prince Kamsa again on this side of the river!' He laughed. 'Who knows, he may even have to retire from warmongering forever. I don't think his men will follow him with any modicum of respect from now on; what do you say?'

Vasudeva smiled. 'He might have some difficulty in that regard.'

Their laughter rose above the treetops as the uks cart clattered and rattled down the bumpy path, mingling with the cries of birds seeking their nests for the night. The news they carried back that night would occasion celebrations across the Sura nation, jubilation at the departure of Kamsa and his plundering army and the prevention of what had seemed to be certain war with the Andhakas.

Sadly, they were mistaken in their assumptions, their confidence misplaced.

The worst was yet to come.

seventeen

Kamsa seethed on the ride homewards.

He could not believe he had been bested by a gowala, a mere *govinda*, a milk-sodden cowherd armed with nothing more than a crook. His head still spun from what had transpired. He rode alone, even his fellow marauders avoiding him for fear that he might take out his frustration and bitterness on them: he tended to be harshest on those he was closest to at such times. The rows upon rows of cavalry and foot-soldiers straggled on towards Mathura, attempting to keep their voices low to avoid incurring their commander's wrath, but not wholly succeeding.

Kamsa heard snatches of talk everywhere, always about Vasudeva and the 'chamatkar' they had witnessed. He knew that the incident would become a great legend over time, and that it had already damaged his leadership badly. He had held his army together by brute force and fear of his own viciousness. They obeyed him because he was their lord and because they believed that none other could stand up to his brutal belligerence in battle. Now that someone had stood up to him, and triumphed so successfully, they had no reason to fear him any more. Yadavas were too independent minded to enjoy the rugged discipline and command structure of a standing army; if he could not hold these men together, they would soon drift back into their traditional occupations. And if he could not keep his core contingent together, the army at large would lose morale as well.

What had happened was an unmitigated disaster. There was no other way to look at it. He was still badly shaken by it. Outwardly, he succeeded in keeping up appearances. Inwardly, he was trembling with shock. How had Vasudeva done it? It was impossible! Yet it had happened in front of his very eyes. He had tested it every which way he could think of, and found no trickery, nothing to indicate maya or sorcery.

But if not sorcery, then what?

The other explanation, the one his soldiers were bandying about, was too preposterous to consider for even a moment. Hand of Vishnu indeed! As if almighty Vishnu would reach down from vaikunthaloka and protect a simple Vrishni clan-chieftain!

But what else could have accomplished such a feat?

He was still lost in his own morose thoughts when his horse whickered and came to a halt, stamping its feet.

Kamsa looked up to see what was obstructing his way.

A sadhu. A penitent hermit clad in trademark tattered ochre robes, resting his weight on a rough staff. But unlike most tapasvis, he had no flowing white beard or the stick-thin body of one who had wasted away through prolonged fasting and self-deprivation.

Kamsa's horse whinnied uneasily and shied away from the man. Kamsa tightened his already strong grip on the reins, pulling the horse's head down, yanking the bit hard enough to cut its mouth to remind it of the consequences of acting up. It settled reluctantly, but he could see its eyes looking off to one side, rolling to show their whites, as if afraid of the man who stood in its path.

Kamsa frowned down at the sadhu. 'Old Brahmin,' he said impatiently, 'get out of my way. Do you know who I am?'

The sadhu looked up at him imperiously with that supremely arrogant Brahminical look of superiority that Kamsa had loathed ever since he was a boy.

Ugrasena-putra, Padmavati-putra, your end is nigh.

Kamsa's horse reacted before he did, bucking hard. It took a few sharp applications of the stick and some forceful twisting of its mouth to keep it from bolting. Only then did Kamsa allow himself to feel the shock that had struck him the instant that booming bass voice had resounded in his ear.

It's the same voice, the one that spoke to me on the field before I attacked Vasudeva.

He was overcome by a powerful urge to spur his

mount on and run the Brahmin over. But the horse was acting very strangely now; it persisted in shying and whickering incessantly despite his repeated warnings to it. It was trying desperately to twist its head away from the old Brahmin. Kamsa raised his stick and was about to administer a harsh reminder of his mastery when he saw something that further chilled his heart.

The old man cast no shadow!

The sun was off to their front and to the right, low in the sky, casting long shadows behind them. The old Brahmin's shadow ought to have stretched from where he stood, down towards Kamsa, leaning diagonally to the left. That was how the shadows of the trees and passing soldiers on either side were falling, moving and distorting as they intermingled. But where the old man stood, with everyone leaving a clear berth for Kamsa to ride along, there was not so much as a whisper of a shadow.

'What are you?' Kamsa cried out, suddenly feeling more apprehensive than he had felt at any other time. The encounter with Vasudeva had shaken him to the core, disturbing him more deeply than he had realized. He understood that this was no ordinary being because he had seen his horse's reaction, the lack of a shadow and the obvious way his soldiers were paying no attention to the old man standing just a few yards ahead – as if they did not see any old man standing there at all.

He suddenly wished he were anywhere but here.

I am Narada, said the Brahmin, *one of the original saptarishis, the Brahmarishis who walked the mortal realm when it was newly created; we were here before men and asuras and amsas and avatars and all other manner of beings. We were giants then and we lived inside the earth.*

Kamsa found himself unable to speak.

The old rishi peered up at his face and nodded, his ancient face creasing in what might have once passed for a look of amusement.

You are not as feeble-minded as some think. You have already fathomed that I am here only in spirit, not flesh.

'Bhoot,' Kamsa said, the word emerging as a croak from his throat, 'preth.'

Narada-muni's face wrinkled in that almost-a-smile again, taking on an almost sinister cast.

Neither ghost nor ghoul. Merely traversing between planes on an errand. Usually, I would use a vortal to pass from one world to the next. But today's errand required a different means.

'Vortal,' Kamsa repeated mechanically. He seemed incapable of saying anything original. A band of his marauders passed on the left, their chatter dying out as they registered their lord standing in the middle of the clearing, staring and speaking to … apparently no one.

A kind of portal that enables one to travel between worlds. But vortals require a physical movement from one universe to the other. They also have specific laws governing them, such as the Law of the Balance.

'Balance,' Kamsa croaked. His horse had subsided and now hung its head to one side, eyes white, mouth frothing. It seemed to have resigned itself to certain death or perhaps even some far worse fate.

So I used a mirror.

'Mirror,' Kamsa whispered, barely audible.

What you see here is merely a reflection of my physical form. That is why I cast no shadow and why, if you were to ride forward now, you would pass through this image of me as easily as through a cloud of smoke. My voice is projected astrally into your brain, which is why you hear me.

'Astrally,' Kamsa said, starting to feel afraid. Very, very afraid.

Suddenly, Narada-muni's face grew sombre.

Enough preamble. The reason I am here, Kamsa, son of Ugrasena and Padmavati, is to impart valuable knowledge and advice to you. I know of your failure against Vasudeva, despite my exhortations to kill him. That is why I have resorted to this method to relay my message to you. Heed my words well, for what I am about to say will serve you well in the days and years to

*come. It may even save your life and enable you
to accomplish the great ambition you harbour in
your heart. The ambition to be the emperor of the
entire world. That is what you desire, is it not?*

This time, Kamsa could not speak even a single
word. He merely nodded vigorously.

Narada dipped his ancient visage in response.

*So heed me well. I shall tell you that which will
change your life and make the impossible possible.
Pay attention to every word I say now, for I am
about to hand you your future on a golden tray.
The world shall unfold before you like a lotus in
water, offering itself freely. You shall be the king
of all prithviloka as you desire. Every dream
shall be realized, every enemy destroyed, every
ambition fulfilled.*

Kamsa was surprised to hear his voice ask hoarsely:
'Why?'

Narada looked just as surprised.

He raised his head, frowning, turning his vast,
sloping forehead into an ancient crumpled leather
map that had been folded too small too many times.

*Why, you ask, impudent fool! I am about to
gift you the secret by which you will rule the world
and you question why I do so?*

He seemed about to lose his temper, the legendary
temper of Brahmarishis. Both Kamsa and his horse
cringed, but Narada visibly regained control of
himself.

It doesn't matter. Some day I shall return, in person, and demand of you guru-dakshina, as is my right, and you shall grant me my wish without hesitation or question. Does that answer your 'why'?

Kamsa, eyes wide with shock and fear, nodded several times more than necessary. Passing soldiers glanced at him curiously, then looked at each other. Their commander was known for his eccentricities and extreme behaviour, but this was unlike even him: standing in the middle of the woods, staring white-faced at nothing, and making absurd gestures! Perhaps defeat at the hands of Vasudeva had loosened the last hinge on the door.

For now, all you need to do is listen and do as I say. Exactly as I say. Precisely as I say. Do you follow me, boy?

Kamsa nodded vigorously again, his chin striking the armourplate on his chest more than once.

Narada nodded, satisfied. Then he began to speak:

The first thing you will do …

eighteen

Days later, Kamsa stood on a rocky escarpment and looked out towards the distant spires of a great city.

Magadha.

A kingdom so rich and powerful and strong at arms that the thought of ever overrunning it by force had never even occurred to him. Yet, because of its strategic position, Magadha was a crucial player in the politics of Aryavarta.

Ever since his mortal father Ugrasena's days of warmongering, Kamsa had heard its name uttered with respect, fear or frustration, often all three in the same breath. He had often fantasized of standing on this very rise, with a great army behind him, akshohinis upon akshohinis spread out for yojanas, sufficient to cast terror into the heart of any king; of falling upon the great city like a bear upon an unsuspecting prey, crushing it before it could utter a single cry or flail out. For that was the only way that Magadha could be taken: by an enormous force and completely by surprise. Anything else would result in failure and ruin.

Now, here he was, alone, exhausted from the long

ride. He hadn't told anybody where he was going. The instant Brahmarishi Narada's instructions were completed, as per those very instructions, he had turned his panicked horse and ridden off without a word, gesture or backward glance.

Several of his rioters had caught up with him shortly after, shouting to ask him what he desired of them. He had waved them back furiously, and, when they still followed, he had shot arrows at them from his shortbow, turning in the saddle and aiming above their heads. They had understood then, and had slowed to watch him ride on.

Had the encounter with Vasudeva not occurred a short while ago, they would almost certainly have tailed him despite his violent objection, if only because it was their sworn duty as well as their dharma to protect the heir to the crown and the king-in-waiting. But the encounter had unnerved them, and his behaviour made them assume he needed some time to himself.

Kamsa suspected they would have set up camp and would be waiting for him to return, and might even send out regular patrols to see where he had gone and to observe him from a distance.

The thought of riding into Magadha on his own, without anyone to back him up, was so far removed from anything he had ever thought or dreamt of, it seemed absurd now. And foolish. He actually feared for his life. The shifting politics of the northern kingdoms made it difficult to be certain of one's relationship with one's neighbours. Without a specific treaty or alliance between Mathura and Magadha, he had no way of knowing if his unannounced, unaccompanied arrival would be regarded as an act of hostility or perhaps even an insult. Arya society thrived on parampara and sanskriti – tradition and culture – and the preparation for a royal visit, as well as the pomp and ceremony of the visit in itself, was an important ritual which enabled both lieges to observe, prepare for, judge and measure one another. The royal processions through the streets of the city were, in effect, a parade for the citizens to view and gauge the visiting king's net worth and military strength. A holiday was always declared to enable all to view a royal visit.

Yet, here he was: alone, bearing no gifts, unannounced, and with unclear politics. He knew almost nothing about the ruler of Magadha apart from the fact that he must be a strong and violently decisive ruler, because he wouldn't be able to hold the reins of a kingdom this strong and unwieldy if he was not. But that was like saying a Kshatriya could use a sword.

Yet, Narada-muni's instructions had been crystal clear: *The first thing you will do is go to Magadha …*

He shivered as that echoing voice reverberated in his memory again. Kicking his horse, he drove it down the slope of the escarpment.

Beast and rider stumbled downwards, leaving a curling trail of dust that rose lazily into the clear light of afternoon. At the bottom of the slope, they broke into a shambling trot that soon turned into a canter, heading towards the city.

Their progress was noted and then marked by shielded, slitted eyes behind curved visors.

As they approached, the tips of arrows fixed in strung bows followed the head of the rider, eager to be loosened and to embed themselves in his skull.

But the orders were clear and had come from the highest level, down through the ranks:

> A single horse and rider will come. Both as pale as milk. They are to be permitted to pass into the city unharmed, untouched. Nobody will speak to the rider except I. Anyone who attempts to speak with him or slow his progress is to be killed on the spot.

Orders were obeyed without question in Magadha. Men were executed for looking too sharply at those giving the orders, let alone questioning or disobeying them.

At the city gates, a pack of dogs that strayed into the rider's path, barking at the stranger, rolled over yelping, then lay still in the dust, their thin bodies riddled with arrows.

People in the streets gave the rider a wide berth, windows were shut hurriedly, doors barred, livestock brought indoors, children shushed.

The soldiers who enforced the curfew – Magadha was constantly under curfew, around the clock, all days and nights of the year – glanced briefly at the dusty, saddle-weary man of obvious royal bearing and garb, careful not to meet his eyes and to look away instantly. Even their horses shied away from the stranger's mount, which was frothing and almost at the end of its strength.

His horse collapsed on a street, eyes rolling back to reveal their whites completely before shuddering one final time and then lying still. The rider kicked it several times, too tired to flay it as he usually would have done back home, then walked the rest of the way. It was obvious that he had neither received food, nor drink, nor rested or slept for several days.

He wandered through bazaars bursting with produce and wares, an explosion of colour and commerce, in open defiance of the curfew. He was too exhausted to marvel at the richness of goods on display or the profusion of choice. As princes were wont to do in those times, he had lived mainly within the circumference of his father's power, the risk of attack or assassination being too great outside his own kingdom for him to travel far. In his childhood years, Kamsa's father had been at war with most of the world, his ferocity tempered only by age and prudence as he had finally given up the campaigns, the conquests and finally even the rivalries and clashes with neighbours, to sign the recent peace treaty. Those long decades of war had made it unwise for Ugrasena's young to be permitted to go very far from Mathura. The end result was that Kamsa had seen very little of the world, and almost all that he had seen, he had either owned or had some power over.

Here, he had no power, no protection, neither any friends or servers.

Had a thousand pairs of eyes not watched him every step of the way, he would have been waylaid a dozen times and killed well before he reached even within sight of the enormous palace gates. Thieves, crooked merchants, corrupt guards ... Magadha seethed with dangers and threats.

Finally, he reached the palace and even his exhaustion and dehydration couldn't stop him from noting that he was neither questioned nor stopped. Spears were turned away, gates opened for him, shields lowered, eyes looked aside ...

At last, he stood in an inner courtyard of the king's private palace, beside a great fountain.

The enormous, carved doors – inlaid with precious gems and decorated with a great sigil worked in battered gold sheets that were so fine as to be embedded in the grain of the wood through great artisanship – swung noiselessly, and were shut and barred with a booming echo.

The first thing you will do is go to Magadha and meet privately with Jarasandha.

He had done as the saptarishi had instructed.

He was in the private palace of one of the most powerful kings of present-day Aryavarta.

He waited to see what happened next.

nineteen

After a fair amount of time, during which the sun passed from one side of the courtyard to the far end, a giant of a man appeared, treading slowly, as if stepping on sharp stones, and stood before Kamsa.

In a shockingly boyish voice, the man said, 'Come.'

He turned and walked away in large strides, legs wide apart. Kamsa understood he was to follow and passed through to another courtyard, this one festooned with silks of every colour and other lavish decorations. The feminine nature of the adornments suggested that he was entering a queen's or concubine's chambers, and he was soon rewarded with glimpses of women.

They sat, lay, stood, and reclined in various poses, some on seats or beds, others on marbled floors, several cavorting in pools and fountains. There were hundreds of women, each one more attractive than the other. Never before had Kamsa seen such variety and range of feminine beauty gathered in one place. He had heard of seraglios, of course, and it was said that once even Mathura's kings had palaces filled with beautiful concubines. But that was in ages past. Now, Ugrasena was loyal to his queen to a fault, and, had Kamsa not been born, Padmavati would have been permitted to cohabit with a maharishi in order to produce offspring. The men of Aryavarta were brothers, husbands, sons, lovers ... never patriarchs. All bloodline and inheritance was through Arya women and they were too proud to ever permit themselves to be used as mere objects of pleasure. Kamsa felt a surge of disgust for this wanton display of womanly flesh. He had no doubt that he was deliberately being taken through these parts of the palace in order to be shown the wealth and power and luxuries of the king, and he resented it every step of the way.

Kamsa passed through the palace of women and then through a number of passageways and corridors and courtyards. It seemed to take forever. He was exhausted from the journey and from the bitterness of his humiliation at Vasudeva's hands, and desired nothing more than to eat and drink himself senseless and sleep for days. But that very humiliation and defeat also drove him on, for he was not accustomed to losing, and Narada-muni's extraordinary words had intrigued him and awakened hope in his breast. He felt that his salvation lay here in Magadha, for surely a ruler this powerful and wealthy could be of use to him, the future emperor of the world, if Narada-muni was to be believed.

Finally, the giant with the boy's voice brought him to another courtyard. This one was bare and bereft of any decoration or sign of luxury. It was little more than an enormous rectangular space with overlooking balconies and what appeared to be doorless chambers on every side. He smelled the rank stench of human sweat, blood, piss, shit and the other unmistakable odours of death and battle, and knew at once that he was in a place where soldiers trained, fought, lived, and died. In a sense, this was home to him, for he lived and breathed war and such places were as natural to him as a mother's breast to an infant.

He stood, blinking in the bright sunlight, and tried to see who was sitting in the shadows of the balconies, watching, but the angle of the sun was in his eyes and he could only see outlines and the gleam of eyes, telling him that several persons were watching from above.

The giant turned to face him, bending down and grabbing a fistful of powdery dirt with which he rubbed his palms as one did to prevent one's grip from slipping in combat. Then he slapped his bulging pectorals, his biceps, his swollen inner thigh muscles, and charged directly at Kamsa.

Kamsa was not taken by surprise. He had been expecting something along these lines ever since he had entered Magadha's city limits. Indeed, he had been surprised that nobody had accosted or challenged him until now. The giant's attack came almost as a relief.

He sidestepped the giant's onrushing advance, turned, kicked at the larger man's legs, dropping him to his knees, then sent him sprawling with a cry of outrage. The giant landed face down in the dust. Kamsa was on his back instantly, grasping his shaven head. The sweaty oil-slicked scalp slipped from his grip the first time but he crooked his elbow around the man's neck, and took firm hold before yanking his arm upwards. The bicep strained as the giant gasped and struggled, feet and arms drumming in furious protest. A cracking resounded and Kamsa felt the massive neck give way. The large body went limp as the man's excretory organs depleted themselves involuntarily. Kamsa lowered the man's head to the dust slowly, extracting his hand, and rose to his feet.

He stood, gazing up at the shadowed balcony, shielding his eyes from the sun which was directly over the balcony and in his eyes.

'Magadha-naresh!' he shouted. 'How many more of your eunuch champions do you wish me to kill before you grant me an audience?'

There was silence at first. Then a soft chuckling came from one of the shadowy balconies. He saw a movement in the shadows and a man's shape took form.

'Mathura-naresh,' a clear mid-pitched voice replied, 'I thought to offer you only a small snack to remove the dust of the road from your palate. Now, if you desire, you may enjoy a fuller repast by feasting on my concubines whom you passed on your way here. They will feed any hungers of the belly you have as well as slake other needs, and bathe and wash you in scented oils and waters and provide you fresh anga-vastras. Then, when you are rested and refreshed, we shall meet again and talk.'

The shadowy silhouette turned away, returning to the darkened recesses of the balcony.

Kamsa saw movement nearby and turned at once to see another eunuch, also a giant, darker skinned than the first one, standing by the archway through which he had been brought to the training area.

'If you will come with me, My Lord,' said the hermaphrodite obsequiously.

Kamsa heard the sound of something heavy scraping on dirt and turned again to see two other eunuchs dragging away their fallen comrade.

'My Lord,' repeated the eunuch by the doorway. 'If you will accompany me …'

Kamsa ran to one of the pillars that went from the ground up to the roof of the training house. He caught hold of the pillar in a crouching monkey action. Using his hands and feet, he pulled and kicked himself upward, propelling his body with practised ease. In a moment, he was on the upper level, and vaulting over the railing of the balcony. He landed with a gentle thump on the wooden-plank flooring and grinned at the several armed men who turned towards him with expressions of surprise. They drew their swords and daggers instantly but he raised his arms carelessly, grinning.

'I wish only to exchange words with the lord of Magadha,' he said, reassuring them.

None of them lowered his blade or moved an inch.

The man who had spoken earlier stepped forward, eyes glinting as he examined Kamsa over the shoulders of his men. 'I have heard of your impatience, son of Ugrasena,' said the king of Magadha. 'But by your rashness, you deny yourself the pleasures of women, wine, food and rest.'

Kamsa shrugged, uncaring of the many blades pointed at him, aware that one wrong move would cost him his life. 'I care not for the pleasures of wine, women, food or sleep. Time enough for all those when I have sated my first hunger.'

The king of Magadha looked at him speculatively. 'And what would that be?'

'To rule the Yadava nations,' Kamsa said simply.

There was a long pause during which Kamsa could hear the sound of bowmen on the balconies on the far side of the training court pointing arrows at him – he could hear the stretching of the bows as they took aim at his head, neck, heart, liver …

Then the lord of Magadha laughed softly and came forward, brushing aside his men as if they were wheat stalks in a field. Their blades went down, their eyes averted, to avoid threatening their master.

The king clapped his hands on Kamsa's dusty shoulders and grinned broadly. 'You are a man after my own tastes, Kamsa, son of Ugrasena. I think we shall get along very well.' And he grasped Kamsa's hand in a vice-like grip, the traditional greeting of warriors, so hard that Kamsa thought his forearm would snap.

'I am Jarasandha.'

twenty

As the dazed, shaken men of Kamsa's contingent drifted back into Mathura, word spread about Vasudeva's 'miracle' and Kamsa's abject humiliation. The return of his proud marauders, now with lowered heads, silent and sullen, sent ripples of shock and confusion through the rest of Mathura's military forces.

As usually happened in such times, the exact details of the incident grew exaggerated out of all proportion, growing more distorted with each retelling. One version claimed that Vasudeva had expanded his body to the size of a sala tree and flicked Kamsa across the field like a gnat. Another recounted the tale of how Lord Vishnu himself, deeply offended by Kamsa's challenge to him, had invested Vasudeva with his powers so he could teach the Andhaka prince a lesson he would remember forever.

When Kamsa himself did not return, the rumours grew out of control. He had lost his nerve, people said. He had lost his mind, others insisted, quoting witnesses who had seen him talking to a tree in the woods and cringing as if hearing the tree speak. His absence was taken to indicate his deep embarrassment.

It was even assumed by some that he had banished himself rather than return to face his soldiers again.

Ugrasena and Padmavati received the news of Vasudeva's triumph with great elation. They sifted through the exaggerations and understood that something extraordinary had occurred at the camp, and that a thousand of Kamsa's men had witnessed it and been deeply disturbed by it. They were not concerned about Kamsa's disappearance. Without saying it in so many words, both king and queen were secretly relieved that he had removed himself from the scene. Dealing with his transgressions had been a difficult proposition for them. By going away, he had resolved the issue. Perhaps he would surface again, but at least for a while, Mathura had a season of rest.

The army, disheartened and disturbed by the humiliation and subsequent disappearance of their commander, began to question its existence. What good was a fighting force whose leader could not face and fight a simple cowherd armed with a crook? What point was there in maintaining the legendary iron discipline and rigorous training of Kamsa's Army if the peace treaty was to be upheld to the letter?

Several akshohinis disbanded, soldiers returning home to their families and fields, glad to be tilling the soil or raising livestock instead of slaughtering innocent Yadavas. They kept their spoils, for those had been earned in the course of duty, and took their pay for the time they had spent in Kamsa's service;

but thereafter, they were happier being farmers and citizens rather than soldiers.

The marauders remained in service, for they were soldiers for life. For them, the only retirement was death, the only holiday granted for recovery from grave illness or grievous injury; the only payment, the spoils of war and the largesse of their commander.

They received word from the spasas who had trailed Kamsa in the woods and learnt that he had gone to Magadha. The spasas had not chanced following him into Magadha – they would not have been allowed to pass as he had – and knew not what had transpired inside the city. They could not even tell if Kamsa lived or not. Ever since he had gone into the great kingdom, he had not been heard from or seen again. They tried to glean information from travellers from those parts, but even the citizens of Magadha knew nothing beyond the fact that their king had granted safe passage to Kamsa and that he had been permitted to enter the palace. Apart from that, not a single scrap of news or information came out of Magadha.

All they knew was that Bana and Canura had also disappeared at around the same time as Kamsa. Some said they had been seen riding south. Others, east. None knew for certain. But they had gone away; that was certain. Everyone assumed that they too had deserted like the rest. After all, as Kamsa's closest friends and advisors, they had committed the lion's share of atrocities and war crimes. In the present mood of Mathura, they would have borne the brunt of the anti-Kamsa wave sweeping the kingdom. The rumour was that they had vanished precisely to avoid this controversy.

After the regular army disbanded, the marauders stepped down as well, disgusted by the breakdown in military discipline and the cavalier, almost festive atmosphere in Mathura. Which is to say, they remained in uniform, occupied barracks, and drilled daily as well, but they no longer patrolled the perimeter of the city or the kingdom's borders. These latter lapses in duty were not their own choice, but on the orders of the king. With Kamsa gone, Ugrasena resumed his duty as their supreme commander, and it was his wish that the marauders be disbanded. They compromised by stepping down temporarily, making it seem as if they were disbanding but, in fact, merely pretending to do so. They remained close to the palace, their fingers on the capital's nerve centre, knowing that if their master returned, he would expect them to be here, ready to serve at a moment's notice.

But with each passing day, their morale ebbed and waned. Held together mainly by Kamsa's obsessive, self-driving ambition, they lacked a cohesive force or motivation now. What if Kamsa never returned? The politics of the Yadava nation were a perpetually shifting quicksand of major and minor interests, some openly conflicting, others intertwined in a complex series of convenient alliances and temporary truces. The longer they stayed loyal to an absent master, the more time they were out of the swirling circuit of contemporary interests.

Already, the resentment that people had felt towards Kamsa's brutalities was being directed towards them, the executors of that brutality. When they went on their twice-daily patrols of the inner city – a ritual initiated by Kamsa, designed to remind the people as well as the regular conscripts of the superiority of the marauders – they were greeted with abuses, jeers and stones flung at them from rooftops. One night, two of the rear enders in their jogging column were pulled away into dark alleys by anonymous mobs and stabbed to death before they could cry out or fight back. It was only a matter of time before full-scale reprisals were launched against them.

Ugrasena and Padmavati debated briefly over how best to take advantage of this unexpected turn of fortunes. Both happily agreed that the best answer would be to invite Vasudeva to ally with them openly and to fix a date for the proposed wedding of the Sura Yadava king with their stepdaughter Devaki.

Devaki's father, Ugrasena's brother Devaka – after whom Devaki was named as was the custom in Arya royalty – was happy to give his consent. He had been most pleased at the prospect of her matrimonial alliance with Vasudeva and the peace treaty, and most apprehensive once word of Kamsa's misbehaviour had threatened both the alliance as well as his daughter's nuptials. A peace-loving man devoted to bhakti and spirituality, he was thrilled at Kamsa's self-banishment and happily threw a grand feast to celebrate the announcement of the wedding date. The city celebrated with them, and when the auspicious date of the wedding was announced publicly, cheers rang out in the streets. It had been a long time since Mathura had something to celebrate.

Devaki and Vasudeva were both thrilled, of course. 'I never dreamt you would accomplish so much so easily,' she said to him when they met in Vrindavan for a walk one evening, chaperoned by Akrur and Devaki's hawkishly watchful daimaa. This was their last walk before the marriage. After this, they would meet only on the day of the wedding when Vasudeva brought his baarat – the lavish groom's procession – to her father's house to claim her.

He smiled, as self-deprecating as always. 'What had to be had to be,' he said simply.

'And I had to be yours,' she said, then blushed at her own audacity.

He nodded. 'And I yours as well.'

Only the watchful eyes of their chaperones prevented them from showing their affection more clearly. Soon, the brief hours of their assignation flew by and it was time to go.

'When I see you again, it shall be as your bride,' Devaki said, her raven-black eyes brimming.

'I shall ask the sun to dim his light, as he will not be able to contest your beauty,' Vasudeva said.

They parted with tears of anticipation. Even the stern wet-nurse, sensitive to her young mistress' depth of emotion, was quietly sympathetic.

Akrur was equally quiet as he drove the uks cart away from Vrindavan, allowing his friend and king to dwell on the assignation at leisure.

Vasudeva looked back one last time at the idyllic grove. The next time Devaki and he visited it, they would be wife and husband. They would have no need of chaperones then, or care for how they showed their affection for each other. They could quaff as much of Vrindavan's famous soma or honey wine as they wished, and do with one another as they pleased.

He smiled to himself, looking forward to that day.

He had no way of knowing then that it would never come.

twenty–one

Jarasandha rode with Kamsa through the streets
of Magadha, which were devoid of people. Even
the merchants and bazaars, traders and whores
and people scurrying through the lanes on urgent
errands were gone.

Kamsa asked Jarasandha why this was so. The men
accompanying the king glanced sharply at Kamsa as if
expecting his host to order him cut down on the spot
for daring to question their master.

But Jarasandha only smiled and told him that the
citizens had cleared the streets on his orders.

Kamsa marvelled at a king who could shut down
the business of an entire city simply so he could ride
through the streets. He thought of mentioning to
Jarasandha that such regal arrogance would never
be tolerated in Mathura or any other Yadava nation.
Then he recalled that Magadha was not a republic like
most Arya kingdoms and kept quiet.

'Do you know anything about Magadha at all?'
Jarasandha asked as their horses picked their way
along narrow, cobbled streets packed on either side
with hovels jammed so close to one another that they
seemed to share common walls. Some were piled three

and four houses high, which made Kamsa think that they might fall at any moment.

He answered his host's question as best as he could: 'Only that you take in those who are outlawed and banished by other Arya nations.'

Jarasandha did not nod or acknowledge Kamsa in any way. He was a quiet, lean man, with the appearance and manner of a munshi rather than one of the most powerful kings in the Arya world. Kamsa thought that had he passed him walking on the streets of Mathura, he might have run him over without even realizing he was someone important. But there was no mistaking the power of his grip, or the casual yet supremely confident way he spoke, and the sense that he saw, heard, and knew everything there was to see, hear and know. The sheer power that he radiated was magnetic. Kamsa had never met anyone whose physical appearance so belied his inner power and strength. He wondered idly how difficult it would be to kill Jarasandha in hand-to-hand combat. He assessed every man he met the same way, that being the reason why he had been able to despatch the eunuch so quickly – he had already noted the man slightly favouring one knee during the long walk through Jarasandha's palace.

Jarasandha's voice was neither deep nor high-pitched, pleasant to the ear, clear enough to be understood even when he spoke quietly, which was almost all the time. In fact, he spoke so quietly that Kamsa kept feeling the need to lean closer. He found himself having to resist this urge several times as they descended the winding hillside road. It would take him a long while to realize that this was precisely why Jarasandha spoke so quietly, compelling others to be quiet around him in order to hear what he said. Powerful men exerted their power in such ways.

'Unlike other Arya cities, Magadha was never the name of a kingdom. It was the name given to the non-varnas.'

'Non-varnas?' Kamsa asked. His interest in most things outside the realm of combat, fighting techniques and war stratagem was negligible. He had thrown one of his first tutors from a high balcony in his father's palace because the man had bored him too much with a lecture on the history of Bharatavarsha. He had been eleven years old at the time. Ugrasena had had considerable difficulty persuading other learned tutors to agree to tutor his son thereafter.

'Any varna that is not one of the four basic varnas,' Jarasandha said, matter-of-factly, 'Kshatriya, Brahmin, Vaisya, Sudra.'

'Of course.' Even Kamsa knew that much. Although he had found that Brahmins and Kshatriyas each tended to put their own varna first when reciting the four names.

'It is possible for a person of any varna to move to another varna through his own work, and through recognition of his new status by his peers of the other varna. There may be any number of reasons for him to want to do so: upward mobility, a change of profession or residence, or the other way around, a diminution of his circumstances, wealth or status. A person may also be compelled to move to another varna if he is unable to fulfil the obligations of his original varna. For example, a Kshatriya who is more devoted to rituals and worship than to the art of war is, subtly or not-so-subtly, advised by his Kshatriya peers to become a Brahmin. Or vice versa.'

Kamsa nodded, even though, being ahead of Kamsa, Jarasandha could not see Kamsa's action. 'Yes, I see,' Kamsa felt compelled to say aloud.

'But what happens when two varnas inter-marry? What of the children produced by that intermarriage?'

Kamsa shrugged. He had never thought or cared about such matters before.

'Theoretically, they could claim either of their parents' varnas as their own. But what do they do until they are old enough to do so? Or even after they lay claim to the varna of either parent, what do they do if that community refuses to recognize or accept them as such?'

Kamsa had no idea.

Jarasandha glanced back at him, compelling Kamsa to sit up straighter and pay closer attention just by the power of his gaze. 'They become non-varnas. Or, to use an inaccurate but more familiar term, out-castes. Although, of course, varnas are not castes at all, not in the sense that our Western brothers across the oceans use the term.

But in this case, one might as well use the term, for, like those who do not fulfil the obligations of their caste in those foreign societies, the offspring of two different varnas in Aryavarta are veritable non-varnas. Out-castes in every sense of the term; they are not permitted to marry, conduct business, seek employment or employ others, trade, cook, clean, reside, or otherwise live within either community. In short, they have to hit the road and keep moving from place to place, snatching a brief respite at each new place by lying about themselves or producing fake bona fides and references, until they are found out or penalized for their deception.'

Jarasandha paused. 'The penalty for claiming to be of a varna other than one's own, in most Arya capital cities, is death.'

Kamsa caught a note of deep bitterness in this last announcement. He listened with more interest. It seemed Jarasandha had a more personal stake in this impromptu lecture than Kamsa had realized at first.

'So where do these non-varnas or out-castes go if they wish to survive, let alone thrive or prosper? Where can they seek employment, residence, enrichment, mates, companionship, and all the rest that life has to offer?'

Without waiting for Kamsa's answer, Jarasandha raised a thin, wiry, muscled hand and gestured at the city. 'Magadha.'

Kamsa blinked. 'You mean ...'

'Magadha means "out-caste",' Jarasandha said. 'There

are other terms for those who fall between varnas: Vandi, for a son begotten by a Vaisya man upon a Kshatriya woman; or Vamaka, which means the same. Or the Kshatriya tribes currently known as Atirathas, Sutas, Ayogas, Vaidehas, Swapakas, Pukkasas, Ugras, Nishadas, Tenas, Vratyas, Chandalas, Karanas, Amvaththas ...' he continued reeling off names for several minutes until Kamsa's head swam.

'Are all of these out-castes?' Kamsa asked, astonished. He had known men by these names, and since Kshatriyas for hire mostly sought employment by their tribe or clan names rather than their birth names, that would mean they had been of these tribes ... out-castes! Several of his marauders were from these varnas – or *non*-varnas as Jarasandha would have it. It was hard to believe.

He mentioned this to Jarasandha who nodded. 'Kshatriyas, being bhraatr united by war, will often help Magadhans conceal their true origins.'

'You mean ...' Kamsa frowned, 'my other soldiers know that some among them are not pure-breed Kshatriyas?'

'Indeed,' Jarasandha said. 'There is an unspoken rule among Magadhans everywhere. When asked point blank what their varna is, they must always answer "Magadh". For if they deny even this title, what do they have left to cling to? You will find that they will always answer "Magadh" and that they will do so with great pride, even if it means imprisonment or penalty of death.' He gestured again at the houses they were passing, less crowded than the ones on earlier streets, evidently a slightly less impoverished section of the city. 'This is their last refuge. Those who become Magadhans understand that the title is more than a varna or a nationality. It defines a person.'

Kamsa mused on the implications. 'You mean that your kingdom is made up entirely of half-castes, mixed varnas and out-castes?' He was more than a little shocked: he was, after all, a Raj-Kshatriya, not merely a warrior varna but a warrior-kings' varna. It was bred into his blood.

Jarasandha laughed. 'Yes. That is what I have been explaining to you, my Yadava friend. But do not fret, we shall not make you impure through contact with us. Remember, the code of the Kshatriyas tells us that fighting brothers are united despite varna, stature, class or sex.'

So it did. But the concept of an entire kingdom – or, well, a city – composed wholly of out-castes was still mind-boggling. Kamsa tried to work through the politics of this situation, then gave up. It was too complicated. And as a prince brought up at the helm of power, he was as chauvinistic about his superiority by birth and entitlement as any high-born Arya; the very notion of being surrounded by an entire city full of out-castes made him ... queasy.

Something else occurred to him, something that his war-oriented mind found easier to grasp: geography. 'But then how did you build this city?'

Jarasandha raised a finger, correcting him. 'You

mean to say, *where* I built this city? For the *how* is self-evident, it was built as all cities usually are. But the location was the main issue. For where do out-castes go? What place is given unto them? The short answer: none. Nowhere. That is why I had to *take* this land, *carve* it out of the neighbouring states to make my own.'

Jarasandha turned his horse abruptly to face Kamsa. 'Until now, we have had to fight and fend off the repeated attacks and attempts by those same neighbours to take back what they consider to be their land. For long have I waited patiently, building my strength, expanding my forces, gathering more and more Magadhs, awaiting this day. Now, at last, I am ready to put into action the next phase of my great plan. To prove Magadha as not just the great city it already is, but as the capital of a great kingdom, the greatest, most powerful Arya kingdom that ever existed. This city that you see around us will be just a minor township in the great kingdom of Magadha that I am about to build, my friend. A minor township!'

Kamsa nodded, impressed. 'A great ambition.'

Jarasandha laughed. 'Far more than just ambition. A reality, awaiting the right moment to be unleashed. And that moment is *now*.'

He pointed at Kamsa. 'All that remained was one final piece of the plan to move into place. And that piece has now arrived at my doorstep.'

Kamsa frowned, trying to understand what he meant. Piece? Arrived?

Jarasandha laughed again, this time echoed by his entourage. 'That means you, my friend. *You* were the final piece I required to complete my great plan. Now that you have arrived, I can put into motion my campaign to build the greatest empire the world has ever seen. And you, Kamsa, son of Ugrasena, shall be its chief architect!'

Before Kamsa could utter a word, Jarasandha turned the head of his horse and rode the rest of the way up a steep, winding road to the top of a high hill, the highest point in Magadha, Kamsa realized as he followed. On his approach to the city, he had seen that it was built on a virtually desolate plain, with sharp crags and dips. He assumed that Jarasandha wished to go to the top of this rise to afford him a bird's-eye view of the city. Kamsa wanted to tell his host not to bother. He had seen enough of Magadha. It's squalor and filth; the crowded, narrow lanes with houses almost falling over one another, falling apart, rather; the stench of human lives; the poverty; the lack of any public sanitation or drainage system ... it had taken every ounce of his willpower not to turn his horse and ride back – or away. He had obeyed the sadhu, Narada's orders; he had come to Magadha and met Jarasandha. But apart from big claims, the king did not seem to have much to offer. How could a lord of out-castes do anything to further his, Kamsa's, career? How could he, Kamsa, accept help from such a person, no doubt an out-caste himself? It pained his sense of self-worth and high-born stature. No. This was a mistake. He would listen to a little more, then slip away at the first chance he got, seeking alliance and assistance elsewhere. There were other enemies of the Sura Yadavas, other political forces seeking to further their own causes and careers. Aryavarta was a seething hotbed of politics and ambition. It would not be difficult to find allies.

Then he topped the rise, close behind Jarasandha's mount, and caught his breath. The king of Magadha laughed as he turned and took in Kamsa's stunned expression. He used his reins and his feet to expertly reverse his horse, making it trot backwards so he could continue looking at Kamsa, who came forward unable to help the dazed look on his face.

'Well, Prince of Mathura, whatever you were expecting today, I do not think this was it!' And Jarasandha turned and said in a louder tone to the large gathering of men awaiting them on the hill: 'What do you say, my friends?'

A resounding chorus of nays and gruff laughter greeted his query.

Kamsa stilled his horse and tried to still his heart too as he looked at the men gathered on the flat, unpaved promontory overlooking the city. Some he recognized at once from gatherings of Arya nations during various concords; others he identified by the sigils stitched onto their breastplate or garment; and others he could not identify at all, but knew at once to be rulers or lieges of some standing from their stance, attire and bearing. There were some two dozen men gathered at that spot and his head reeled as he gazed at each one in turn, their moustached, bearded or clean-cut faces grinning or smirking in response to his stunned expression.

Kings, they are all kings, every last one of them.

Kamsa and Jarasandha dismounted, their horses led away by waiting hands.

'Yes, Kamsa,' Jarasandha said, as if reading his mind. 'You see gathered here today the most powerful royal caucus in all Aryavarta. These are all lieges who have sworn allegiance to me. Together we propose to build the greatest empire this mortal realm has ever seen.'

'With you as emperor, of course,' Kamsa said cunningly, showing he had not been completely disarmed by Jarasandha's well-mounted surprise. He grinned boyishly to undercut his own sarcasm.

Jarasandha laughed. 'I like this boy more and more. Yes, of course I shall be emperor. For I control not just a substantial fighting force now, but every out-caste, half-caste, or even those who feel unwanted or unassimilated in any community will gladly ally with me at a moment's notice. Do you know what a great portion of Arya communities is made up of such people?'

Kamsa nodded, conceding the point. Varnas were not iron-clad, and were never intended to be so. But sadly, those who fell between them or did not satisfy the requirements of their own varna, were often shunted aside or openly shunned by their own, leading to discontent and inequity. He had often used these inequities to serve his own selfish purposes. Jarasandha was doing the same, but on a much, much greater scale.

He seeks to recruit every out-caste in the world! That would give him the greatest army ever assembled, not to mention spasas and allies secretly embedded within every court, every community, every army.

'And where do these fine chieftains come in?' he asked, indicating the who's who of Arya royalty assembled around them.

Jarasandha smiled. 'Each has his own motive for allying with me. Everyone gets his fair share. As will you. For instance, you want to rule all the Yadava nations, do you not?'

Kamsa swallowed, trying not to show his eagerness and almost succeeding. 'I could do that on my own,' he said, trying to act nonchalant.

Jarasandha chuckled and beckoned someone forward. 'I think not.'

Kamsa started as Bana and Canura appeared, smiling cautiously in greeting. 'Well met, Lord Kamsa,' they said in turn. 'We have always served you loyally, and will continue to serve you—

'In exchange for their own fiefdoms, of course,' Jarasandha added slyly.

Kamsa stared with growing rage at his war advisor and second-in-command. 'You are both half-castes? And you spied on me all this while?'

Their faces lost colour and they stepped back,

wary of Kamsa's temper. Jarasandha came forward, interceding.

'Calm down, my young friend. Were you to try and root out all my spies from your midst, you would be left with a very poor fighting force indeed. Speaking of which,' he said, smartly changing the topic and diverting Kamsa's attention, 'I believe you have almost no fighting force left now. Is that not so, Bana?'

Bana nodded nervously, keeping his eyes on Kamsa and his distance from his former master as he spoke. 'Aye, sire. The army has disbanded. The marauders are falling apart, losing men daily. And Vasudeva has been given charge of Mathura's security.'

'Vasudeva?' Kamsa's anger was instantly diverted, his outrage roused. 'How can *Vasudeva* be given charge of *my* forces? He is not even an Andhaka!'

He moved towards Bana as he spoke, his first impulse as always to batter and punish the source of the news that caused him discomfiture.

Jarasandha stepped forward smoothly. While lean and lithe, he moved with a panther-like grace that spoke of powerful, well-oiled muscles and a wealth of experience in close combat. Combined with his intense eyes that seemed to bore into you and quiet tone, he came across as a lethal predator who had no need of showing off his strength in order to subjugate.

Kamsa instinctively took a step back. It was the first time he had ever done that for any man in his life.

'All is well. This is to our advantage. You can claim that he deviously insinuated himself into your father's good graces ...' he paused, keeping his eyes fixed on Kamsa's, unblinking, 'or your mother's bedchamber ...'

Kamsa flinched, his fists coming up at once. Ever accustomed to expressing his anger at the very instant it exploded, he was unable to control it quickly enough. Jarasandha's insulting insinuation coming immediately on the heels of Bana's disturbing news was too much for his limited self-will to control. He exploded.

Jarasandha's hands caught his fists in grips as tight as iron vices, clutching them without so much as a downward glance. He moved closer, close enough for Kamsa to smell the pungent, sweet odour of tambul nut on his breath. 'A *king* uses whatever he must, whatever he can, in order to further his cause. I speak not of violating your mother's body, merely sullying her name. The accusation would be levelled at your enemy. Is it truly so hard to swallow?'

Kamsa stared at the piercing grey eyes that looked up at him from a height at least half a foot lower than his own. He recalled his old battle master cuffing him as a boy and telling him that the greatest warriors needed not height or great musculature or even elaborate weaponry; that, in fact, they were almost always short, lithe, of small build and deceptively childlike in appearance. *'Tis not what you have, 'tis what you do with it that counts*, old Venudhoot had said, before hawking and spitting a gob of phlegm in the dust of the training field. Kamsa had learnt everything he knew about hand-to-hand combat from the old teacher before he had finally bested him on the wrestling akhada and broken his neck. He had been fourteen then and had never had a fighting master thereafter.

Now, it seemed he had one.

He looked into Jarasandha's eyes and understood what this new master was telling him. He was not insulting his mother, not really. He was merely laying out a strategy. One that would lead to Kamsa climbing the first step on his road to ruling the Yadavas: he was telling him how to become the king of Mathura.

twenty-three

'Dvivida, Pundra, Dhenuka, Karava, Baka, Kirata, Pralamba, Putana, Mustika, Karusha, Akriti, Meghavahana, Bhauma, Vanga, Dantavakra, Bana, Arista, Paundraka, Canura, Bhishmaka, Bhagadatta, Purujit, Kesi, Trnavarta, Agha …'

The list of names of kings reeled off the tongues of Jarasandha's aides, Hansa and Dimvaka, in quick succession like honey off a bear's tongue. Even Kamsa was impressed. He guessed that such a show of royal strength was rarely seen outside of an Arya kings' summit.

They must surely represent half the power of Aryavarta. Kamsa then smiled wistfully and corrected himself: *we. We must surely represent half the power of Aryavarta.* Add Jarasandha's own hidden forces of half-castes, quarter-castes, and other embedded supporters awaiting his command to rise, and it was the most formidable single power ever assembled in Arya history. With such a caucus, Jarasandha could become the emperor of the world, not just Aryavarta. Kamsa felt a rush of joy and power such as he had never experienced before – not since the days when he had discovered the joys of slaughter on the battlefield.

Hansa and Dimvaka, each speaking from what appeared to be a carefully rehearsed and orchestrated script, spelt out the domains each king would govern as part of the agreement signed with Jarasandha. Kamsa, unable to write his name clearly in Sanskrit or even commonspeak, had let one of the aides write his name on the list of signatories and seconded it with the impression of his thumb, ignoring the pretty calligraphy of the others. What use did a king have with writing, art, music and all that nonsense? He desired only power. And for what Jarasandha was offering him, he would have given the Magadhan king his mother's *corpse* if he desired, not merely her name sullied by rumour. What use was a mother who did not stand up for her son, after all? His heart had hardened towards everyone back home on hearing the news from Mathura: they were carrying on as if he had been an oppressor and tyrant, not the liberating hero he truly was! The fools! Allowing Vasudeva to run Mathura! Were they utterly blind and brainless?

After the formalities were done, Jarasandha rose again.

'My kings,' he said. 'We are all of an accord. Time now to cast the die; to start out upon the long path that will take us to our shared destiny.'

He gestured to his aides. Dimvaka, the larger and stronger of the two, picked up what appeared to be a sigil on a pole. He raised it high above his head, muscles heaving, and waved it to and fro. The red flag flashed in the evening sunlight, probably visible across the length and breadth of the city below.

At once, in response, a great roar rose from below.

Jarasandha gestured to the assembled allies. 'Come, see for yourself the launch of our great juggernaut.'

Kamsa joined the rest at the edge of the promontory, careful not to step too close to the rim. He did not trust any of his new allies enough not to suspect them of trying to shove him over. After all, the fewer of them there were, the greater each one's kingdom. But there seemed to be none of that petty rivalry here. Seeing how politely and graciously they moved and made space for one another, he instantly felt ashamed of his bumpkin-like behaviour. These were real kings already. He was merely a rough boy who liked killing and power so much that he wanted nobody above him to tell him what not to do.

He caught Jarasandha watching him with that sly, knowing gleam in his cat-grey eyes. He nodded curtly, pretending to look down, but he knew that Jarasandha had caught his moment of self-loathing and weakness. The Magadhan seemed to see deep within his soul with those eyes.

The next moment, he looked down, and forgot everything else.

Magadha was being set ablaze.

Riders were racing through the city, riding like madmen with blazing torches in hand, setting light to houses, rooftops, hayricks, wagons …

A dozen fires were already blazing furiously. After the heat of the day, the close-packed houses were taking light like tindersticks. Soon, the whole city would be a morass of smoke and ruin.

'But why?' he said, before he realized he was speaking aloud. 'Why would you do such a thing?'

Heads turned to glance at him. Several faces wore sardonic, sympathetic expressions for the young novice who had yet to learn so much about politics and kingship. Others glanced scornfully at him before turning away with a shake of their heads. He knew that there were some who questioned if he even deserved to stand among them in this alliance. After all, he was the only one who was merely a crown prince, and a shamed and self-banished one at that, not a king in his own right. But Jarasandha had no such contempt or scorn creasing his smooth features.

'I told you, Magadha is not a city or a kingdom; it is a word that means out-caste. No-caste. Non-varna. This gathering of hovels you see below ...' he gestured expansively, 'was merely a temporary refuge; not a permanent abode.'

'But still ...' Kamsa wrestled with words, trying to frame his thoughts in a way that would not make him seem too ignorant and naïve. 'How can you burn your own houses? Your own people?'

Several kings snickered. Kamsa turned red with anger and embarrassment. Jarasandha put a hand on his shoulder, reassuring him. 'The people are safely away; and all the warriors and fighters ... in our forces.'

Kamsa swallowed and turned his head, listening. 'But ... I can hear them screaming ... on the wind.' He glanced down. 'You can see them too. There are people there ... dying in the fire.'

Jarasandha shrugged. 'Only the very young, the very old, the infirm.'

One of the older kings, Bhagadatta, grunted and quaffed a large goblet of wine, the spill staining his white beard crimson. 'Women, children, olduns, infants, sick men ... of no use to an army on the move.'

Kamsa stared at Jarasandha, who nodded. 'From now on, we are an invading force. Ever moving, unstoppable, undefeatable. Like the great god Jagganath who was a relentless force of nature, ever moving onwards. By killing their families, their loved ones, burning their houses and leaving them nothing to come back to, I remove every distraction that my soldiers might have in the campaign ahead. Now, they have nothing left to do but fight, win, destroy; and if they triumph, rebuild a new city, raise new families. This is the Magadhan way. First destroy. Then rebuild.'

'One must burn the grass in order to grow it anew,' said a younger, sly-looking monarch named Meghavahana who kept fingering a large emerald ring on his heart finger.

Jarasandha continued speaking softly: 'Once the city is burnt, we shall descend again, and take our places at the helm of our forces assembled outside the gates of the city. My army will lead, with the others bringing up the flanks. We shall cut a swathe across Aryavarta like the greatest herd of uks ever seen, bulls rampaging across the land, and when we pass, we shall leave none standing. We shall take what we please, do as we will. We are warriors one and all, we are kings.'

Kamsa nodded, understanding. And now that he understood, he could even take pleasure in the sound of the screams, the cries and wails of the dying, desperate, abandoned ones. As the smoke rose and the city blazed, and the kings around him drank and jested and bickered and talked, he felt a sense of pride and accomplishment. To burn his own city, put his own weak and infirm to death, what an epic warrior and commander Jarasandha was! He had never known one like him before. He looked at his new friend, admiringly, fondly, and felt proud that he had made such an ally. He found himself unable to take his eyes off this magnificent man, this incredible leader.

Jarasandha glanced at him from time to time and smiled slowly.

When it was time, they descended the hill, brushing aside the stench of burnt corpses and houses. Horses bore them through the gutted streets. Kamsa gazed in morbid fascination at the sights that met his eyes: mothers and infants clutching one another in the last throes of agony, burnt black. Old men sprawled across pavements, infants curled into foetal balls in the agony of burning. Everywhere he looked, he saw a charnel house; burnt corpses leering down at them from the scorched remains; twisted bones and cracked skeletons oozing putrid juices. The kings rode on without a care, the hooves of their horses crushing the charred skeletons underfoot, sending up a terrible percussion as they galloped through the devastated city. The kings laughed.

Kamsa thought it was easy for them to laugh. These were only low castes to them, not real Aryas. He wondered how they might feel if it had been *their* cities turning to ash, *their* women and children and olduns trampled underfoot … He thought they might not be laughing as generously then. He caught Jarasandha glancing at the backs of the heads of the other kings and knew then that the Magadhan was thinking the same thing.

He does this to prove that he will go to any lengths to succeed, Kamsa thought with a flash of insight. *For only through his own cruelty and example does a leader command the fealty of his followers. By showing how far he can go, Jarasandha has outmatched them all before the war has even begun. Now, they know that they dare not cross him. For what might not a man do when he is willing to slaughter his own in order to succeed?*

He smiled secretly to himself, pleased to have gained this insight into Jarasandha's strategy.

He spurred his horse and rode on, following his new teacher and guide. To the end of the earth, if required.

twenty-four

Kamsa bellowed a warning as he galloped forward and threw himself off his horse.

He fell upon the pair of assassins, bringing them down to the ground, where all three of them sprawled, the two attackers struggling, twisting, vying furiously to stick their knives into him as they rolled in the dust. He tasted blood and knew that one of their knives had slashed his lip and cheek. He felt hot blood spilling down his neck. He ignored it and grasped the assassin's neck. With some surprise, he found that it was a girl, her head shaven and disguised with a scarf. She bit into his forearm, drawing blood. He roared and threw himself back, slamming himself onto the ground as he used the force to jam her head in a death-lock. He felt her neck crack satisfyingly and released her, just as the second assassin flew at him with a dagger curved like a bull's horn. This one was barely a boy. They struggled in the dust for a few seconds, then Kamsa swung the boy down with a sudden, jarring impact, smashing his shoulder and loosening his grip. With a second swift action, he rammed the hilt of the curved blade back towards the boy, through the assassin's own chest, punching through the bone and into his heart. With a moan and a gurgle of blood, the boy died.

Kamsa rose to his feet, looking around warily, ready for more attackers. But there were none. Jarasandha dismounted his horse, examining the dead assassins quickly. Behind him, the city they had just ransacked echoed with the clash of fighting and the screams of the dying. Kamsa leaned against a brick wall broken by a downed elephant. The beast's tusks lay close enough for him to touch. The house upon which it had fallen lay exposed to the sky, filled with muddy water from a huge cistern that had broken and spilled nearby. Chaos reigned.

'Gandaharis,' Jarasandha said, even as Hansa and Dimvaka came up at a gallop, dismounting and joining their master. They stood with swords drawn, ready to fend off any further enemy, but it appeared that there were none left. After a three-day siege, the city had betrayed itself, Jarasandha's Magadhans rising from within to slay their lords and neighbours before opening the gates to let in their emperor, to whom they had secretly sworn allegiance. 'Do you know what this means?'

Kamsa shook his head, catching his breath. He was almost too tired to stand on his own. He had no recollection of when he had last slept, and only a hazy memory of eating some kind of roasted meat the previous night, or was it two nights ago? His body ached all over, bleeding from a dozen or more superficial wounds, and his hip felt as if it had been dislocated badly. He had lost count of how many he had slain, and he neither knew the name of the city they had just ransacked, nor the kingdom. There had been too many cities and kingdoms these past several days. Life had turned into one battle after another, siege followed by battle, battle followed by skirmish, rally followed by attack ... war was his only food and drink; rest, a forgotten friend; sleep, a lost lover.

'It means my fame has spread to the farthest corners of Aryavarta,' Jarasandha said proudly, taking the scarf of the girl assassin as a souvenir. He tucked it into his waistband, along with the curved dagger, after he had wiped it clean on the dead boy's garments. Neither the boy nor the girl looked older than ten years, and their striking resemblance made it obvious that they were siblings. It was their apparent frailness and youth that had enabled them to reach this close to Jarasandha, clutching one another and stumbling along, pretending to be weeping survivors. But Kamsa had not been fooled. He trusted children least of all. After all, had he himself not been a butcher of a boy, remorseless in killing?

'If Gandahar wants me dead badly enough to send assassins this far south,' Jarasandha mused, 'it means our campaign is making them quake even across the Himalayas. They fear that once I am done subjugating the subcontinent, I will turn my eyes further north.' He grinned, displaying blood-flecked teeth. 'And indeed I shall. But I shall not stop at Gandahar. I shall go farther north, to the limits of the civilized world.

Beyond Gandahar lie Kasmira, Kamboja, Parada,
Rishika, Bahlika, Saka, Yavana, Parasika, Parama
Kamboja, Huna, Uttara Kuru, Uttar Madra, Hara
Huna, Tushara, Pahlava ...'

Kamsa frowned at the unfamiliar foreign names,
though he recognized many of them from his poring
over his father's maps as a boy. Geography had always
been of great interest to him: he understood the
concept of land and the fact that he who dominated
the land owned all that stood upon it. That was true
kingship, not this munshi's business of taxation and
levies and lagaans. *What good is calling a place your own
if you cannot walk the land and command the obedience of
those who live upon it!* his father had growled once at his
advisors, back when Ugrasena had been a warrior king,
not just an old man governing a dwindling domain.

Kamsa swayed slightly, light-headed and
disoriented. Jarasandha looked up at him and said
gently: 'My friend, you deserve some rest. You have
saved my hide for the third time in as many days.'

Kamsa shrugged self-deprecatingly. 'Someone has
to keep an eye on our future emperor.'

Jarasandha smiled his quiet smile. 'And you have
done that very well. So well, in fact, that I think it
is time for you to rest those tired eyes on something
more comely.'

Kamsa frowned, unable to fathom Jarasandha's
meaning.

Jarasandha clapped his hand on Kamsa's shoulder,
making him wince: he had been slashed there by a

passing spear. 'Come, let us leave my Magadhans to enjoy the spoils of war. It is time I showed you what we are fighting for.'

They rode away from the ransacked city, the orchestra of cries and screams dying away in the distance. Kamsa was too tired to even ask where they were going. He let his horse follow Jarasandha's, noting that except for the ever-present Hansa and Dimvaka, nobody else came with them. That was unusual in the extreme.

After three days of rough riding, they passed over a final rise and Jarasandha unfurled the vastra he had wrapped around his face, on his aides' advice, to protect his face as well as conceal his identity.

'Behold,' he said.

Kamsa stared at the city below. Incomplete though it was, little more than a skeleton partly fleshed and barely clothed, its epic ambition, architectural magnificence and sheer audacity was breathtaking. He had seen nothing like it, nor heard of such a city. Ayodhya, Mithila, all the mythical cities paled before the freshness and beauty of this wonder rising from the desolate wilderness. 'It is Swargaloka,' he said, dazed.

Jarasandha laughed and clapped him on his back. 'I call it Girivraja. It shall be the new capital city of the new Magadha. Centre of the world!'

They rode together through the wide avenues of the city, Kamsa marvelling at how precisely each broad road ran from north to south, east to west. He gazed up in wonder at the magnificent towers, the great mansions, the superbly carved facades, the sculpted pillars and arched windows ... the sheer opulence and luxury of the place. Every street was a beehive of activity. They passed workers carrying materials, hammering, sawing, cutting, chiselling, polishing, raising pillars, carving ...

'Vishwakarma himself must have designed it,' Kamsa said, referring to the architect of the devas. He had never seen such house designs or patterns before. It was like something out of a story about gods and heaven.

Jarasandha pointed out the hills rising around the city, upon each of which watchtowers were being built, connected by a great wall that ran around in an enormous circle. A forest of Lodhra trees overran the hills and the surrounding countryside, rendering the city near invisible unless one approached within a hundred yards of the tree-protected wall, while the towers could spy anyone approaching from a yojana away. The hills were named Vaihara, Varaha, Vrishava, Rishigiri and Chaitya and they were almost high enough to be considered mountains. Jarasandha explained that although this meant that once enemies broke through the walled cordon, they would be able to look down upon the city, the cleverness with which the architects had used the natural wood cover and rock formations afforded numerous defensive points for the city's guardians. And, of course, no enemy could ever come close enough in the first place.

Moreover, because the city was at the site of the ancient hermitage of Gautama, he of great fame, it was a highly auspicious location as well. 'After all,' Jarasandha grinned, 'even we half-castes do care about such things.'

Finally, they came to a hamlet nestled in the very centre of the city, with an artificial lake and the under-construction structure of a great palace overlooking the lake. Gardeners were already hard at work laying out sumptuous gardens around the complex. Here, the construction was busiest, and the richest materials in evidence.

They dismounted as Kamsa looked up at the richest palace he had ever seen. It made his father's palace look like the oversized cowshed it had once been.

'Home,' said Jarasandha, gesturing in a manner that suggested that it was as much Kamsa's as his own.

twenty-five

Kamsa was wonderstruck by the beauty of Jarasandha's palace and his rising capital city. The Magadhan had been right. It was one thing to be fighting a vicious war campaign for supremacy of the subcontinent and quite another to actually see some of the fruits of that labour already being polished and prepared for one's repast. After the brutality and relentless bloodshed of the battlefield, this was like coming home.

Kamsa wished he could pick up the entire palace and the city and carry it on his back all the way to distant Mathura. How the Yadavas would ogle and exclaim! Clansmen would come from hundreds of yojanas away to gape at the sight! The simple gowalas and govindas of the Yadava nations had no comprehension that such luxury and beauty could even exist, let alone be *possessed* by such men as they.

And here I am, Kamsa thought, *allied with the emperor of the civilized world.*

For he had no doubt that Jarasandha's campaign would succeed. Already, their victories were becoming legendary, their onslaught relentless and unopposed. Or, rather, they were opposed but feebly, futilely. No army could dare oppose the Jagannath-like progress of Jarasandha's great coalition. Even Kamsa had no idea how many akshohinis his friend and ally commanded; where the king of Magadha was concerned, truth and rumour mingled freely to produce that inseparable compound one could only call legend. All that was certain was that the juggernaut rolled on and, day by day, the greatest empire the world had ever seen was being stitched together like a patchwork quilt held tightly by Jarasandha's brilliantly conceived network of affiliations and alliances.

Many Arya kings had held rajasuya and ashwamedha yajnas, going forth with Brahminical rituals to lay claim to larger tracts and kingdoms. In time, they had lost all the ground they acquired when other Arya kings did the same. None had ever before had the foresight and political mastery to put together such a superb coalition of vested interests, each supporting the other in a seemingly impossible yet unquestionably sturdy web of solid structures. Kamsa had begun to realize that Jarasandha's brilliant plan might not just see him seated emperor but keep him on that hallowed throne for generations to come.

Political alliances are the bedrock, military victories the foundation, and the loyalty of the people the structure of a house, Jarasandha had said to Kamsa one night over a meal. *An emperor must have all three to stay an emperor.* He did not need to add: *And I do.*

In a sense, he mused as they reclined on welcoming, satin-cushioned seats and were served wine and fruit by comely servants, Jarasandha's campaign of conquest was being waged much the same way his magnificent new capital city was being built: brilliant architecture executed with painstaking craftsmanship and artistry, by loyal and dedicated workmen.

Kamsa's thoughts were diverted momentarily as two of the most beautiful women he had ever seen approached demurely, clad in luxuriant garments and jewellery that clearly set them apart from the palace staff. Assuming they were Jarasandha's wives or concubines, he averted his eyes. Though never one to shy away from ogling another's woman, he would never transgress upon the territory of this friend. For the first time in his life, Kamsa had a true friend, the first man he truly respected.

'Kamsa,' said Jarasandha, 'meet Asti and Prapti. They are the jewels of my heart.'

Kamsa murmured a rough greeting, sketching a polite namaskar. He was startled when the two women knelt beside him and began bathing his dusty, chapped and cut feet with warm, scented rosewater. 'What … what are you doing?' he asked.

They looked up at him with doe eyes, openly flirtatious, yet politely demure. 'Arghya, Mathura-naresh,' they said together in a single singsong chant. Then giggled.

Kamsa looked at Jarasandha for an explanation. Jarasandha grinned. 'My daughters speak as eloquently with their eyes as most women do with their tongues. Their eyes are saying that they like you very much. They would be pleased to have you as their husband.'

'H ... husband?' Kamsa had not stammered since he was a little boy. He sat upright, staring first at the two beautiful girls, then at his host.

'Yes, a legally wedded husband. I would be honoured if you would consent to accepting the hand of one of my daughters in marriage and becoming my son-in-law. Tell me, which one do you prefer?' Jarasandha frowned as he tried to evaluate his daughters' assets objectively. 'Prapti has the best child-bearing hips and lushest body. But Asti has the sweeter nature.' He shook his head. 'I dote equally on them both. It is impossible for me to choose. You must decide for yourself. Which one do you prefer?'

Kamsa swallowed nervously. Both women had finished the ceremonial washing of his feet and were awaiting his answer. He saw from their pointed glances that while immaculately mannered, they were not shy in the ways that counted. There was mischief in the warm brown eyes of the one with the riper body. And a promise of sweet nights in the other, more slender girl, who had cool grey eyes, reminiscent of her father's steely pupils. He bit his lip, trying to find the right thing to say without causing offence. 'Both are so beautiful ...' he said hesitantly, 'I cannot decide ...'

Jarasandha spread his hands. 'Then you shall marry both. So be it. It is decided. You are a man of large appetite; my daughters will be more content with one Kamsa than two of any other man. The wedding shall be organized tonight.' He clapped his hands, summoning Hansa who was only a few yards away. 'Make the arrangements.'

'Tonight?' asked Kamsa, astonished. This was all happening much too quickly for him to keep pace.

'We do have a war to wage,' Jarasandha said apologetically, peeling a grape with expert fingers. 'After we finish the first phase of our campaign, you shall have leave to enjoy the company of your new wives. I shall see to that myself. But for now, one night will have to suffice. We shall return to the front lines tomorrow morning. A good commander cannot leave his forces unsupervised for too long.'

The wedding was a blur of colour and pomp and pageantry. Despite the incompleteness of the city, Jarasandha was able to put on a display of royal extravagance more fantastic than Kamsa could ever have imagined. The night that followed was short, rituals and ceremonies taking up most of the moonlight hours. He barely had an hour alone with his new brides, although they wasted no time in making good use of it. He was yawning when he stepped out of his bedchamber to follow Dimvaka through the winding corridors the next morning at dawn.

At the wedding, Jarasandha had introduced Kamsa to his son Sahadeva. Kamsa had barely begun to wonder why, if Jarasandha had a son, he was not on the battlefield with them, when Jarasandha explained that the entire city they had seen, with all its beauty and splendour, was Sahadeva's doing. 'Some are warriors on the field,' the father said, 'others build empires out of wood and stone.' The implication was self-evident, but there was not a trace of irony or disappointment in Jarasandha's tone. He had clearly accepted his son's choice of vocation and was at peace with it.

Even so, Kamsa could not help feeling a surge of jealousy when he clasped hands with the handsome, almost girlish Sahadeva, whose hands were softer than any man's he had clasped before, hair curled in delicate twirls around his effeminate, not unattractive features. He had never known that Jarasandha had a son. Good that he was only an architect, a builder, and an artist, not a warrior.

In his heart and mind, Kamsa had come to think of himself as Jarasandha's true son. For the Magadhan was, in every sense, the father he had always desired and never had. The father he respected and loved, and who acknowledged and praised him in return.

I would give my life for him, he thought fiercely as they rode out from Girivraja the next morning. He loved the man he was following more than he had ever loved anyone or anything before. He had not protested or debated when Jarasandha asked him to marry his daughters who happened to be beautiful and everything a man could desire, but he would have done the same had they been wart-ridden and ugly in the extreme. Jarasandha had only to ask him to ride his horse off a cliff and he would do so without question, trusting that there would either be a river below to break his fall, or the sacrifice of his life was necessary for his friend's cause. No act was too gruesome, no sacrifice too great.

In the days and weeks that followed, his resolve was put to the test and only strengthened and tempered further, as steel is tempered by fire followed by ice over and over again until the layers of beaten metal bond permanently. Even Hansa and Dimvaka, perpetual protectors of the emperor and eternally by his side, were hard-pressed to match Kamsa's ability to spot and deflect assassins, attacks, murder attempts and outright assaults. No Kshatriya in the coalition fought as fiercely, no warrior risked as much, no leader achieved as many victories. As ruthless in carrying out as he was in deflecting assaults, Kamsa grew from the hot-headed Yadava prince who rode into Magadha to a finely tempered commander of men in battle. Mathura iron, never known for its temperance, now as solidly bonded as Mithila steel.

Finally, a day came when Jarasandha turned to him and said, 'It is time for you to go and stake your claim to your own domain.'

Kamsa knew at once what his father-in-law meant, but pretended he did not understand. 'This is my domain, by your side.'

Jarasandha slapped him lightly on the cheek, a gentle admonishment. 'You would be an emperor's lackey all your life? You are destined to be a king, and a king of your own domains. Remember what you asked for when you came to me. The reason why you formed this alliance, signed the accord. All the others have carved out the kingdoms they desired. Only you remain by my side. It is time for you to go home and command the Yadava nations.'

Kamsa hung his head unhappily. 'Let me stay a while longer.'

'If you stay a day longer, you will stay forever,' Jarasandha said gruffly. He cuffed Kamsa across the ear, too gently to hurt but firm enough to convey his insistence. 'Go. Show me your face again only when you have become lord of all Yadavas. Put all that I have taught you to good use. Make me proud.'

Kamsa left, his heart aching and feeling as if he were leaving home to go out into the wilderness, while, in fact, it was the other way around.

Jarasandha watched him go and said softly to Hansa and Dimvaka who flanked him as always: 'We have watered and nourished and nurtured enough. Now, let us see whether the seed we sow in Mathura shall bear sweet fruit or not.'

Kaand II

A peace accord is a piece of parchment sealed with wax and signets. A wedding is a union of families sealed with frolic, food, and love. Ministers and politicians preen and pose at the former and everyone tries to claim credit, even those who have not contributed at all. At a wedding, everybody has the time of their life and each person deserves equal credit.

Mathura roared, whistled, clapped and cheered as Vasudeva and his four brothers emerged with their new brides. The feasting and celebrations, spanning several days – weeks actually – had culminated today. Mathura herself resembled a bride. The city had played host to the Andhaka kingdom and to her siblings, the Sura and Bhoja nations as well. It had been too long since the Yadavas had known such unfettered joy, and they made the most of it. As passionate, boisterous, large-hearted people, they revelled in the feasting and in the relaxing of inhibitions. Released from the fetters of clan and inter-kingdom rivalry and violence, all Yadavas joined in with equal fervour, sharing food and wine and good humour as if this were the last celebration on earth and they the last revellers.

In the Andhaka pavilion, a host of richly garbed and bejewelled royalty joined its few hundred voices to the roar of the lakhs thronging the avenues, streets and by-lanes. The gathering was the kind that few had seen before in their lifetime. People were cheering from places as far away as Gokul – a tiny village where Vasudeva's dearest friends, Nanda and Yashoda, resided – for many in such outlying areas could not afford the expense and time spent on the long journey, nor leave their fields and kine unattended. Instead, they festooned the entire length of their tiny villages, and thus the Yadava nations, with their joy at the union.

Vasudeva's parents, Sura and Marisha, were looking radiant. His sisters were present too: Pritha (better known as Kunti – a name derived from her adoptive father Kuntibhoja's name), Srutadeva, Srutakirti, Srutasrava and Rajadhidevi. Vasudeva's brothers – Devabhaga, Devasrava, Anaka, Srinjaya, Syamaka, Kanka, Samika, Vatsaka and Vrika – were joyously celebrating the occasion since, along with Vasudeva, four of them had married Devaki's sisters – Kamsavati, Kanka, Surabhu and Rashthrapalika – which meant that the festivities and happiness were multiplied tenfold.

Apart from five daughters, Ugrasena had nine sons – Kamsa, Sunama, Nyagrodha, Kanka, Sanku, Suhu, Rashthrapala, Dhrishti and Tushthiman – of whom only Kamsa was missing. Kamsa's brothers were nothing like him in nature or outlook, and

Ugrasena had wisely given each of them a substantial state to govern independently, thereby keeping them away from the centre of power as well as apart from each other. With each brother a minor king in his own right, there was no petty rivalry to spoil their relationship. This meant that there was no acrimony soiling the gruff voices of elation that they were adding to the festive clamour with enthusiasm.

Ugrasena's brother Devaka had four sons: Devavan, Upadeva, Sudeva and Devavardhana; and seven daughters: Santideva, Upadeva, Srideva, Devarakshita, Sahadeva, Devaki and Shritadeva. Devaki's sisters surrounded her like diamonds clustered around a white solitaire, sharing their sibling's joy as well as flirting openly and outrageously with their brother-in-law, for among Yadavas, a sister's husband was second only to one's spouse.

Then there were the patriarchs and matriarchs of the Andhaka dynasty, a veritable genealogy in the flesh: Ahuka – Ugrasena and Devaka's father – and his ageing sister Ahuki were in attendance at the festivities. Ahuka and Ahuki's father Punarvasu was there, still standing proud and tall and with a great deal more darkness in his hair than white. Punarvasu's father – Ugrasena's great-grandfather – Avidyota, and his wife were present, and even the great patriarch of the nation, Anu, was present. That made for five generations of Andhakas all together in one place! At well over a century, Anu was too old to walk on his own, and was carried on a royal seat, cackling with delight, for he loved weddings almost as much as he loved his soma. Unfortunately, Andhaka himself – not he whose name now belonged to an entire nation, but the seventh descendant of that original Andhaka – had passed away only a few winters earlier. He was sorely missed, but a hundred-and-fifty years was a passable age to gain moksha, and his memory graced them all.

These, of course, were merely the immediate royal family, which, if you counted the spouses, children, and entourages, numbered several hundreds.

On the Sura side too, there were as many if not more. Families begat tribes which begat clans which begat nations, and there was not a soul in the three Yadava nations who did not know some relative, however distant, related to any stranger he happened to meet. Akrur even had a formula that he applied to each new person he met. He would ask them to recite their genealogy seven generations back, which usually covered living forebears, since all Aryas married young and became parents in their adolescent years with just a few rare exceptions. Before the litany of seven names could be completed, he would pounce on one he found familiar and excitedly point out his relationship to that forebear, finally tracing how the stranger and he were directly related. It turned out he was related to everyone at the wedding! He remained as enthusiastic even when Vasudeva gently pointed out that as Yadavas, one and all, ultimately they were all related to each other.

And the people ... Which kingdom does not relish a grand royal wedding? That too one that serves to cement the relationship between nations, and brings some much-missed peace? Even in the short months since the extraordinary incident at the army camp and Kamsa's subsequent disappearance, Mathura's air had started smelling of a garden in full bloom, with the former fetid stench of the dungeons fading out of most citizens' memories. Whatever doubts or hesitation anyone might have had were set aside for the duration of the wedding. The Sura wedding invitees who had arrived with Vasudeva as part of his wedding procession had grown so accustomed to Vrindavan's honey wine that it was all they drank night and day. In the quarters occupied by the wedding guests, the revelry had raged morn to night, then all night long.

It was with a great effort that Vasudeva himself succeeded in remaining relatively sober during this period. He alone could not easily forget how precious this occasion was, how hard-won this joy, and how each peal of laughter or whistle and cheer had been paid for with innocent blood.

Another issue that plagued his mind was the infuriatingly erratic but incessant flow of news from distant regions: news of a great war campaign being waged by the demoniac Jarasandha of Magadha and his many allies. Accurate news was hard to come by, for few survived or were able to flee this far to tell their tale, but from the fragments that had drifted this way, he had formed a rough outline of a terrible invasion in progress. It was made worse by the knowledge that Aryas were waging war against fellow Aryas on such a scale. Even the most tenuous accounts and rumours agreed on one thing: the scale of bloodshed was epic, the slaughter massive.

Vasudeva's brothers, his allies, the Council, all shook their heads and stroked their beards sadly and commiserated with the plight of fellow Aryas in those distant lands. But they also thanked the devas that *their* misery had ended so fortuitously with the departure of Kamsa and the success of the peace treaty enforced by Vasudeva. It did no good for Vasudeva to remind them that the storm that raged in their neighbour's yard could easily turn and ravage their own tomorrow; or that Kamsa had only gone away, not died a mortal death. Yadavas were positive in their outlook and never cared to dwell on the worst. People of the moment, they seized the day and every little joy it brought. It was the only way to gain some satisfaction and joy from an uncertain life.

But now, Vasudeva himself had succumbed to the enormous swell of sheer delight sweeping him along. How could he resist? What pomp, what splendour, what majesty! It was a wedding that would have honoured a god! His head swam to even count the many rich treasures he had been gifted, and his heart filled with pride that he had been able to afford the queen's dowry he had given the Andhakas in return. To quote Devaki's favourite phrase: Truly, today, they were both rich. They were rich in pleasure, love, goodwill, and in coin and kine!

Vasudeva savoured the warmth of the sun on his face, the fragrance of the blossoms, the colour and pageantry of the pavilion, the uplifting roar of the crowd and the delectable soma. Ahead was the uks cart, the uksan painted gaily as was the Vrishni custom, the driver seated and waiting to cart them away. It was time to go home and unlock the door to the future.

Vasudeva turned to his bride to assist her up the cart. Her face peeped out of the deep-red ochre wedding garments, bashful and demure, as if she had only just picked him out of a swayamvara line-up and was suddenly contemplating the implications of going home with an absolute stranger for a husband.

He winked at her, and she turned a deeper shade of red but winked back with a coyness that thrilled him. Ah, he would have children by this woman, a prodigious flock that they would raise together to be the joy of the Yadava world. Five, ten, a dozen bonny children! And that was the number *she* had spoken too, shyly, with eyes averted, but with a mischievous twinkle in them.

His bride safely ensconced upon the uks cart, Vasudeva sat beside her. The crowd achieved a new level of ecstasy as dhols, kettledrums, conch-shell trumpets and all kinds of musical instruments, vocal performance, and accompaniments – including the joyful baying of hounds, neighing of horses, lowing of kine, and trumpeting and foot-stamping of elephants – combined to create a deafening wave of sound that threatened to raise the cart and carry it all the way to his doorstep. He laughed till tears poured from his eyes in joy, and put a hand gently on the shoulder of the driver of the cart, speaking into the man's ear to tell him he could start the long, slow procession. It was customary for one of the bride's brothers to drive his sister and her groom home in order to extend the bride's familial connection as long as possible. He assumed that the man was one of Devaki's nine brothers; it hardly mattered which one.

The man turned his face to Vasudeva and, suddenly, it mattered a great deal.

The man driving the uks cart was none other than Kamsa himself.

two

Vasudeva's brothers, each seated with his bride in an identical uks cart drawn by painted uksan and driven by one of Devaki's brothers, shouted to him to get a move on. Vasudeva heard their voices as if from a great distance. His attention was focussed on Kamsa's face.

The prince of Mathura looked so different, he even tried to convince himself that it was one of Kamsa's *brothers*, not the man himself. But there was no mistaking that heavy brow, those almost colourless grey eyes, the jutting jaw and mien of menace. The face was sun-darkened, as were the burly arms gripping the reins; the body had filled out, grown more muscular, bulging powerfully beneath the incongruous, gaily coloured anga-vastra. There was something different about the man that went beyond just the physical muscularity. It was as if Kamsa had grown years in the few months he had been absent. Not that he had aged. If anything, he seemed more vital and vigorous. It was an overall drawing in of energies, a focussing of psychological and physiological strengths, a sharpening and a tightening.

It is, it is … Vasudeva groped to understand what he saw, even as his mind raced wildly through the myriad implications and possibilities that Kamsa's reappearance entailed … *it is*, he realized at last, *as if Kamsa had gone away into the wilderness alone, and had undergone a rite of passage that had made him a man.*

Yes. For the face that turned to look back at Vasudeva was not Kamsa the spoilt brat accustomed to having his own way in everything, or even Kamsa the brutal bully who viewed the entire Yadava world as his playground. It was the face of a man who had recently matured and grown into the full possession of his adult faculties.

Kamsa had left a boy, returned a man.

Vasudeva had no idea what this man intended, or what he might do. He could not read his eyes, his face, or fathom his inner spirit.

The question was, would the man act as the boy had done, or …

And in that *or* lay an infinity of possibilities.

Vasudeva felt a hand on his back, prodding him gently, insistently.

It was his bride, one hand holding her coverlet in place to maintain the custom of modesty, while urging him eagerly to start on the journey to her new home.

He swallowed and looked at Kamsa.

To his surprise, his brother-in-law merely smiled slyly and began driving the uksan forward. The crowd roared with delight, its excitement reaching an apogee as the princesses and their new husbands

clattered away on the carts. Children ran alongside
the carts, yelling, laughing; those too old to be out
on the streets watched, beaming, from their houses;
those on the streets cheered uproariously. The sound
of drums and music could be heard all across the city.
Beside him, Vasudeva heard his new bride laugh with
pleasure, an open-throated laughter that should have
gladdened his heart as well.

But all Vasudeva could think of was: *Kamsa is
back.*

What did he mean to do? Surely he wasn't going to
drive Devaki and him home like a good brother!

That would be too much to expect from *this*
brother-in-law.

No, Kamsa must have something in mind. Why
else would he have appeared unexpectedly, on their
very wedding day, and taken his place on the uks cart
as if he was just fulfilling his brotherly duty?

Vasudeva looked at the broad back. Kamsa had
changed so much that even the crowds did not
recognize the crown prince at first glance. Those who
noticed him at all assumed he was one of his brothers
– after all, there was a striking resemblance. Did the
external change reflect an inward one as well? What
were Kamsa's intentions?

Vasudeva did not have to wait long for the
answer.

Suddenly, a sound broke the din of cheering and
celebration – a sound that almost seemed to be part
of the overall cacophony at first.

It was the sound of a woman screaming.

It was joined by other screams, both male and female.

Slowly, the din in the great square began to die out as people realized that something was amiss.

As the cheering and yelling and whistling dwindled, the screaming grew more audible.

Then, even the music stopped.

And the terror began.

three

After leaving Jarasandha, Kamsa had not ridden directly to Mathura.

His new ally had promised him an army of his own when he returned, the better to help him take charge of his homeland and weed out the rebellious elements among his own forces. It was to collect this fighting unit that he had gone after taking leave of Jarasandha.

During the months they had fought together, Jarasandha had taught Kamsa a great deal about warfare, battle strategy, governance, dominion, and related matters. He had mentored Kamsa more effectively than any tutor had until then. Unlike the gurus Kamsa had had as a boy, Jarasandha's teachings were hard-won ground truths, ripped raw and bleeding from the reality of his life and adventures. Kamsa's own enthusiasm enabled him to learn more effectively. Instead of the sullen resentment or sneering indifference he had shown to earlier gurus, he received every mote of wisdom from Jarasandha with admiration and respect.

True education comes about through insightful *learning*, not from being *taught*. The greatest lessons are those gained through self-awareness and realization, not merely rote learning. This is especially true for a Kshatriya for whom practical knowledge was the most valuable and often made the difference between life and death, unlike the memory-testing scriptures that Brahmin acolytes were required to parrot almost from the time they could speak.

Kamsa had learnt his lessons well with the king of Magadha and among those lessons was the crucial insight that while any good leader could rule a kingdom, it took an extraordinary one to continue to rule it. His encounters with Vasudeva and the shocking failure he had experienced on both occasions had shown him the importance of relying on more than brute force to defeat his enemies. The news of his army's disbandment and the subsequent dissolution of the marauders made Kamsa realize the necessity of an elite unit that would serve him with absolute loyalty. His own countrymen and clansmen, while great fighters, were too independent minded. He needed a group of prime soldiers who would obey and serve him unquestioningly, unto death.

For this, Jarasandha had given him the Mohini Fauj: An army of eunuchs named after the avatar in which Vishnu the Preserver had taken the feminine form in order to deceive the Asuras.

Mohini – a woman who was in fact a man, and vice versa.

Mohini Fauj – a motley collection of boys taken from enemy camps and kingdoms during Jarasandha's many raids and invasions, clinically emasculated and trained into superb fighting units. The eunuchs had no nationality, no family, tribe, clan, faith or affiliation. They lived and fought purely for the honour of the Kshatriya code, and to serve their commander. Their only means of proving their self-worth was through fulfilling the wishes of their commander.

Jarasandha had raised a particular unit to obey Kamsa as their leader. For them, Kamsa was god incarnate, the ultimate being, one who could do no wrong. By implication, all those who opposed him were evil incarnate and must be destroyed. Their world was neatly divided into these two convenient compartments. Kamsa = Good. Kamsa's Enemies = Evil. As simple as that. They were indoctrinated so deeply that they could not comprehend any world view that challenged it. In short, it was simpler to kill them than to attempt to argue them out of their conviction that Kamsa was god.

And killing them was not simple at all.

The dregs of their communities, witness to the most horrific war crimes, abuse, atrocities, brutalities and every other variation of human cruelty, they had had every drop of humanity drained from them through a training regime designed by Jarasandha himself, a regime of such sustained, vicious and inestimable indoctrination that only the hardiest, most indestructible specimens could survive it. Those that did survive were deemed to have excelled, because survival against such odds as Jarasandha stacked against those pathetic eunuch-orphans *was* excellence in itself. They came out as lethal killing machines, superbly conditioned and honed to fighting prime, obeying only Kamsa, committed to destroying all others regardless of the risk to their own lives and well-being.

Jarasandha had demonstrated how his Mohinis could be ordered to maim themselves, commit suicidal actions and endanger the lives and limbs of their fellows at a single command. He had squandered several Mohinis just to demonstrate this fact. Those that survived with mutilated bodies or severed limbs had to be executed because a Mohini had to be utterly self-sufficient and ruthless to a fault. Even Kamsa was not privy to the training regime, or to the process of indoctrination, as these were personally supervised by Jarasandha and none but he possessed full knowledge of all the details and methods employed.

It did not matter. What mattered was that he had been handed a fighting force of such formidable power that no other force comparable in number could survive an encounter with his Mohinis. If anything, they could be put up against a force far superior in number, position, or means, and while they might not always triumph against impossible odds, they would cause such damage to the enemy as to render his victory hollow.

It was this Mohini Fauj that Kamsa had gone to collect from the remote wilderness camp where they were spending their days in endless training and preparation. Jarasandha had not permitted the Mohinis to be used in his own army, or to serve anyone else but Kamsa himself. At one point, Kamsa had wondered aloud about a situation in which he commanded them to wage battle against Jarasandha. Would the Mohinis comply? Would they remain loyal to him?

'You would cause me great losses,' Jarasandha replied, answering the question quite seriously and without taking offence. 'But eventually, your Mohini Fauj would be wiped out to the last individual.'

Kamsa had chuckled and said that if the Mohinis were able to get to Jarasandha himself before being cut down by superior numbers, it wouldn't matter if they were wiped out. After all, the ultimate goal was to kill the enemy's leader, was it not?

Jarasandha had smiled and said that Kamsa had a great deal to learn about warfare. Those were the initial days of their friendship.

'The purpose of war is not merely to kill one's opposing king or commander, it is to render that kingdom or force incapable of attacking you again. It's not enough to cut off the head, it's more important to sever the limbs and puncture the vital organs.'

Kamsa had frowned, not able to extrapolate the application of this anatomical metaphor to actual warfare. Jarasandha had shrugged, saying Kamsa would understand in time. 'But to answer your question about the Mohini Fauj,' the Magadhan said, 'they might succeed in causing me great losses before being cut down to the last man, but they would never succeed in harming me personally.'

Kamsa had chortled and suggested that Jarasandha was saying that because he couldn't concede that his forces could ever be defeated.

'No, my friend,' Jarasandha had said good-naturedly. 'I say that because while my Mohinis will indeed obey you unto death, they do so not because they are loyal to you, but because they are loyal to me. You see, they obey you *because I tell them to obey you*. They obey me *because they are trained to obey me*. That is a crucial point. If, by some unhappy mischance, you were to order them to attack my army, they would do so, but they would stop short of causing me any personal harm.'

Kamsa frowned and asked how that was possible if the Mohinis thought of him, Kamsa, as god incarnate.

Jarasandha smiled his calm smile and said, 'They think of you as god incarnate, but of me as god in person. You are my incarnation. I am god himself!'

It turned out that Jarasandha could name any man or woman as his avatar or amsa and the Mohinis would worship that person as their master thereafter. But Jarasandha himself always remained their true god and commander.

After that, Kamsa never asked any theoretical questions regarding the loyalty of the Mohini Fauj. He simply accepted the gift he had been given and used it as best as possible.

When he returned to Mathura, he had taken the Mohinis with him.

Now, he raised his whip and spun the lash, once, twice, a third time, giving his aides the predetermined signal to start the 'festivities'. It was time to let Mathura know that its crown prince was home.

four

A t first, Devaki could not comprehend what she saw.

The procession had just begun moving. She had even prodded Vasudeva impatiently to continue on their way. After days of ritual ceremonies and feasting and celebration, days and nights spent with more people than she had ever had around her in her life, she wanted nothing more than to be alone with Vasudeva.

My *husband*. The words warmed her heart, made it glow.

She was happier than she had ever been, looking forward to the rest of their life together. As the uks cart trundled forward, she laughed, raising her hands to wave gaily at the crowds, at the children running alongside, at her sisters in the carts following them...

That was when she saw the woman attack the soldiers.

Soldiers of both Ugrasena's and Vasudeva's armies were lining the avenues, ostensibly to keep the crowd back and clear a path for the wedding procession, but also to keep the peace. Fat chance of that with the populace wild with joy and venting years of pent-up energy on this tumultuous event.

Most of the soldiers wore a festive look, with the citizens having smeared coloured powder on their faces as well as each other's, and made no attempt to curb their smiles. Both armies mingled freely, chatting, exchanging views on the wedding, the food, the grand arrangement, boasting of which wedding party had celebrated the most, consumed the most honey wine, eaten the most sweets – basically behaving like brides' and grooms' relatives at a wedding feast.

Devaki's gaze happened to fall upon a woman approaching two soldiers from behind. The woman in question was dressed in garb as gaily coloured as the rest of the crowd, but it was the way she moved that caught Devaki's attention. She had a litheness about her that was almost like a dancer about to perform an acrobatic step.

As Devaki watched – half her attention diverted towards bestowing her brightest smiles upon the throng, her hands flailing to acknowledge and return the cheers of the ecstatic crowd – she saw the woman raise her hands. Something she held in each hand flashed brightly in the morning sunlight. Something metallic and highly burnished, with sharp edges. The objects flashed as the woman moved her arms with great grace and speed, and the two smiling soldiers abruptly lost their smiles and collapsed where they stood.

The next moment, the woman was lost in the crowd. But not before Devaki saw the things she held in her hands rise again to catch the sunlight. This time they did not flash *as* brightly, for they were covered with something dark and reddish. But she knew at once what they were. Blades. The woman had just killed those two soldiers, cutting them down from behind like sheaves of wheat.

Devaki caught another glimpse of flashing steel elsewhere and turned her head.

She saw another woman hacking down another soldier, then a second, then a third, and yet another. This other woman too moved with a fluid, effortless grace that was no less than any classical dancer, swirling, flowing, slashing … She swung and soldiers died.

Suddenly, there were flashes of steel everywhere as far as she could see, winking in the sunlight, visible even through the dense, colourful crowd.

Flashes of steel.

And splatters of red.

Then the screams began. First a single woman, as she stumbled over a dead soldier and reacted instinctively.

Then several more as they found other dead soldiers.

Then the puzzled shouts of men as they found corpses too, or glimpsed other soldiers being killed.

Slowly, the din and cacophony of celebration died down, even the music faltering, then halting, then dying out altogether.

Suddenly, a terrible silence fell.

In those few moments, Devaki heard the sounds of slaughter: The liquid thud of knives hacking through flesh and bone. The choked death grunts of dying soldiers. The swishing and tinkling of garments as the female killers went about their deadly work, incongruously clad in festive garb.

Then a new cry rose from the crowd.

'Assassins!'

At once, a new mood swept the enormous collective. A mob is like a body of water. Spill fragrant essence into it and it will turn lavender and aromatic; spill offal and it will soon be covered with a layer of scum and reek. The same crowd that was ecstatic with joy only moments ago, was now terrified.

Soldiers were dying across the city by the hundreds. Andhaka as well as Sura soldiers. The soldiers killed were only a fraction of the whole force, but the vast number of soldiers untouched by the violence could barely comprehend what was happening, let alone identify the ones responsible.

For one thing, the killers were women, clad like normal Mathura women, and therefore virtually indistinguishable from the rest of the crowd. They killed, then hid their weapons beneath their voluminous garments and moved to their next target, working with chilling efficacy and ruthlessness. Nothing the soldiers had experienced had prepared them for such attackers. How could they fight the enemy when they could barely tell them apart from the tens of thousands of ordinary female citizens?

For another thing, the crowd was drunk on celebration and joy; emotions ran sky-high, and the moment the killing began, people overreacted. Some began attempting to flee, causing stampedes. Others tried to apprehend the killers and, in the process, got themselves killed, or grabbed the wrong women in their haste. Chaos broke out. The only ones who benefited from the chaos were the killers themselves. Moving through the crowds, killing at will, they reaped a terrible harvest. Safe on the uks cart, Devaki saw blood and slaughter and stampedes all around. She saw children run down by panicked crowds attempting to flee. She saw soldiers draw their weapons and hack blindly at the crowds around them, confused and angry at their comrades' death. She saw citizens take hold of the assassins, only to be hacked down brutally in a moment. The celebration had turned into a slaughter. The wedding procession into a funeral procession. The cheers and whistles and cries of joy turned to screams of terror and howls of agony.

Devaki clutched Vasudeva's anga-vastra and yelled to make herself heard over the din. 'Do something, My Lord! Stop this madness!'

But Vasudeva did nothing. He only sat there, watching the terror spread like wildfire.

She gaped, unable to understand why her husband wasn't doing anything to stop the madness, or at least shouting to control the crowd. She could see the look of horror on his face, the shocked gaze which meant that he was registering everything that was going on. 'Vasudeva!' she cried.

He turned to her, slowly. She was moved by the infinite sadness in his gaze. As always, his face made her feel that she was looking upon some exalted force.

He stared at her silently for a moment, then lowered his eyes in sadness.

'My Lord,' she sobbed. 'Your people are dying!'

She realized her mistake and corrected herself: '*Our* people are dying!'

He did not respond in words. Only raised his eyes sadly again, looking over his shoulder at her brother at the head of the cart.

Frowning, she looked in the same direction.

She recognized him, somewhat darker and more leathery, the body more muscular and manly, but it was him.

Finally, comprehension dawned that it was *he* who was driving the cart.

And suddenly, she knew why Vasudeva was not doing anything. Why he *could not* do anything; why her wedding day had turned into a nightmare.

'Greetings, sister dearest,' said Kamsa, grinning amiably. 'Allow me to offer my heartiest congratulations on your nuptials … and commiseration, for you will not live to enjoy a long and happily married life.'

five

Kamsa was thrilled at how easily his plan had been put to action.

Along with Bana and Canura, he had hatched the idea of infiltrating the city and striking when Mathura was most vulnerable: during the royal wedding. With the kingdom in the grip of wedding revels, and visitors arriving by the tens of thousands from all corners, it had been easy for him to enter the city. Procuring suitable garb had posed no great challenge either, with the markets filled with traders and craftsmen from all across the Yadava nations offering wares and services for sale. Not that he had needed to purchase anything; his forces had simply taken what they wished, but they had been cautious enough not to do anything that would attract too much attention. Once they had secured the appropriate garb from houses lying empty – the inhabitants busy carousing during the wedding feasts – his Mohinis had mingled with the crowds and awaited the start of the procession.

As for Kamsa taking his place on the uks cart, it had been simplicity itself. He had just kept enough of his face concealed by his head-cloth to confuse the guards into assuming that he was one of his many brothers and clambered aboard. His brothers never suspected because once they saw him seated on the leading cart, they assumed he was this or the other. They were merry in their cups as well by then, after all.

His greatest advantage lay in the fact that no one expected him to be at the wedding. It was inconceivable that he would appear at such a time, that too in so surreptitious a manner. It had never been his way. The Kamsa of yore, the younger, brasher Kamsa, would have simply charged in: galloping, roaring with fury and hacking down or riding down anyone who obstructed his path. These devious subtleties were Jarasandha's teachings bearing fruit.

Once the procession had begun to move, he had given Bana and Canura the signal to direct the Mohinis to get to work; and they did so with the same ruthless ease with which he had watched them hack down enemy warriors during the training skirmishes Jarasandha had set up for his viewing pleasure. The sheer tumultuous chaos of the wedding, the enormous crowds, the emotional fever-pitch, and the silent, *deadly* smoothness with which his Mohinis moved through the city, killing Mathura and Sura soldiers alike, thrilled him. It was almost artistic in its speed, precision and acrobatic beauty.

There, a Mohini slashed her blade under the guard of a Mathura soldier, pirouetted, then pierced the abdomen of a Sura soldier who was rushing at her in a blind rage; then swished around in a third spin, her swords disappearing into the folds of her garment. The next instant, she was lost in the crowd, head lowered, working her way discreetly to her next target as the horde of horrified witnesses around her tried to make sense of what had happened.

Here, a small band of soldiers formed a protective cordon around his cart – putting their bodies and their lives at stake for the royal couple they sought to protect – as a Mohini came sprinting from their flank, ducked under their slow, defensively raised lances, and slashed briefly but with killing perfection at each of them in turn, not killing at once, but mortally wounding. The entire cordon collapsed as one man, bleeding to death in agony as the uksan, unable to stop in time, stomped over their prone bodies, and the wheels of the cart lurched and heaved as they crushed the dying men underneath.

Everywhere, the same dance of death was being performed.

Kamsa glanced back at his sister, gratified at the expression on her face and on that of Vasudeva's as well.

'Well, sister, how do you like my wedding gift?'

Devaki's face stared back at him. 'Wedding … *gift?*' she repeated, uncomprehending.

Kamsa gestured broadly, indicating the city, the crowds, the screams, the chaos, the dancing Mohinis slaughtering hapless Yadava soldiers by the dozens, the hundreds, the stampedes, the terror – the madness and beauty of the whole scene. 'A great performance, is it not? Have you seen such artistry from our classical danseuses? I think not. I trust you are pleased with this great demonstration.'

'Abomination!' she spat, recovering her senses. 'How could you do such a thing? During your own family's celebrations?'

Kamsa laughed. '*My* family's celebrations?' He clucked his tongue at the uksan, guiding them past a pile of writhing bodies left in the wake of a stampeding horde; most of them were very young children. He ignored the pitiful cries of those left broken and bleeding in the pile. 'No, Sister. You confuse politics with family. This is merely part of the Sura plot to take control of Mathura. You are merely a bonus!'

Devaki made a sound of despair. 'Stop it at once, Kamsa. Call off your mad dogs! Stop this mindless killing.' Tears spilled from her eyes, causing her kohl to streak. 'I beg of you, Brother. Lay down your arms. This is an occasion of peace and brotherhood!'

Kamsa grinned at her. 'You have been thoroughly brainwashed, Sister. I am merely doing now what our enemies would have done very soon to us anyway.'

Vasudeva spoke up, cautious but unafraid. 'You are killing your own Kshatriyas as well as mine, Kamsa. Are they your enemies as well?'

Kamsa shrugged, avoiding looking directly at Vasudeva just yet. 'They are either *with* us or *against* us. By standing with *your* men, they show themselves to be *your* men. Therefore they must be put down. I intend to clean out the rot from Mathura completely this time. Oftentimes, to save a healthy body one must sever an infected limb. I fear that my kingdom's military is badly in need of overhauling.' He lashed the whip at a foolish woman joining her hands together and begging the lords on the cart to help save her dying sons. 'It is time we brought some fresh blood into Mathura. And now is as good a time as any.'

Everywhere he looked, he was pleased to see the plan proceeding perfectly. Yadava soldiers were no match for the ruthless efficiency of his Mohini Fauj and were falling like flies. Within seconds, he would be clear of this crowded avenue and proceed to the next part of his plan, which was to—

Kamsa!

He dropped the whip. His head pounded with excruciating agony. '*Guru!*' he cried involuntarily, calling out for Jarasandha as he often had during the preceding weeks when in situations of extreme risk or pain, appealing to the only man who had ever treated him as a father ought to treat a son, the only real teacher, master, preceptor he had ever acknowledged as worthy of commanding his attention.

Jarasandha cannot help you. This is your bane to break. And break it you must. Or it will break you!

'WHAT ARE YOU BABBLING ABOUT?' he cried, not caring that he was shrieking the words aloud, or that both Devaki and Vasudeva were exchanging glances and staring at him, as were several of those in the crowd who were not too preoccupied to recognize the altered but still recognizable face of their crown prince.

Devaki, your sister, will bear the male child that will be your undoing. Kill her now, or she will grow the seed of your destruction within her womb.

Kamsa writhed in agony. On the earlier occasions that Narada had spoken to him, in his mind as well as in spectral form in the forest, there had been only a gnashing sensation, like a deep rumbling of thunder too close to his head for comfort. But this time, it was as if the thunder was inside his head, crashing and resounding across the battered walls of his brain. '*I … am taking control … of my destiny …*' he said, panting when he finished the brief statement. It was a statement he had learnt from Jarasandha. This part of his plan was aimed at taking control of his own destiny instead of waiting for it to be handed to him the way he had waited all his life. He had a plan, a beautiful, perfect plan. And the first part of the plan was going masterfully. 'My Mohini Fauj …'

Your Mohini Fauj will not save you from the One who approaches. Once He sets foot upon this mortal plane, none will succeed in opposing Him. Not even your great guru. The only way to protect yourself from Him is to kill the woman who will bear His mortal avatar in this lifetime. Kill Devaki.

'*But* …' Kamsa said, unaware that he was rocking from side to side like a drunkard in the seat of the uks cart, or that even his Mohinis had stopped their slaughter to stare at him in consternation. Bana and Canura were watching him as well, open-mouthed with astonishment.

With a mighty effort, he raised himself up and roared to the skies. 'WHAT CAN A SINGLE MORTAL CHILD DO TO ME? WHO IS HE? I FEAR NO MAN! I AM KAMSA!'

Silence fell across the avenue as all stopped to listen and stare. Into that silence, Kamsa heard the voice of the bodiless one speak like thunder out of the clear sky, and this time, not just he but everyone around him heard the words as well: as clear as a peal of booming thunder on the heels of a rage of lightning.

He is Hari incarnate. Vishnu reborn. If you are Kamsa the Great, then he is the Slayer of Kamsa!

six

Devaki cried out as Kamsa grabbed her by her hair and dragged her to her feet.

Vasudeva stood as well, the uks cart shuddering under the shifting weight of the three of them, but was careful not to make any sudden or threatening movements. It was obvious to him that Kamsa was a man already far beyond the verge of madness. If he had doubted it before, he knew it for certain now. The last several minutes, spent watching Kamsa debate and rage against an invisible voice, was not the reason Vasudeva doubted Kamsa's sanity. He too had heard the voice speak, had heard its brain-crushing thunder and felt its formidable menace. It was not that reaction that made him question his brother-in-law's mental stability. It was something else, something much deeper, more subtle, something he had glimpsed even on that day in the convocation hall when Kamsa threw the barbed spear at him ... But there was no time to dwell on such subtleties now.

Kamsa held Devaki up by her hair like a rag doll. She screamed and wept copiously – not because of fear, but due to her shame at being treated thus.

Devaki was a strong woman, brought up in the Arya tradition that regarded women as the true leaders of their clans. To be treated in this fashion by *any* person was inconceivable, let alone by one's own brother on the day of one's espousal.

Kamsa seemed to care nothing for the humiliation or pain he was causing his sister. His eyes were wide, the whites showing all around, the pupils mere pinpricks, face engorged and red with blood, a vein pulsing in his temple, the muscles and tendons of his powerfully muscled neck, shoulders, arms and chest bulging and straining as he held his sister up high, as if displaying her to the world.

Everywhere – across the great square and the avenues approaching it, on rooftops and windows, casements and verandahs, from the palace and from the streets – horrified eyes watched the drama unfold. Even the Mohinis, swords dripping blood, had paused in their slaughter to wonder at what was about to happen. The dying and the wounded groaned and cried out, unattended, as every citizen – shaken to the core by the shock of the brutal assaults, and now by the bestial behaviour of the crown prince – gaped at the dreadful tableau unfolding on the cart at the helm of the procession.

'This woman?' Kamsa bellowed, his voice carrying like a lion's throaty roar across the square. 'This woman would be the cause of my destruction? My own sister?'

His voice revealed his outrage and hurt. It was

difficult to believe that a man like Kamsa could be hurt emotionally; but, of course, he was no less vulnerable to the arrows and barbs of human pain than any person. If anything, Kamsa was more sensitive than most, imagining slights where none had been intended, humiliation where none existed. As a young boy, he had spent many hours and days brooding over things his companions or playmates had mentioned casually or in play, refusing to rejoin their games or pastimes, often venting his anger on his pets, horses, kine and servants until he was old enough to take out his anger upon those who caused him these hurts, gradually working his way up the scale until the day he had flung his old tutor out of a palace window to his death. He harboured a self-righteous sense of outrage about his temper fugues, an air of being treated unfairly by an unjust and biased world. And never was it so evident as now. Even after his many atrocities and brutalities – after he had crept deviously into his own kingdom's capital on the very day of his sister's nuptials, wreaking havoc and causing mayhem all around – here he was, eyes brimming with tears of indignation, holding up his blood-kin as if she was something less than human, heartbroken at her betrayal! Thus are the wicked utterly convinced of their own righteousness, and thus are those who believe themselves the most upright often the least capable of upholding their own lofty principles.

'Kamsa,' Vasudeva said gently, careful not to provoke him further by action or vocal inflection.

'Devaki means you no harm. She loves you as you are her brother. Look at her. See for yourself. She is a woman unarmed and intending no violence.'

Kamsa turned his mask of fury upon Vasudeva, and it took all of the Sura king's self-control to keep himself from flinching. It was indeed like looking upon a mask rather than a man's face, so distorted and bloated by fear and hate was Kamsa's visage.

'Are you in your senses, Vrishni? Did you not hear the saptarishi's words? She will bear the child that will destroy me! Her womb will carry my slayer into this mortal realm.'

Vasudeva kept his head lowered, deliberately crouching a little to keep his considerable height below Kamsa's eye level, his own eyes cast downwards rather than looking directly into Kamsa's. He was keenly aware of how tightly Kamsa's hand was wound around Devaki's hair, and of the drawn sword in Kamsa's other hand that needed only an instant to strike a death blow.

'But she is just newly wedded to me, barely just a wife, let alone a mother. How can there be any child in her womb? Do you think she and I would violate the sanctity of our customs and traditions thus? Never! Whatever the voice may say, Devaki does not bear you any harm, nor does she bear any child that could possibly harm you!'

Kamsa was in no mood to listen. He turned his flashing eyes towards Devaki again, the poor woman squirming and writhing in pain, for Kamsa had her in a grip that not only held her up by the roots of her hair but also twisted her neck and torso agonizingly.

Vasudeva saw that were Kamsa simply to wrench his hand in a certain action, he would break Devaki's spine and neck as easily as one might snap a dry twig by twisting it suddenly. Given his musculature and strength, the sword was redundant; Kamsa was capable of killing Devaki with barely a wrench of his wrist.

The crown prince of Mathura heaved and said in a tone of infinite suffering: 'What you say matters not, Vasudeva. *She* is the one who will some day bear the instrument of my death. The only way to protect myself is to kill her now, before she slips out of my grasp and fulfils her destiny. I was warned *now*. There must be good reason why I was instructed thus at this point in time and not tomorrow or ten years from the morrow. I must obey.'

Kamsa raised his sword with the ease of an accomplished warrior, tossing it up in the air and catching it easily. He then gripped it in his right hand, with the point inwards, like a dagger. His massive back muscles clenched as he brought both arms closer to each other in a pincer-like action, the sword now poised directly above the weeping Devaki's breast. She stared up in misery at the weapon of her annihilation, crying out for mercy. Vasudeva felt his whole world tremble on the brink of an abyss. It was impossible to believe that only a short while ago, his new bride and he had been about to embark on the first journey of their newly wed lives. What evil twist of fate had turned their joy into terror so abruptly?

He knew that being subservient and obsequious would not serve any longer. He must penetrate the veil of conviction that Kamsa had wrapped around himself. And he must do it at once. Otherwise, the sword would pierce the breast of the woman he loved and his world would lie bleeding upon the uks cart.

Vasudeva raised his head, drawing himself to his full stature, speaking in his normal voice. Despite his gentle nature and love of all living beings, he was a chieftain, a general, a king among men. He spoke now, not as a gowala, a cowherd, a husband or even a brother-in-law. Simply as a king. His voice rang out clearly across the sea of stunned faces filling the square.

'So you serve a *voice* then? *That* is Kamsa's lord and master? A disembodied voice that only *you* can hear and which speaks inside your head?'

He did not curb the scorn in his tone, the natural cynicism in the phrasing. He sought now not to appease but to provoke, to draw ire upon himself. Words were his only arrows, his voice the only bow.

Kamsa's back tensed, his arms flexed. Almost without realizing it, the arm holding the twisted mass of Devaki's hair in its fist loosened a little. Not enough for Vasudeva's wife to be free, but just enough to give her a moment's relief. She gasped, hitching in her breath and hope. Kamsa turned to look at Vasudeva, head lowered on his powerful neck, eyes glowering like those of the wound-maddened boar deep in the Vrindavan forest. Vasudeva still bore the scar of that boar's left tusk on his calf where the beast had cut open a gash. He had never forgotten the malevolence with which the boar had watched him from the leafy depths of the undergrowth, challenging the two-legged intruder to face him in his domain. Vasudeva had been seven years of age. He had killed the boar, but not because it had wounded him; he killed it because it had killed three other children and two grown men and had become a menace to their village.

Kamsa's eyes glowered in the darkness of his own face. He raised the sword, fingers deftly manoeuvring the blade till it was once again held in a forward grip. Now the point was aimed directly at Vasudeva's right eye.

'I serve no master. I have no lord. I am Kamsa,' he said, the words exploding from his heaving lungs and bursting from his mouth with frothy spittle. 'You dare call me a slave?'

Vasudeva had done no such thing, but that was Kamsa's way – to exaggerate everything in order to emphasize how unjust and unfair the other person, or the world, or the universe at large was to him, Kamsa. Because, of course, he, Kamsa, was the centre of all creation.

Vasudeva stood up to that gaze, meeting Kamsa's fevered eyes without blinking. He used Kamsa's own paranoia against the man. 'A voice speaks, you obey. If you are not its slave, why do you obey? How do you even *know* whether what the voice tells you is true?'

'Because it has spoken before, and what it said came to pass!' Kamsa said, still holding the sword pointed at Vasudeva. 'I have no time to bandy words with you, Sura. The voice has told me that this woman will be the cause of my destruction. I believe it. I do not care if you believe or not. I will kill her to protect myself.'

'And be known as a woman yourself!' Vasudeva's voice rang out loud and clear.

Kamsa stared at him.

'You command an army of womanly warriors.' Vasudeva gestured at the Mohinis. 'You raise your sword against an unarmed woman, your own sister, no less. What will itihasa say about you in times to come? It will say that Kamsa was a woman among men, a eunuch who recruited others of his kind, who did not dare to face warriors with weapons; he chose only to kill by stealth, deception, and attack defenceless women of his own house!' Vasudeva raised his hand now, pointing his finger at Kamsa. The tip of the finger barely inches from the tip of the sword. 'You will be known as a craven without dharma or honour.'

Kamsa roared with fury, bristling with such rage that he was momentarily rendered speechless.

Vasudeva moved closer, into the arc of the upraised sword, close enough for the edge of the blade to be almost touching his own neck, the blade itself poised over his shoulder. He looked directly into Kamsa's eyes, challenging him openly. 'Too craven to fight *me* as a man.'

Mathura held its breath as Vasudeva stood before Kamsa, his neck bared to the edge of Kamsa's sword. One sideways cut of that muscular arm and the blade would bite into Vasudeva's neck and sever his most vital vein. The Sura king had no defence, nor a weapon of his own to counter Kamsa's. He faced certain, instant death.

Yet, Vasudeva stood ramrod straight, eyes unblinking, face fearless and set in the equanimous manner of a warrior who faced death daily and accepted its inevitability. For Vasudeva was a true warrior, not a mercenary thug like Kamsa who fought for personal gain and selfish motives, but a Kshatriya of the highest order, serving only the cause of dharma. Not just a *soldier* of dharma, a *sword* of dharma. And what does one sword have to fear from another?

It was Kamsa's hand that shook. It began as a tremulous quiver, just a single ripple of his etched-out muscles, as if the sword had grown too heavy for him to hold straight. Then the entire arm began to shudder and shake, and then the elbow bent at the crook and the sword descended, falling out of Kamsa's numb grip to clatter on the wooden planks of the uks cart.

The rest of him shuddered as well, a quaking of his entire body that bent him over double, bringing him to his knees in a posture curiously like supplication. His other hand, grown as numb as the first, released his sister involuntarily, and she fell, gasping with relief, on the cart. Kamsa shook and shivered like a man in the grip of a malarial fever, and from his mouth came a trickle of drool … and a single word …

None but Vasudeva heard that word.

Then, Kamsa buried his head in his own lap, his arms held out by his sides, twitching of their own accord. To all those watching, it seemed as if he had surrendered to Vasudeva, and was now repentant for his sins. It was a profound moment for all those who witnessed it. A moment of great clarity. For in that moment, every Yadava knew the truth: Whether by divine miracle or by dint of superhuman power, Vasudeva could not be defeated by Kamsa in single combat. This was the third and final encounter between the two men, and even the most sceptical supporter of Kamsa or hater of the Suras and Vrishnis could no longer deny the stark evidence of their senses. Kamsa could not kill or harm Vasudeva. 'Not so much as a hair on his head,' people would say with pride and wonder afterwards.

Vasudeva looked to his bride. Devaki lay crumpled in a heap, crying a little but mostly just in shock from the violence of the episode and the proximity to death. Vasudeva gently cradled her in his arms. She looked up at him and, while she said nothing, her light-brown eyes – the colour of freshly threshed wheat from a good harvest – spoke eloquently. His own eyes read them easily. He knew that she was telling him that he should have killed Kamsa much before this day; that her brother was a monster, a demon, a rakshasa among men, and deserved no more than to be put down like one. She was pleading with him to do so even now. Her eyes cut away from him, seeking out and finding the sword that Kamsa had dropped, and which now lay only a foot or two from Vasudeva. She looked at the sword then raised her eyes to him, then looked pointedly at Kamsa. Words could hardly have expressed it any more clearly.

Vasudeva's heart filled with a great sorrow. He knew that Devaki was right. Pacifist though he was, he was no fool. Had Kamsa never returned to Mathura, there would have been no need for Vasudeva to go after him and seek his destruction. But now that he had returned, making his intentions so clear to one and all, celebrating his return with a chilling dance of blood and death, laying violent hands upon his own sister, Vasudeva's wife, he was no more a potential threat. He was a tangible enemy.

And the voice. It had said that Devaki would bear the child that would kill Kamsa. Vasudeva had heard it, even if Devaki had not. He had also heard Kamsa's utter conviction that everything the voice said to him was true. He had called it 'saptarishi' and who was to say that it was *not* a saptarishi speaking to him from some ethereal plane? Far stranger things had occurred in Aryavarta of yore. What mattered was that Kamsa believed the voice and it had pronounced that Devaki's son would prove to be the death knell for Kamsa. Now, Kamsa would kill Devaki; or, if he didn't wish to see his wife murdered in cold blood, Vasudeva would have to kill Kamsa.

Devaki looked up at Vasudeva, waiting.

When Vasudeva made no move, she took the initiative. Reaching out, she picked up the sword and turned it around, inverting it so that the hilt faced Vasudeva, and offered it to him.

As soon as she did this, the watching crowd broke out of its stupor.

First one citizen shouted hoarsely: 'Aye!'

Just that single word, so clear yet terrible in its surety.

Then: 'Kill him!' This from the woman who had begged Kamsa for mercy and aid before he stopped the uks cart.

'Kill the prince!' cried another. A chorus of ayes followed this one.

Then a young boy's voice called out: 'Lord Vasudeva, save us!'

And the dam broke.

With one voice, the entire populace shouted for Vasudeva to kill Kamsa, to slay their crown prince, to destroy the monster, put down the rakshasa, kill, slaughter, murder, finish.

Vasudeva looked around, not sure whether to be pleased or saddened. Pleased, for it was evident how dearly the people loved him. Sad, because it was their own crown prince they wanted killed. He gazed at the sea of upturned faces, shouting mouths and pumping fists.

Amongst the crowd, he could see Kamsa's mercenaries, confounded by the developments of the past several minutes and unable to decide what to do next. At least the killing had stopped for the time being. He also noticed the soldiers of both Andhaka and Sura colours moving in discreetly to ring Kamsa's warriors. He saw Kamsa's allies and aides, Bana and Canura, looking around in dismay as they took in the obvious fury of the crowd. It was one thing to infiltrate a happy and celebratory crowd of wedding voyeurs and take them by surprise and quite another to stand in the thick of a raging mob that knew exactly who you were and wanted you dead. Right now, the people's attention was on Kamsa. The moment Kamsa was slain, they would look around to seek out his soldiers and, judging by the intensity of their anger, they would flay them alive for the deaths they had caused today.

Vasudeva raised a hand, requesting silence. The din faded, reluctantly but respectfully, and he was able to speak.

'I know you desire this, and I do not say it would be wrong. What Kamsa has done today is sufficient to condemn him forever. Even so, I cannot take his life summarily.'

Querulous cries of outrage rose from all around. Vasudeva raised a hand again.

'I signed a pact of peace with your king not long ago. Regardless of how many times and in how many ways your own prince and your own soldiers – his erstwhile marauders – may have broken that pact, *I* cannot do so. I will not do so. I have upheld the sacred accord signed and sealed between me and your king Ugrasena all these many days, and I shall do so even today. Kamsa shall be taken to your king to be judged by him and brought to justice as your king sees fit. It is King Ugrasena's prerogative, not mine, to judge him and punish him with whatever danda he sees fit.'

Out of the corner of his eye, Vasudeva glimpsed Bana and Canura sidling away backwards, seeking to make good their escape.

Raising a hand, he pointed directly at them, drawing everyone's attention to them. Both men froze, aware of the hundreds of pairs of eyes upon them now: angry, vengeful eyes.

'However, the men Kamsa brought with him today – the ones who butchered so many innocent bystanders and honourable soldiers as they stood at their posts – these men are outsiders and I, being the king of the Sura nation as well as the co-protector of the Andhaka nation, have as much power to pronounce judgement upon them as King Ugrasena. Seeing the grave threat their freedom poses to each of us gathered here, I deem it fit to try them here, try them *now*, and stop them from carrying out their vile plans.' He paused, raising the sword to point directly at Bana and Canura. 'Apprehend them at once, dead or alive.'

With a terrible roar, the crowd moved to do his bidding. The Mohinis, unable to understand the dialect of Mathura or the Yadava tongue fluently, were unable to comprehend Vasudeva's words. However, they sensed that something was amiss, and several were ready to act. But this time, they were hemmed in tightly. It was difficult to pirouette and spin and dance acrobatically with flailing swords when one had barely a foot of room to stand in. The crowd converged on them like a pond swallowing pebbles, and while several succeeded in causing more deaths and wounds before succumbing, they all went down without exception.

Vasudeva watched grimly as the crowd meted out the punishment they felt Kamsa deserved upon the mercenaries who had done his bidding.

'Is it just?' Devaki asked him. 'To condemn ordinary soldiers, even mercenaries, to death thus? While sparing my brother simply because he is a prince? Is this not unfair and unequal treatment? Are not all men to be treated equally under dharma in Arya law, in your own words?'

Vasudeva nodded. 'I do not spare Kamsa because he is a prince. I spare him because he is an Andhaka, and I have signed a pact that states that I will not kill any Andhaka.' He pointed at the crowd, slaughtering the assassins one by one. 'Those men – or whatever they are – may be equal under dharma. But they are not Andhakas.'

Devaki caught his arm, pressing herself against his side so she might whisper into his ear. 'If you will not do it, let me,' she said. 'Give me the sword; I shall kill him. We cannot let him live.'

Vasudeva caught her hand gently before it could take hold of the sword and take it from his hand. 'We must let him live and let your father judge him under law. Or we would be just as demoniacal as he.'

She looked up at him, and in her eyes he saw her acceptance but also her anxiety.

eight

King Ugrasena's court was filled to bursting. There was barely room to stand. Hundreds more waited outside the sabha hall and the palace grounds and the streets outside were packed as well. The entire kingdom waited to hear the outcome of Kamsa's trial.

A flurry of excitement rippled through the crowd as King Ugrasena entered from a private entrance and took his place upon the royal dais. Queen Padmavati was by his side. Vasudeva and Devaki were present as well, as were Kamsa's brothers and their new wives. The ministers of the court, the preceptors, the purohits, the Brahmins, there seemed to be no one who wanted to miss the trial. In many ways, it was a curious echo of the same collective that had gathered at this same venue for the sealing of the peace accord.

Ugrasena waited for the court crier to reel off his long list of antecedents and titles before taking his seat. Everyone else remained standing, but Ugrasena knew that he would not be able to get through this procedure on his feet. He could barely get through it at all. He glanced at Vasudeva, wondering what alien metal the man was made of. Had he been Vasudeva's age and in his position, he would have struck down Kamsa where he stood without a second's hesitation. There was no law, no dharma and no Arya court that could possibly condone all the evil that Kamsa had unleashed upon his own people as well as their neighbours.

The months of Kamsa's disappearance had been among the most blissful of Ugrasena's later years. He had even begun to hope that his son was dead, lying slain on some foreign battlefield, or murdered in the dark filth of some alley behind a drinking house or place of ill repute. The change in his queen had been palpable as well. After suffering the shock of learning the truth of what Kamsa had been up to, she had grown into a pale shadow of her former self. While no longer the stunning beauty he had married over two decades ago, she had at least been carrying her age gracefully, which was more than could be said about himself.

Now, he decided, it was time to end this travesty once and for all.

'The facts of the trial are unquestionable,' Ugrasena said. 'This morning, we have heard them all, reported by the most reliable witnesses possible.' He glanced warmly in Vasudeva's direction. 'I shall not dither or delay justice any further. Dharma dictates that Crown Prince Kamsa be given the sharp edge of the fullest extent of the law for his many crimes against humanity.'

A murmur of approval passed through the gathering.

Ugrasena went on grimly, ticking off the points of his judgement one by one as the court munshis raced to keep pace with his recitation. Later, the purohits and scholars would rephrase and clean up his pronouncement to ensure that the official record was properly pompous and officious enough to be fit for posterity. Right now, he used brevity and incisiveness to convey his points sharply and quickly, concerned more with getting over with it than with the beauty of phrase.

'First, I strip Kamsa of his crown. No more is he crown prince.' That was crucial under law, for a crown prince was, by virtue of his position, not subject to any judgement of any court of the land. In fact, since the king was himself the chief dispenser of justice in a Yadava republican court, the crown prince was the chief-justice-in-waiting, so to speak. A court could hardly rule against one of its own senior officials. By stripping Kamsa of his crown, he had removed that legal hurdle.

'Secondly, I divest Kamsa of all his royal titles, possessions, lands, property and anything else of value that he may currently own, may have owned in the past or may claim to own in future, under my authority as his pitr as well as the king of the Andhaka nation. As all possessions of the royal family are merely community property given to them for their use, Kamsa's possessions belong to the

Andhaka nation, and the Andhaka nation hereby takes them back.'

With his wealth, inheritance, property, servants, soldiers, in short, *everything* gone, Kamsa no longer possessed anything of value with which to buy support or raise military opposition; neither would any heirs that Kamsa might have appointed or produced biologically, of which Ugrasena was not aware. Again, a point of law, but a crucial one to avoid future complications.

'Now, Kamsa is an ordinary citizen, subject to ordinary laws. As such, I find him guilty of multiple counts of abuse of the peace accord between our nation and the Sura nation. I also find him guilty of numerous instances of assault, murder, conspiracy, rioting, and other crimes.'

Ugrasena paused, eyes sweeping the rapt faces of the gathering. After a long time, he felt strong, in command, as if he was truly king again.

Kamsa had emasculated me, he thought bitterly. *Unable to fully accept the truth of his misdeeds or punish him myself, I had lost all confidence in myself as a ruler.*

That was another debt he owed Vasudeva. By his honourable actions and decisions, exemplified by the brilliant manner in which he had apprehended Kamsa rather than simply executing him, he had reasserted dharma in Mathura. It was a powerful message and one that Ugrasena intended to underline now.

'For all these crimes, I, Ugrasena, king of the Andhaka tribes collected into one nation under Sri the Eternal, Isa the Supreme, and Narayana the Infinite, condemn Kamsa to be executed in the public square in front of the palace.'

He raised his rajtaru, pleased to note the steadiness of his grip and the firmness of his voice. 'Such sentence to be carried at once.'

The rapping of the rajtaru on the floor of the dais boomed and echoed throughout the sabha hall.

nine

Padmavati sighed as Ugrasena pronounced the judgement. As a mother, her heart broke to hear such a sentence. Not because she disagreed, but because she lamented that her son, her flesh and blood, should have brought himself to such a pass. What had she done wrong? Should she have nursed him longer as an infant? Cared for him personally rather than have the daimaas look after him? Been stricter in her punishments? She was wracked with self-doubt, questions, anxieties and guilt.

The people suffered from no such dilemma. The roar of approval that greeted Ugrasena's sentencing made that clear. The enthusiastic cheers and shouts that echoed through the sabha hall, the palace and the streets could not be called jubilant – for which kingdom enjoys the execution of its own crown prince? – but it was certainly coated with relief. Nobody had doubted that justice would be done, but after long years of being at the receiving end of Kamsa's atrocities, and the ugly disputes, feuds and other conflicts, the people's faith in the king had slipped a little.

Today, that faith was renewed with vigour.

Shortly after, Padmavati stood at the balcony overlooking the courtyard of the palace. As with the sabha hall, every inch of space was packed with eager citizens wishing to witness the execution of the former crown prince. Never before had such an event occurred. She prayed it never would.

Beside her stood Ugrasena, discreetly leaning on a royal crook that was not visible to the crowds below: a king had to keep up the appearance of strength, even if he was ailing and frail. Vasudeva and Devaki stood with them. Kamsa's other brothers and sisters and their spouses stood nearby. The atmosphere was grim and heavy and fraught with a certain tension that she understood: not tension for the event, but a kind of tense anticipation, awaiting the end of the event, so they could breathe freely again. Even Kamsa's brothers, blood-kin though they were, displayed the same impassive expressions, waiting for the danda to be carried out, and the black sheep of the family to be eliminated. Growing up, Kamsa had made enemies of them, one and all; and the chief reason why Ugrasena had chosen to send them out to govern other regions of the kingdom was to avoid their coming into mortal conflict with Kamsa. Padmavati could see no vestige of love or regret on any of their faces, and this made her sad as well. What had Ugrasena and she done to produce a son so unloved and hated that an entire kingdom, including his own family, now looked forward to his execution?

For the people, there were far stronger implications of today's event. This execution would change the history of the Yadava nations forever. It would prove that no one was above dharma. It would reaffirm their faith in an idea – of a republic – that had been faltering for years.

Padmavati forced herself to look down at Kamsa. He had been pressed into a kneeling posture on the execution platform below, his head resting upon a wooden block. The executioner, a giant of a man who was in reality a shepherd of the mountain tribes – the only community that undertook to perform such executions – stood patiently beside him, a large mace leaning against his thigh.

Oddly enough, Kamsa had done nothing, said nothing throughout the brief trial and sentencing. He had simply knelt thus, as he knelt now, head bowed, long hair unfettered and falling across his face, concealing any expression or trace of emotion. In no way did he betray any other response or feeling. He did not utter a single word or make a sound.

She supposed that he was filled with remorse for his misdeeds and overcome by guilt and shame. She hoped that was the case. It would have been too terrible to bear had he ranted and raved and called out for mercy or abused his accusers. True, he had the right to do so, but it would only have made people pity him. Weakness among Yadava Kshatriyas was unforgivable. They would have mocked him, scorned him ... *hated* him for not accepting his death like a

Yadu. This way, he would at least die honourably, executed by official danda, punished under dharma. He could even be cremated officially, his ashes scattered in the Yamuna as those of his ancestors had been. *And soon, my ashes will fall into the river as well,* she thought, sadness pressing against her heart like a cold fist, *for how will I live with the shame of this?*

The magistrate presiding over the execution looked up at the balcony. Ugrasena raised his rajtaru, the signal to begin. The executioner lifted the mace over his head, his powerful hands hefting the massive length of iron, dimples appearing in his shoulders and back. Unlike the maces carried into battle, this tool was not plated with steel, silver, gold, or even copper or brass. No filigree work adorned it, no shaping altered its menacing bulk. It was simply a black pillar of iron with a bulbous head thrice as large as a grown man's, pitted, scored and dented in several places from use. She wondered how many condemned men the mace had crushed to death, whose blood would mingle with her own, for the blood that ran through Kamsa's veins was her blood.

With the head of the mace lifted as high as his muscled arms could raise it, the shepherd steadied himself to take careful aim. He was known to accomplish his job in a single blow, and Padmavati prayed that he would do so today as well. She could not imagine the cruelty of a man half-crushed, half-dead, lying on the wooden block, suffering.

'Be merciful; make it quick. He is my son after all,' she prayed. For her, whatever he may have done, it all came down to a single point: Kamsa was her son. And she could not find it in her heart to wish him cruelty even now.

The mace hovered in the air for a moment, then began its terrible descent. A sound rose from the crowd, an instinctive natural sound that originated deep in the chests of the onlookers and rose to their throats as a wordless growl. As the mace descended, the growl rose to a roar and exploded.

The deadly tool crashed down, hard enough to smash a skull to pulp, to end life instantly, to shatter bone and mash flesh and splatter blood.

The executioner grunted with the effort.

But instead of meeting skull and flesh, the mace was met by an upraised hand. At the very instant that it began to fall, Kamsa's hand shot up and, with unerring instinct, met the head of the mace with its palm. It was not entirely uncommon; men were known to panic and attempt to save themselves at the last instant. The mace ought to have smashed the hand along with the skull, without its descent being affected in the least.

Instead, Kamsa's outstretched hand slapped against the head of the mace, successfully halting its purposeful approach. Stalled mid-hurtle, the mace stayed there: an inch above Kamsa's head.

A gasp rose from the watching crowd. Incredulity. Disbelief. Shock. Such a thing had never happened before. The executioner stared down, baffled. He then tried to haul the mace up again, intending to bring it down and do the job properly the next time. He had assumed that he had not wielded the mace correctly the first time; that was the only explanation which made sense.

But though the executioner struggled fiercely, his corded arms, shoulders, back and neck muscles straining until they stood out in etched relief, the mace did not budge.

Then, Padmavati saw Kamsa's fingers begin to close upon the head of the mace, the balls of the fingers pressing *into* the solid iron bulb.

And the iron yielded.

Kamsa's fingers dug into the metal like a child's fingers squeezing a ball of mud. The executioner stared in disbelief, then lost his grip on the mace and backed away. Nothing in his entire life had prepared him for such an occurrence. People across the courtyard gasped and cried out in shock, pointing.

Kamsa rose to his feet. He was holding the mace by its head. He looked down at it and slowly closed his fist, crushing the solid iron bulb as easily as the mace ought to have crushed his head moments earlier. Then he tossed the mace aside – directly at the executioner. A hundred kilos of iron struck the man in the chest, shattering him. He fell off the execution platform, landing on his back on the stone courtyard, broken beyond repair. People screamed now, unable to comprehend what was happening. Perhaps the oddest thing of all was the way Kamsa looked at his own hand, flexing the fingers, and then stared at the dying executioner with the mace embedded in his chest, *as if he is …* Padmavati groped … *as if he's as shocked at his own feat of strength as everyone else!*

Kamsa seemed to accept his new-found strength at last and raised his head, looking around at the watching crowd. His hair fell into his face, concealing most of his features. Only one eye glared out, bulging, red-veined, the pupil reduced to a pinpoint; and brilliant white teeth flashed in the dark shade of his hair-curtained face. He lifted his heavy-lidded eyes and gazed up at the balcony. Padmavati flinched as his eyes sought out and found her. She thought she saw him grin by way of greeting; then that terrible wild-eyed gaze passed on to find his father. There it stayed. She sensed Ugrasena standing his ground, neither flinching nor showing any reaction that might give Kamsa any satisfaction, but from the trembling of his hand upon the crook that helped support him, she knew that the effort cost him dearly.

Kamsa chuckled.

Padmavati suddenly realized that Kamsa had expanded in size. Instead of his normal height of two yards, he was a good yard taller now. In fact, he was growing even as she watched. She had barely taken her eyes off him, to look at her husband, and found him a head taller when she looked down again. Now, he was twice his height, his width expanding proportionately. Now, thrice his size … She heard the platform creak as his weight increased as well, now four times, then five times. Kamsa then started growing exponentially, rising like a coiled cobra expanding to its full height. The crowd gathered in the courtyard screamed and shouted in terror, unable to make sense of this new phenomenon.

And Kamsa continued to grow.

ten

'YADUS OF MATHURA!'

The voice boomed like a peal of thunder mingled with a grinding metallic sound. Ugrasena's ears throbbed painfully with the impact of the sound. Beside him, Padmavati clapped her hands over her ears. Devaki did likewise. In the courtyard, people reeled and fell back, stampeding to get away from the monstrosity that stood in front of the palace. Elsewhere, horses reared and whinnied in panic, elephants trumpeted in anger, kine lowed in protest, babies howled in dismay.

The being that had been Kamsa just a few moments ago now towered above the height of the palace, with just the head measuring a hundred yards in height. It was the width and thickness of a mansion. Dust clouds, raised by its movement, boiled and seethed around it, lending it an air of sorcery, as if some conjuror had tossed down a crystal ball of magic powder and this impossible thing had emerged. The puranas told of such things: creatures that altered shape at will, grew in size or diminished in stature as they pleased. But this was no creature out of a puranic tale. This was Kamsa!

'BY CONDEMNING MY MORTAL BODY TO DEATH, YOU HAVE RELEASED MY TRUE FORM. UNTIL TODAY, I TOO HAD JUST PREMONITIONS AND GLIMPSES OF MY TRUE IDENTITY. BUT BY BRINGING ME TO THE POINT OF DEATH, YOU HAVE UNLOCKED MY TRUE NATURE. THIS IS WHO I AM. NOT A MERE MORTAL LIKE YOU. LOOK UPON ME AND WEEP, FOR I AM YOUR DESTINY. I AM YOUR DEATH. I AM YOUR OVERLORD!'

Ugrasena sucked his breath in, struggling to support his weight on the crook. He realized that he had inadvertently been leaning back, causing his balance to fail. He reached out and grasped the balustrade, using it to prop himself up. It no longer mattered if anyone saw him; nobody had eyes for him any more, or for anything else except the giant rakshasa that loomed in the palace courtyard.

Yes, a rakshasa, for what else would you call this being! His mind shuddered, desisted from accepting what he was experiencing with his own senses. It was something straight out of the scrolls that recorded ancient tales and forgotten legends.

Grotesque, malformed, hideously shaped and bulging out from unexpected places, it appeared to be more a war machine than a living creature. Its size was the feature that was least unusual about it. Its massive muscles were an epic parody of Kamsa's physique. Its feet were ringed with a fuzzy down that was more goat- or sheep-like than human. It took a step forward, crushing the remnants of the execution platform to splinters, and the earth reverberated with the thud of the impact. When it spoke, its tongue protruded, a violent, swollen purple tongue crawling with life. Were those *serpents* weaving in and out of the flesh of its tongue? And the eyes, those terrible bulging eyes with the pinpointy pupils – there were living things squirming inside its eyeballs as well, wriggling to and fro and falling ... to land with a sickening plop on the courtyard far below, each the size of a finger, trailing a blood-red, mucus-like residue.

Despite this macabre transmogrification, there was no question that the being was Kamsa. That face, swollen and fat with hatred and rage; those eyes glittering through the curtain of filthy ropes of hair; the overall shape of those features; that body, the way it moved and walked and turned its head ... even the voice, thunderous and with its undertone of gnashing metal, was still recognizably Kamsa's. As the creature spoke – almost to itself at times – with curious lapses into a kind of self-questioning tone, Ugrasena realized that the being was discovering its true self even as they were viewing its transformation.

'*TOO LONG HAVE I ENDURED IN THIS FRAIL, MORTAL FORM. TOO LONG DID I STAY IMPRISONED IN THAT PUTRID CAGE OF MORTAL FLESH AND BONE. THIS IS THE DAY OF MY RESURRECTION. YET I DO NOT THANK YOU, FOR THIS TOO WAS*

ORDAINED, AS WERE ALL THE THINGS
THAT HAVE PASSED AND THOSE THAT ARE
YET TO HAPPEN.'

The giant took another step, this time stepping right onto a section of the crowd of onlookers who had come to witness the execution. Ugrasena saw a dozen innocents crushed like ants beneath the giant foot. Kamsa did not even realize that he had ended their lives. All he had done was shift his weight from one foot to the other.

Ugrasena realized that he had to take charge of the situation somehow, or at least attempt to do so. The being was not killing people ... not by its own volition ... at least not yet ... Perhaps if he kept it talking for a while longer, he could pre-empt some violence.

'Who are you?' he cried, his voice cracking with age and emotion. 'You are not my son Kamsa. What are you? Identify thyself, creature!'

Kamsa turned and looked down at him. The yard-thick black lips curled to reveal ivory-white fangs. *'WHO AM I? WHY, I AM THE ONE YOUR WIFE NAMED KAMSA. DO YOU NOT KNOW WHY SHE NAMED ME SO? ASK HER THEN. ASK HER WHY SHE NAMED YOUR FIRST-BORN KAMSA!'*

Ugrasena frowned. What was the creature talking about? Surely, it was raving. Then he glanced at Padmavati and saw the way she stared up at the rakshasa, her face drained of all colour, and realization dawned.

'My Queen,' he asked her, 'what does this monster mean? Can you explain?'

Padmavati looked at Ugrasena. In her eyes, he saw a terrible truth.

She knows what the rakshasa means. She knows!

'My Lord,' she said, 'this is a creature from the netherworld. A being out of myth. It seeks only to delude and confound you. Do not believe anything it says.'

But her voice rang false and her face betrayed the truth.

Ugrasena hobbled over to where she stood, the crook striking the marbled floor of the balcony with a sharp crack. 'Speak the truth,' he commanded. 'I demand it.'

She blanched and turned away. But he caught her arm and pressed upon it.

Slowly, with her head lowered, and tears starting to trickle, she said, 'He was named after Kala-Nemi.'

'*INDEED*,' said the giant towering above the city, its voice carrying to the farthest corner of Mathura, its terrible form visible from every place in the city. There was a tone of glee in its voice now; as if it had finally unlocked a great secret, something it had sought for long. '*AMSA OF KALA-NEMI. HENCE, K-AMSA! FOR THAT IS WHO I WAS IN MY PAST LIFE UNTIL THE SURYAVANSHI IKSHWAKU KSHATRIYA KING OF AYODHYA DEFEATED ME AND THE BRAHMARISHIS VASHISHTA AND VALMIKI CONDEMNED*

ME TO CENTURIES OF IMPRISONMENT. KALA-NEMI.'

Rama Chandra of Ayodhya had defeated this being? Yes, Ugrasena recalled hearing some tales of his derring-do from his preceptor as a boy. Never did he expect to see the stuff of those fireside tales and bedtime stories come to life in this way.

He raised his crook, pointing it angrily at the giant.

'What is it you seek here now? Why have you returned to prithviloka? And why did you choose the body and form of my son as your receptacle?'

The bulging face stared down at him. Ugrasena saw now that there were things moving beneath the surface of the rakshasa's *skin* as well, all over his body. Tiny, writhing forms in a variety of shapes, like insects of various kinds – centipedes, millipedes, roaches, bugs, and other crawling creatures – moving here and there, causing the beast's skin to ripple and bulge at unexpected places and in unsettling ways. He swallowed nervously, not letting himself think of the impossibility of fighting such a being. What weapon could he use against it? How many warriors would it take to lead an assault? Where and how would they strike at it? Could it be wounded? Killed? How?

'YOUR SON?'

The being that had once been Kala-Nemi and was now Kamsa issued a sound that made even Ugrasena cringe with pain. It was like a horse coughing right into one's ear.

The being dribbled as it spoke, its spittle as alive as the rest of its existence. Several writhing forms spattered onto the balcony and coated it in a slimy white fluid. Ugrasena saw one crawling at his foot and brought the crook down upon it, impaling it. A tiny scream of agony reached his ears. He resisted the urge to void his guts over the balcony railing.

'I AM NOT YOUR SON, UGRASENA. I HAVE NEVER BEEN YOUR SON. I AM NOT BORN OF MORTAL MAN. AGAIN, ASK YOUR QUEEN IF YOU DO NOT BELIEVE ME. ASK HER WITH WHOM SHE LAY IN ORDER TO CONCEIVE ME. IT WAS NO MORTAL MAN, LORD OF MATHURA. IT WAS CERTAINLY NOT YOU!'

As the being laughed, spewing living saliva, Ugrasena glanced at Padmavati. She had fallen to the ground, her face buried in her hands, weeping bitterly. He felt sad for her, but also anger and disgust. Could it be true, then? Her reaction suggested it was. What did it matter now anyway? The crisis that faced him, that faced them all, was far greater than a mere question of paternity. The future of their entire race was under threat now. He could be an angry husband later, in the privacy of his bedchamber; right now, he was still king of Mathura. And as king, he needed to know the enemy's intentions.

'Tell me then,' Ugrasena said. 'What is it you desire from us now?'

Kamsa looked down at him, then up at the sky, then around. From that height, Ugrasena guessed that the giant could surely see the whole of Mathura, as well as much of the surrounding countryside.

He could probably cover the entire kingdom in a few hours if he leaps and runs. And he could destroy it in days if he wishes.

Finally, the giant completed his examination and looked down again. Ugrasena glimpsed that same hideous smile. *'ONLY WHAT I DESERVE,'* Kamsa said with unexpected simplicity, then added: *'TO RULE THE YADAVA NATIONS FROM NOW UNTIL THE END OF TIME, FOR I AM IMMORTAL AND THIS REWARD OF ETERNAL LIFE IS GIVEN UNTO ME AS MY JUST DESERTS FOR PAST SERVICES RENDERED.'*

He seemed to pause and think for a moment, then his face brightened grotesquely as he beamed with insane delight. *'YES. IT IS SO. I AM YOUR NEW KING AND, AS OF THIS MOMENT, I CROWN MYSELF KING ETERNAL. BOW TO ME, MATHURA. BOW … OR DIE!'*

eleven

A pall of dread hung over Mathura. The Yadavas set great store by signs and omens, all of which were ominous. Calves were born stillborn or deformed. Milk was curdling everywhere in the kingdom; even freshly drawn milk lay in frothy lumps in the pail. A mysterious illness swept the kine population; many believed that it was engendered by the vile effusions the giant Kamsa had exuded. Hundreds of thousands of heads of cattle died and more continued to die in the weeks that followed. Sown fields were picked clean of seeds by birds. Crops ready for harvesting were suddenly found devastated by rodents, vermin or fungi. Yokes cracked, uksan's legs broke and they had to be put down, horses went mad and attacked their own syces, elephants went into masti outside of season, rampaging through the villages, causing havoc. One moment the sky would be promisingly overcast, the next, it would turn cloudless. A river broke its banks and washed away an entire village even though it was late summer, almost autumn; there was no logical explanation for the deluge. Other rivers dried up overnight, leaving fish gasping and dolphins flailing pitifully on the riverbeds. The villages they served reached drought-like conditions despite a record monsoon. Strange phenomena appeared in the western and eastern skies, as if the sun was about to rise at midnight, or had just set at midday. Brahmacharya acolytes who had been able to recite thousands of Vedic shlokas found themselves perfectly blank-headed, barely able to stammer a few lines. Water drawn from the sweetest wells came up foul and rancid. Newborn babes found no milk in their mothers' breasts; others choked in their cribs and died of unknown ailments. People saw their dead ancestors move about amongst them, warning of impending doom, urging their descendants to migrate to distant lands. Soothsayers, astrologers, priests, madmen, philosophers, poets, cowherds ... all agreed that a great and terrible disaster was imminent. Many predicted that the extinction of the Yadava race was nigh. Nobody laughed or disagreed.

The reign of Kamsa had begun.

twelve

Kamsa smiled as the masons worked. He had reduced himself to his normal size, but still seemed somewhat larger than before. Vasudeva had observed that each time he expanded into a giant and then regained his human form, he appeared a little changed. Once, he noticed something creeping beneath the skin of Kamsa's arm, sluggishly, as if unable to move as energetically in human flesh as it would in a bigger, rakshasa body. Slowly, as Vasudeva watched discreetly, it seemed to be absorbed back into the arm. On another occasion, Kamsa's face reduced to normal human size along with the rest of his body, but the eyes themselves remained rakshasa-like, the contrast between the human face and rakshasa orbs horrifying to behold.

Vasudeva wondered if something in Kamsa's substance changed each time he underwent the transformation. If, perhaps, eventually, Kamsa would become all-rakshasa, with no trace of the human left.

It was a chilling thought. Kamsa was already the terror of the land. After the day of his execution – 'the day of my rebirth!' as he called the day, demanding that it be made a public holiday in Mathura to be celebrated by all Yadavas henceforth, on pain of death – he had initiated a pogrom of terrible efficiency. His aides-de-camp, Bana and Canura, had miraculously survived the battering by the crowd on Vasudeva's wedding day. They had been scheduled for execution following Kamsa but were freed and reinstated to his side, and had been proclaimed mahamantris by him. There were seven mahamantris already in place at the royal court, and since no more than seven could hold the post at any time, Kamsa had killed the other seven, leaving only Bana and Canura to manage the day-to-day administrative affairs of the kingdom. He had also slaughtered the rest of the court officials, nobles, and others who had either opposed him in the past, disagreed with him privately or publicly, or offended him inadvertently. When each one was brought before him for 'trial and sentencing' under the new 'justice system' that he had initiated, he seemed unable to recognize several of them, but shrugged and gave the command for execution anyway.

The new execution platform, constructed overnight to replace the old one that Kamsa had shattered as a giant, soon turned red with the blood shed over its planks. Nobody came to witness executions any more, for, often, Kamsa would point randomly at the crowd and say that he recognized a woman who had once giggled when he was passing by, or a boy who reminded him of a long-ago playmate who had won a race against him, or some such whim, and the person would be dragged up to the platform and executed then and there. All grist for the mill.

Now, he was overseeing what he termed the 'restriction of facilities' for the 'former' king and queen Ugrasena and Padmavati. Since he had declared himself King Eternal, Ugrasena and Padmavati were redundant; their very presence an offence to the current sovereign.

Arya tradition required Raj-Kshatriyas to spend the third, autumnal phase or 'ashrama' of their lives, vanaprastha ashrama, in the shelter of the forest. In point of law, Kamsa was correct. By tradition, Ugrasena ought to have retired to a hermitage in the forest by now, Padmavati accompanying him voluntarily as was the custom, and have been available to his children and former citizens as a mentor and advisor, the physical remove from active politics and prohibition against owning property or accumulation of wealth ensuring that he could never become a political rival to his heirs. Ugrasena was well past the age. In fact, he was on the verge of sanyasa ashrama, the phase of complete renunciation when a Raj-Kshatriya devoted his energies and remaining lifetime to the contemplation of godhead, preparing himself for union with the infinite power of Brahman, the all-pervasive. The only reason Ugrasena had remained on the throne until now was because he had known that Kamsa was ill-prepared to take on the task of running the kingdom. That, and the enduring strife between the Yadavas had kept him on the throne, draining his dwindling strength in statecraft when he ought to have been enjoying the fruits of his long life and considerable accomplishments.

Kamsa reasoned, in the convoluted thought process that he had developed since his 'rebirth', that since Ugrasena had failed to take vanaprastha ashrama at the prescribed time, regardless of his reason for flouting tradition, he had consumed part of Kamsa's birthright. Kamsa reminded those listening that he was not Ugrasena's son, but Padmavati's. Since Arya dynasties and society were matriarchal, he was the heir to the throne and, as Padmavati's eldest son, entitled to reign. Since Ugrasena had deprived him of his entitlement, he had committed treason against Kamsa, the rightful king, and as such, Kamsa was justified in doing whatever he pleased with him. This was a gross simplification and distortion, of course. In point of law, if Ugrasena could be proven to have transgressed by wilfully denying his heirs and the kingdom their rightful change of liege – which was clearly not the case here – then, in that unlikely scenario, Ugrasena might perhaps have been banished into permanent exile, to spend his last years in the wilderness, never to return to Mathura. Under the circumstances, this would have been a merciful sentence as well as the right one under dharma.

But Kamsa had chosen instead the sentence he was now overseeing.

Vasudeva watched with great sadness as a hundred masons, bricklayers, stone workers and other artisans and craftsmen worked feverishly to complete the task given them. They were building a wall around the private chambers of Ugrasena and Padmavati – not the entire palatial mansion, which was a veritable palace in itself, and which they had formerly occupied, but a tiny section of the same, barely more than an apartment. It was, in fact, the apartment that housed Padmavati's maids and was, as such, grossly unfit for a queen, let alone a royal couple. It had been stripped of any 'luxuries' and filled instead with dirt, assorted plants, and even insects and rodents specially brought from the woods and set loose inside the rooms. The roof had been painted half blue and half black. A hole had been made high up on a wall, and a pipe trickled water from this hole into one of the chambers, which in turn spattered on the muddy floor beneath, turning it to mush, and it was apparently up to the occupants to provide a pathway for this 'river' to flow neatly through their 'domain'. There were no facilities for the two occupants to use as a toilet; merely two medium-sized chambers filled with this assortment of filth and vermin. Two tiny windows set high near the ceiling let in whatever little light and air could find its way into that claustrophobic space.

This, Kamsa said proudly, was to be their vanaprastha ashrama. Their forest abode!

And to ensure that they remained within this space as surely as they would have remained in an actual forest, he was having it walled in. Even an elephant would have a hard time breaking through the two-foot-thick stone wall he was getting built, rising from floor to ceiling. No door remained to enter or exit the 'forest world'. From time to time, some raw vegetables – herbs and roots and tree bark, and the occasional fruit – would be pushed in through the high windows or the water pipe to perhaps be found and eaten by the residents or, if they were not quick enough, their fellow inhabitants.

Kamsa turned to Vasudeva and said cheerfully: 'There; it is done. Isn't it marvellous? They shall be so happy in their forest world. So restful! I think they will become true yogis in no time at all.'

Vasudeva had tried his best to plead on behalf of the imprisoned king and queen, begging with Kamsa to give them even just a clean apartment with daily meals and facilities for their toilet. But Kamsa had acted as if he did not hear him, and had extolled the virtues of his 'brilliant' plan in a succession of self-aggrandizing compliments. Vasudeva had known that were he to press the point, Kamsa's anger would turn upon him. Yet, he had tried and tried again, risking his life and not caring. What Kamsa was doing was simply executing a death sentence upon his parents: a slow, agonizing death sentence that would be implemented through starvation, disease, pestilence, deprivation, or all of these. But Kamsa had neither budged an inch from his plans nor had he lost his temper at Vasudeva. If anything, he seemed to have grown remarkably fond of Vasudeva, treating him like family, displaying a disturbing warmth and affection that was in stark contrast to his earlier hostility. This was enough to make Vasudeva's insides churn with disgust. He hated to have to stand by and watch Kamsa commit these atrocities, let alone be treated as if he were complicit in these crimes and sins. But for Devaki's sake, he held his peace.

Now Kamsa clapped a hand on Vasudeva's shoulder. 'Come now, brother-in-law, let us retire in private. I wish to have a few words with you. It is time for us to resolve our situation.'

thirteen

Devaki paced the halls of her chamber, waiting anxiously for Vasudeva to return. Under the new martial law imposed on Mathura, women were not permitted to travel unaccompanied by a man outside their homes. Even when they did travel with their menfolk, they were compelled to be clothed from head to toe in garb that must not be found provocative in any way, and their faces veiled. If found violating any of these conditions, the woman in question would be regarded as chattel and thrown into one of the many danda-ghars that had been built specially for this purpose … to be suitably punished by Kamsa's soldiers for as long as they saw fit. There were stories, fearfully whispered, of mahamantris Bana and Canura deliberately lifting the veils of women they passed by, and, if the faces they saw pleased them, accusing the women in question of violating the law by having 'enticed' them through provocative gestures, words or simply the way they walked. It was straight to the danda-ghars for those poor unfortunates. The lucky ones were too ugly, too old, disease-stricken, or otherwise unappealing. Naturally, to avoid falling prey to this gross injustice and misogyny, women virtually had stopped travelling outside at all. Even Devaki had no choice but to stay indoors. In Kamsa's Mathura, nobody was above the law, not even his own sisters.

Devaki heaved a sigh of relief as she saw Vasudeva's familiar, neatly pressed hair as he passed across the courtyard of their house, disappearing below the balcony on which she stood. She spun around as his footsteps sounded on the stairway and the instant he appeared at the top of the stairs, she went to him, eagerly. The sight of his face, pale and drained of all strength, shocked her. She instantly glanced behind him, then over her shoulder at the courtyard once more, fully expecting to see Kamsa's soldiers – the new army, they called themselves – come with him to bear both of them away for immediate execution. Each day since the ill-fated day of Kamsa's 'beheading' had been spent in expectation of that moment. Seeing Vasudeva's face, she feared it had arrived at last.

But there were no soldiers, only Vasudeva, sinking down into a seat, holding his head in one hand, eyes wet with emotion.

'What is it, My Lord?' she asked. 'Pray, tell me. Is it execution for both of us? Has he condemned us at last? He has condemned and executed almost everyone else by now. Why not us as well? Tell me, Vasudeva, is it execution?'

He looked at her at last, his hand finding hers and stroking it passionately. 'No, my beloved. It is worse. Far worse.'

She stared at him, wondering what he meant. What could be worse than execution?

He told her.

And it was so. There *were* things far worse than merely having one's head crushed to death or being put to death in any fashion, however slow or quick. Her young life and limited experiences had never allowed for such possibilities; but that did not mean they did not exist.

By the time he finished explaining the terrible, horribly unjust terms of Kamsa's 'solution', she was shaking. Her head turned from side to side, trying to deny it all, to pretend she had never heard it. But the tears that fell from her eyes to splash hotly upon her hands contradicted that gesture. Finally, she broke down, sobbing bitterly, chest heaving as he put his arm around her, comforting her. Even in her deep distress, she could feel Vasudeva's pain as his eyes shed tears too. Together, they held each other and wept.

'It is a nightmare,' he said at last, 'and like all nightmares, it will end. But for now, we must live through it. Do you understand, my love? We must live through it.'

She nodded, then shook her head stubbornly. 'Why? Why not just …' She could not complete the thought, but her meaning was evident.

He shook his head firmly. 'Because someone must stand up to him. Some day, his time will come to an end. If we end our lives, how will we stand up to him when that time comes?'

'What if his time never ends? What if he really *does* rule forever, as he says he will? *King Eternal!*' She spoke the phrase scornfully, directing her emotion at the cause of her misery.

'No living thing is forever. Anything that is born must die. Kamsa was born of mortal woman. He is a rakshasa and possessed of great power. But some day, he too will end. Or be ended. And we shall be the instruments of that ending.'

She looked up at him, wondering at his conviction. 'We shall kill him? Is that your plan?'

He nodded. 'Perhaps. I shall certainly try. Although I fear he may have grown too strong for any mortal man to kill. Still, I intend to make an attempt.'

Her heart clenched at the thought of losing her husband. 'When?'

'When I go to him with our first …' He swallowed, looking down, unable to say the word. 'Until that time, I shall do exactly as he says, hoping that perhaps, against all odds, he relents, perhaps even sets us free to go home to my people. But if he dares to try to harm our first …' again, he seemed unable to say the word, '… then I shall kill him.'

Devaki was silent. She recalled their conversation in Vrindavan when she had urged Vasudeva to kill Kamsa and he had refused. She did not begrudge him that refusal, nor his refusal to see that Kamsa was no mortal man but a rakshasa. She respected the fact that Vasudeva was his own man and made his own judgement and choices. But she feared that the time for that mode of action had passed. She feared that things would be different this time. Quite different. Though she wasn't sure how.

But she said nothing. Perhaps she was wrong. Perhaps Vasudeva would succeed. Perhaps he would not even need to take that last, desperate step.

Perhaps …

Devaki shook her head, trying to clear it. As she did so, she felt her belly stir and instinctively put a hand to her stomach.

Vasudeva looked at her, concerned. 'Are you well? Do you require anything?'

She shook her head. 'No. We are quite well. Healthy. All is as it should be.'

He was silent for a moment, contemplating the irony of that statement. 'How long?'

She had done the mental calculations already and was prepared with the answer. 'Late summer … no, later, probably during the month of Bhaadra.'

Less than six months from now, thought Vasudeva.

They fell silent then, contemplating the future, the possibilities.

Darkness fell as they sat there. Kamsa had denied them servants or aides, allowing them only a house that was guarded by his sentries day and night. Nobody could enter or leave except Kamsa and his emissaries. They could leave only when summoned by Kamsa himself. It was home imprisonment, no doubt about it, but it was a far cry from the miserable incarceration to which he had condemned Ugrasena and Padmavati.

Vasudeva kissed his wife's forehead and thanked the devas that Kamsa had not treated them as he had his own parents. The thought of Devaki suffering thus through the term of her pregnancy was unbearable. This way, she could at least bring the child into the world safely and hygienically.

And then?

He had said that he would kill Kamsa if he attempted to harm their first-born. He had meant it. But he did not think *this* Kamsa was subject to the same limitations as the Kamsa who had faced him on the three previous occasions when he had been unable to harm or kill Vasudeva ...

But I have never attacked him. What would happen when I try?

There was only one way to find out: the hard way.

Six months. He would find out in six months.

They sat in the gathering gloom of dusk and waited together.

fourteen

The eunuch stood in front of Kamsa's throne. This was a very different sabha hall from the one Ugrasena had presided over. A very different throne as well. This was part of the new palace that Kamsa had designed to suit his purposes, part of the new Mathura. It was a new world, after all, refashioned in his image, to serve his needs and intents; and altering its appearance was important to him. He had never liked the gaily coloured pageantry of the Yadavas, the attempt to mirror all the emotions and shades of life in garments, accoutrements, art, décor, architecture, and everything else that was man-made. What about death? Was *that* not a part of life? Was it not out of his own death that Kamsa had been reborn? One age must pass in order for the next to begin, the way the day died every sunset to give way to the night, as one lifetime ended in order for the aatma to transmigrate to the next. Death was an essential part of the cycle of existence. And what was the colour of death? White, of course. Sterile. Utter blankness. Emptiness. Void. A blank scroll upon which one could write anything one desired, create new worlds, erase old ones.

And so he had had everything painted white. The walls, the floors, the ceiling, every garment, even the tapestries had been painted over with lime. The statuary, the houses of the city, and everything else that was coloured was coloured white.

Kamsa had introduced a compulsory dress code for all citizens and, of course, that was white as well. Nobody was permitted to sport so much as a dot of colour anywhere upon their person – apart from their natural brown skin, of course. Speaking of skin, those who were fairest were to be regarded as superior to their darker bhraatren, with a grading scale that logically followed, the darkest, blackest-hued Mathurans to be shunned and considered unclean and untouchable, fit only for the most lowly, menial tasks: the cleaning of cesspits, the disposal of carcasses, the slaughter of diseased beasts, the performance of executions, and so on. Kamsa himself permitted only fair-skinned and beautiful people within the royal precincts, which was also the only part of the city where women were permitted – encouraged, even – to move freely, dressed as they pleased, even under-dressed if they so desired, or rather, if *he* so desired. White was right. White was might. White was wonderful. This was Kamsa's world. A White world.

The eunuch was dressed in black.

It offended Kamsa.

He contemplated having the eunuch stripped, then flayed, then fed to his pets. Anyone who displeased him was thrown off a balcony, to be eaten by the beasts that roamed the courtyard at the back of the palace. They rarely went hungry. Just that morning he had been compelled to have a serving boy thrown into the courtyard for ... for? Well, he couldn't recall exactly why he had had the boy thrown down, but it must have been for good reason. And even if he *hadn't* had a reason, he was King Eternal; he could do as he pleased.

He had got men and women thrown down on far flimsier grounds than not wearing white.

Like this eunuch.

The fellow was tall and strongly built, like all Mohinis. Apart from the fact that Jarasandha picked only the tallest, biggest specimens to be recruited into the fauj, the built of the Mohinis was the result of the special diet and exercise regime that he kept them on. The eunuch was dusty from the long journey, and clearly exhausted. But he stood straight, eyes steady and unwavering, waiting for Kamsa's answer to his message.

Kamsa had forgotten what the message had been.

'What was it that Jarasandha said?' he asked, irritated that he should have to ask again. Clearly, the courier had not delivered his message with sufficient clarity the first time, or Kamsa would not have forgotten it so easily. Incompetence was such a disease these days.

'My Lord,' the eunuch said, bowing his head again as he repeated his missive, 'Lord Jarasandha enquires after your well-being and asks if you require his assistance in governing your kingdom.'

Kamsa frowned. 'Assistance?'

The courier dipped his bald head, a shiny spot gleaming through the layer of road dust – that must have been the spot where the man touched his head with his folded hands while bowing in the Magadhan fashion. 'My master offers to provide military aid, financial aid, or anything your Lordship desires.'

Kamsa waved away the offer with a sneer of contempt. 'I require no aid or assistance. This is *my* kingdom, I am quite capable of ruling it myself. Besides, your lord might not have heard but, of late, I have discovered my true nature. I am reborn.'

The eunuch bowed again before speaking. 'My lord is aware of this. He wishes to congratulate you upon your rebirth and to wish you much success in fulfilling all your ambitions.'

Kamsa nodded. 'Good, good. Now, is that all Jarasandha sent you to say? Because if it is, I have other matters to attend—'

'There is one last thing, My Lord.' The eunuch sounded apologetic.

Kamsa looked down his nose at the man, imperiously. Something worm-like and slimy emerged from his right nostril, coming into his field of vision. He ignored it. After a moment, it dropped and fell with a small plop to the floor, where it began squirming its way across the polished floor, leaving a trail of slime.

'Well?'

'My lord says to take the prophecy seriously.'

Kamsa raised his eyebrows. 'Prophecy?'

'The prophecy of the eighth child.'

'Ah! My sister's eighth child. Yes, I am aware of that prophecy. After all, it was delivered to me by Saptarishi Narada. I would hardly forget it.'

'Of course, My Lord. Emperor Jarasandha merely wishes to ensure that you realize the—'

'Did you say "emperor"?'

The eunuch bowed. 'Aye, your majesty. My master is now the declared the emperor of Aryavarta, with his capital at Magadha. The new Magadha, that is.'

'Yes, I know about the new Magadha. I saw the city while it was being built. But "emperor of Aryavarta"? Really?'

The eunuch simply bowed in response, remaining silent.

Kamsa thought about that for a moment. Emperor of Aryavarta. What did that make him, Kamsa? A mere king? A rajah? Or a maharajah? Why couldn't *he* be emperor of Aryavarta too? All he had to do was go forth and conquer the rest of the Arya nations. It would not be difficult at all, not *now*, with his new army and his newfound powers. But that would mean leaving Mathura, leaving the Yadava nations. And the Yadus were itching to rise up and rebel against him, the fools. He could not afford to leave Mathura just yet. Also, Jarasandha had now declared himself emperor. He would not like it if Kamsa did so too. There could hardly be two emperors! Kamsa would have to fight Jarasandha in order to claim sole emperorship. He did not wish to do that. Jarasandha was like a father to him. Also, he was the only person Kamsa feared more than himself.

'What were you saying?' He had lost the thread of the courier's missive again.

'The *eighth child*, My Lord. It will be your undoing. You must ensure that it is never permitted to be born.'

Kamsa nodded, distracted by thoughts of empire and emperorship. 'Yes, yes. I have already seen to that.'

The eunuch persisted: 'My lord Jarasandha urges you to slay both the woman and her husband immediately. It is the only way to be sure.'

Kamsa looked at the eunuch coldly. He felt more worm-like things wriggling down his nose. He felt other things squirming and crawling and creeping about his body as well. Getting upset did that to him, it fed his parasites, helping them breed and flourish. The eunuch had finally succeeded in upsetting him by daring to tell him what to do, rather than delivering his message and keeping quiet as he ought to have done.

He began giving the order for the eunuch to be thrown to the beasts, then paused. This was not one of his lackeys or servants, or even a citizen of Mathura. This was one of Jarasandha's personal guards. The elite of the elite within the Mohini Fauj. Jarasandha's most trusted inner circle. He might not look kindly upon Kamsa feeding the man to wild pets.

Then again, Jarasandha had declared himself emperor of Aryavarta. While Kamsa was still just king of Mathura, at best king of the Yadavas.

He gave the order for the eunuch to be fed to his pets. He ignored the man's shocked admonitions as he was dragged away, as well as his threat that Jarasandha would not be pleased.

So what? If Jarasandha did not like Kamsa's treatment of his courier, he could come himself and sort it out with Kamsa. He might be emperor of Aryavarta, but here in Mathura, Kamsa was king. King Eternal!

He plucked out a particularly troublesome parasite from his nostril, stared at it with honest curiosity, then crushed it between his thumb and sixth finger – the new finger which had recently grown between his thumb and forefinger. White slime dripped from his hand. He wiped it off on the armrest of his throne just as a soldier came in to inform him that Chief Vasudeva was here to see him, at Kamsa's own request.

fifteen

Vasudeva cradled his newborn son in his arms. Precious, precious child. Fruit of his and Devaki's love. The most beautiful creature upon prithviloka – in all the three worlds. He wanted only to cradle him and love him and cherish the boy until he grew into manhood. This child was the fulfilment of their life, the symbol of their love and happiness. He ought to walk through perfumed gardens, bathe in cool rivers, frolic with kine and dogs and playmates, be schooled in the Vedas and sit wide-eyed while listening to the great legends and mighty epics; be nursed, fed, clothed, educated, bred and groomed to be a lover, a brother, a husband, a mate, a friend, a citizen, a chief, a king. He deserved all the wonders of the earth and everything upon it. His name was Kirtiman.

Vasudeva held out his hands, holding the newborn carefully in both hands, and offered him to Kamsa to see.

'My Lord,' he said, fighting to keep his voice level and all emotion at bay, 'as you commanded, I have brought to you my first-born son. This is your nephew. A beautiful, perfectly formed boy. Look upon his beauty with your own eyes. We have named him Kirtiman.'

As Vasudeva spoke, Kamsa moved from the throne to lie upon a cushioned bed. Female attendants had begun removing his garments and pouring scented oil onto his back. Now, as Vasudeva raised the infant up, Kamsa grunted and turned his head a fraction, glancing carelessly down. The attendants began massaging his back, kneading the muscles expertly and rubbing the oil into his skin. Vasudeva tried not to look too closely at the places where unspeakable things bulged and protruded and writhed beneath the skin, or peeped out from Kamsa's nostrils, ears, or even his eyes; but the female attendants seemed unperturbed by these parasitical abominations. They even seemed to find them out and press down harder on those spots, as if trying to crush the moving parasites beneath the skin. The sight filled Vasudeva with disgust. He fought to retain his composure.

'Why does it not cry?' Kamsa asked.

Vasudeva was at a loss for words. 'My Lord?'

'Babies cry. They bawl. Why does this one stay so silent? Is it without tongue?'

Vasudeva swallowed. A trickle of sweat escaped his hairline and ran down his temple to his ear. 'My Lord, babies cry only when they are in need, or when something troubles them. Our Kirtiman is a peaceful, contented child. He does not cry because nothing troubles him yet.'

Kamsa grunted, turning his head away, shifting slightly to allow the masseuses better access. They continued their kneading and pressing and – Vasudeva was certain of it now – seeking out of parasites to press and kill all over Kamsa's body, not just on his back. Apparently, this was a daily ritual.

Vasudeva waited for several moments. When nothing further was forthcoming, he began to think that perhaps Kamsa had fallen asleep. He dared not speak again. Better to wait in silence. If he had fallen asleep, Vasudeva might be able to slip away quietly. Kirtiman would be hungry soon, and Devaki was anxiously waiting back home, on pins and needles. Every moment that Vasudeva remained away must be agony for her.

Just when he grew certain that Kamsa had fallen asleep, the rakshasa said, 'Make it.'

Vasudeva had no idea what Kamsa was talking about. 'My Lord?'

Kamsa turned his head again, his eyes staring down at the infant in Vasudeva's arms. 'Make it cry.'

Vasudeva swallowed. Two more beads of sweat burst free from his scalp and trickled down. He was sweating profusely now, though it was relatively cool and quite breezy in the palace.

'Yes. Make the little creature cry. Make it bawl. Make it howl with terror. That way, I will know that it fears and respects me. I take this calm silence to mean that it is content unto itself, that it neither acknowledges nor fears me. That is gross disrespect.

I do not tolerate such behaviour from my citizens, let alone my own nephew. It must be taught manners.'

It. *It*. As if he spoke of an inanimate object, not a human being. Though he had heard Vasudeva speak his name clearly. *Kirtiman. My son. Not an 'it'!*

'My Lord...' Vasudeva felt a tear brimming in the corner of his left eye. He fought to blink it away, to prevent it from spilling forth. 'This is your nephew, my first-born. As promised, I have brought him to you. As you can see, he is a harmless little baby. He can do you no harm at all.'

'The prophecy says otherwise.'

Vasudeva struggled to find words that would be brilliant and incisive in their logic, glittering diamonds of intellectual rigour, perfect gems of eloquence. Words were all he had to convince Kamsa, to plead with the rakshasa for his son's life. 'The prophecy ... if it was a prophecy ... spoke of the *eighth* child of your sister. The eighth. Not the first. This is her first-born.'

Kamsa sat up. He gestured. The masseuses moved back at once, heads lowered, eyes averted. Another gesture and they stepped away, as he leveraged himself off the cushioned couch and stood. His body gleamed with oil, red splotches marking where the parasites had been squashed beneath the skin in various spots. The first ones were beginning to turn pink, lightening in colour as the body absorbed them into itself.

He is growing less and less human each passing day. More and more into a rakshasa, Vasudeva could not help thinking.

'I received another message today,' Kamsa said. 'It warned me to take the prophecy seriously. It advised me to kill my sister as well as you. That way, there would be no way the prophecy can come true.'

Vasudeva felt the bundle in his hands grow lighter with each passing moment, as if Kirtiman were turning to air, to dust, to ash …

'But the sender of the message did not know that I have already tried to do that, in my attempts to kill you earlier. And we both know how that went.'

Kamsa grinned unexpectedly, like a man sharing a guilty secret with an old friend. Vasudeva, taken by surprise, tried to summon up a smile in response. But Kamsa's expression told him that he had not been very successful. Sweat and tears mingled on his face, streaming down freely now.

'I am unable to kill you, Vasudeva,' Kamsa said casually, stepping down from the royal dais, taking each step very slowly, each corded muscle in his lower body showing prominently. 'I do not know why. It does not matter why. I cannot do it. That is a fact. So the only way is to kill Devaki; and end the prophecy.'

'No!' Vasudeva blurted out. 'You cannot! You must not! She is your sister.'

'She is the bearer of my doom,' Kamsa said calmly, now standing on the same level as Vasudeva, just yards away. He moved towards Vasudeva, his eyes on the babe in his brother-in-law's arms.

'I beg you!' Vasudeva cried. 'Spare Devaki. Please. Spare her life. I will do anything you say!'

Kamsa stopped before him. He was within reach of the baby now, only a yard away from Vasudeva. He looked down at the infant, then at Vasudeva's face. 'She means a great deal to you, does she not?' He sounded almost kind, gentle even.

'She is my world.' Vasudeva wept. 'She is my life.'

Kamsa considered this for a moment. Then said quietly: 'Give me the child.'

Vasudeva raised his eyes. He looked into Kamsa's eyes. Rakshasa eyes. No more human. Perhaps they never had been human. He searched for words but there were none left to be uttered. Kamsa's meaning was crystal clear.

Vasudeva handed the bundle to Kamsa. The child. The peaceful, gurgling, uncomplaining boy. Beautiful boy. Boy of a thousand dreams; a brilliant future. Some woman's lover, husband, brother; some man's friend, companion. He handed over his own life to Kamsa and felt his heart diminish as he did so. A part of it was gone forever, never to return.

Kamsa grasped the child by the leg. He held it up to look at it, like a carcass on a butcher's hook. Like a beast hung upside down to be drained of blood. Like a dead thing.

'Slayer of Kamsa?' he said scornfully. '*This?*'

He turned his head this way, then that, examining the now-wailing babe intently.

'So,' he said, 'it *does* know how to cry after all!'

He laughed.

And then he swung the child around, over his head.
With great force and speed.
   Once.
   Twice.
   Thrice.
   And then released it.

sixteen

With a great roar, Vasudeva rushed at Kamsa.

Even the rakshasa was taken by surprise. Not many had dared oppose him since his rebirth. Even fewer had dared attack him. His demonstration of his powers on the day of his execution and rebirth had ensured that. Who would dare to go up against a rakshasa capable of expanding his size a thousandfold; large enough to crush entire hills, uproot whole forests, toss herds of elephants like pebbles? Only the doomed or utterly desperate. Both had tried. And failed. The swift ease with which Kamsa had despatched those first few comers had cemented his reputation. He was unbeatable, someone who couldn't be killed. Better to try running away from him than attacking him.

But none of them had been a king. A senapati. A Raj-Kshatriya.

Vasudeva was all these things.

Like all true pacifists, he was a great warrior. A master of weaponry and tactics, attack and defence, combat and strategy.

He had hoped, prayed, and begged for his newborn son's life.

But he had failed to save Kirtiman.

Now, he had no choice but to attempt a violent assault.

He came at Kamsa when his back was turned and was poised at an angle that made it hardest for Kamsa to respond quickly. He deliberately roared to attract the rakshasa's attention towards himself, even as he then changed his approach and attacked from the other side. He raised his right hand at first, showing a bare fist ready to pound Kamsa. However, his actual attack was using a rod of wood with a sharpened metal point. Denied all weapons, he had used his cowherd's crook and part of a cooking vessel to fashion a makeshift one: a two-yard-long rod with a tapering metal point, not unlike a spear, but with the triangular edges sharpened to a fine keenness. He held it in his left hand, low and out of Kamsa's field of vision. By roaring and waving his right fist as he rushed at him, Vasudeva compelled the rakshasa to act in anticipation of a blow from his fist.

Instead, Vasudeva came from the left, wielding a spear, aimed upwards in a trajectory that, if completed, would pierce Kamsa's torso just below his ribs and enter his vital organs, either injuring him grievously, or killing him outright. It was intended to be a killing blow. Vasudeva's only hope was to attack and kill the rakshasa before he could expand his size. If he failed, or if Kamsa found time to expand himself, then not even a hundred Vasudevas could face him, at least not without weaponry and assistance, whether human or divine.

His feint worked perfectly at first. Still laughing at the ease with which the brother of the prophesied slayer had been despatched, Kamsa was not expecting an attack, let alone one so cleverly planned and executed. When he heard Vasudeva's roar, he assumed that the Sura king had finally lost his wits and was foolishly attempting a futile assault. He swung around, intending to easily block the fist and hammer a blow at the side of Vasudeva's head that would – then he recalled that the blow would have no effect on Vasudeva. That nothing he did could harm Vasudeva directly. Well, he could still block the fist and any other blows Vasudeva threw at him. He had been strong enough to take a beating even as a human. As a rakshasa, he could take much more than Vasudeva could dish out.

But then Vasudeva changed tack. And did it so cleverly and quickly that Kamsa had no time to react. He was still turning to block the fist when Vasudeva suddenly seemed to slide a whole yard to Kamsa's right; the next instant, he was right beside Kamsa, driving what appeared to be a spear-like weapon into his body.

Under ordinary circumstances, it was a brilliant, audacious move. One that would have succeeded. Kamsa would have been mortally wounded, unable to fight effectively, perhaps even killed at the first blow. And everything would have changed right there and then.

Instead, Kamsa discovered something incredible.

The spear came straight at him, broke through his skin, and entered his body. He distinctly felt the sharp jag of pain as it pierced skin and penetrated flesh, scraping against his lowest right rib; then entered his liver, skewering it like a piece of meat to be roasted; before punching through his back and emerging again, with a small explosion of blood and gristle.

Vasudeva stepped back, already preparing his next assault. Mortal blow or no, a warrior always prepared to follow up. Too many fights were lost because one party assumed the other was downed when, in fact, it was not.

Kamsa looked down at the spear sticking out of his body. He realized that it wasn't a spear at all. It was Vasudeva's crook. The same crook that had shattered his sword, a mace, several arrows and sundry other weapons at the war camp. It was sticking out of his chest now.

He reached down and snapped it off. It broke quite easily, given his new rakshasa strength.

Then he reached behind with both hands, groped once or twice, found the spear point, grasped it, and pulled the weapon out of his back. It came free with a further burst of bodily fluids and a sucking, crackling sound. He brought it around and looked at it. The metal spearhead had bent and twisted during its progress through his body. It looked like a bad imitation of a spear rather than a real weapon.

He tossed it aside. It clattered on the polished floor, sliding a good many yards before it came to rest beneath a wall splattered with the remains of his nephew.

He looked at Vasudeva.

Then he put his hands on his hips.

And he laughed.

Vasudeva stared at him in astonishment.

Kamsa pointed down at his own chest, still laughing.

Vasudeva looked down. And saw the open wound closing of its own accord, the organ regenerating instantly to regain its form.

Kamsa turned around, showing his back to Vasudeva, showing how the exit hole in his back was closing – it had closed already – and the wound healing by itself.

Then he turned back and spread his arms wide. His chuckling reverberated through the large, white sabha hall.

'I thought you understood,' he said to Vasudeva. 'When I said I was immortal, it meant I cannot be killed. Not by a mortal at least. That is why I am King *Eternal*. I will *live* forever and *rule* forever.'

In two swift strides, he was at Vasudeva's throat, grasping it with a single hand. The hand expanded, filling with rakshasa blood to grow several times the size of Kamsa's body, the rest of which retained its human size. Vasudeva coughed and struggled as the hand lifted him off the ground to hover a yard in mid-air, feet kicking and flailing uselessly.

'That one I grant you as a learning experiment, brother-in-law,' he snarled. 'The next time, I will break our pact and kill Devaki. Do you understand? *Answer me!* DO YOU UNDERSTAND?'

With a supreme effort, Vasudeva managed to croak out a mangled 'Yes!'

Kamsa released his grip and let Vasudeva drop to the ground. Immediately, his hand began to reduce, returning to its normal size.

'So long as you uphold our pact and bring Devaki's newborn children to me each time, I shall let you both live under my protection. Those are the terms of *my* peace treaty. Uphold them. Or face the consequences.'

seventeen

The human mind and heart are only equipped to feel so much pain and sorrow. Beyond that point, it is simply more pain, more sorrow. Not bigger, greater, grander, just more. Anyone who has experienced the death of a loved one knows this to be true. The tear ducts can only produce so many tears at a time. The heart can grieve for only so long. Anything beyond that is simply more of the same. After a time, the mind grows numb. The heart hardens. The spirit withers and starts to die. *This is life*, says that part of us which enables us to survive holocausts and hurricanes, war and bereavement alike, *live through this*. And so we do live. We go on. We survive. We endure the unendurable and come out the other side, blinking, dazed, shocked and stupefied, but still alive. Still breathing. The heart, hammered by grief, still beats on, pumping life through our veins, keeping us alive. The lungs expand and contract. The brain still fires sparks of thought and reflex. The eyes still see, the ears still hear, and the sun rises and sets, the earth turns and the stars shine on, and the universe proceeds the way it has always proceeded … unhindered.

Through the terrible years that followed, Devaki was kept alive by just two thoughts: The first was Vasudeva's entreaty at the very outset, on the very evening of the day he had been forced to make the awful pact with Kamsa. *Live through this*, he had said. And the simple power of that command struck a deep chord within her. For it was true, despite all else. If they did not live, they would already have failed, without Kamsa needing to lift even a finger against them. And if they failed by giving up, by letting themselves die, or by killing themselves, Kamsa would surely have succeeded. And then what chance would Mathura have? Or the Yadava nations? Or Aryavarta as a whole? For what Kamsa was doing to Mathura, Jarasandha and his allies were doing to the rest of the civilized world. No, whatever happened, they must endure, they must survive. After Vasudeva's attempt on Kamsa's life and his failure, they realized that their best interest lay in upholding the pact. It was the only way for them to survive, to live, to go on.

The second, and most powerful of all, was the knowledge of the eighth child. The one yet to come. The one who was prophesied. *Slayer of Kamsa.* She mouthed the words silently to herself each time she felt her womb quicken with child and during the subsequent months of pregnancy. *You will come and save us, Slayer of Kamsa.* She called him by that title for it was the only name she knew to call him. Or her. All she knew was that the eighth child she would bear would bring about the doom of Kamsa. And if

Kamsa could be defeated, surely Mathura could be saved ... the Yadu race freed of its yoke of oppression ... and in time, Aryavarta rid of the evil of Jarasandha and his allies. The eighth child spelt hope. The future. Infinity.

And how could she give birth to the eighth child if she did not survive?

More than survive.

For a mother could not simply pretend. She must care. Thrive. Prosper. For what she felt, thought and experienced, her unborn child would feel, think and experience as well. So she must be strong and resilient and happy and healthy in order to produce children that were all those things, and more. She must *live*.

I am rich today, she had said once to her father, the father she had not seen in over six years now. And she was rich even now. Rich in the love of her husband and companion. Rich in hope. Rich in promise. Rich in prayer and faith and conviction.

For six years, Vasudeva took her newborn children to Kamsa.

And six times in as many years, Kamsa murdered the babies: held them by their feet, swung them overhead, and smashed out their tiny brains on the walls of his palace.

Six times. Six years. Six lives.

Innocent, beautiful, perfect, wonderful lives. Snuffed out. Destroyed.

Of all the crimes he had committed, all the injustices, all the atrocities and brutalities, surely that was Kamsa's worst offence? To kill innocent babies the very day of their birth? For no good reason.

And now, she was about to bear a seventh. The seventh. Where had the years gone? They had gone to the same place that her dead babes had gone. Into the mouth of Sesa, the serpent of infinity, its coils winding around the Samay Chakra, the great Wheel of Time upon which all Creation revolved. And once Sesa took hold of anything, it never returned. What was gone was gone, what was dead was dead, past was past.

Think only of today and of tomorrow, Devaki. The eighth child comes. Slayer of Kamsa.

But this was the seventh. The seventh, not the eighth.

Even if, somehow, the eighth was born and survived the wrath of Kamsa and lived to grow to adulthood and fulfil the prophecy, that would come later. This next one would only be the seventh. The prophecy had said nothing about the seventh killing anyone. So it would surely go the way of the first six.

Somehow, this realization broke her heart more than the grief she had lived through each year for the past six years.

Not another one, Devi. Not this one.

She prayed to the Goddess, her patron deity, with fervent ardour. Before her mind's eye flashed the several avatars and amsas of the Goddess: Durga, Bhadrakali, Vijaya, Vaisnavi, Kumuda, Candika, Krsna, Madhavi, Kanyaka, Maya, Narayani, Isani, Sarada, Ambika … and so many more she did not even know the names of. Resplendent, omnipotent, magnificent in feminine shakti, they appeared before her one by one and seemed to meld into her own essence, like layers upon layers of thinly beaten metal joining together to form a single blade.

Something happened within her womb.

She cried out.

A great heat surged within her. It grew to an unbearable degree, threatening to consume her alive in a single flash. White light tinged with blue at the corona exploded behind her eyes. She heard a great roaring, as of the ocean. And felt as if her stomach were being turned inside out.

She blacked out.

When she returned to consciousness, she found Vasudeva cradling her head in his lap, anxiously examining her. He had dripped water into her mouth and cooled her head and throat with a damp cloth. Her body was bathed in sweat as if after a high fever.

And her belly was as flat as it had been months earlier.

She touched it, needing to feel the truth for herself before allowing her faith to overwhelm reason. Then she knew it had not been just a hallucination.

'He has gone,' she said. 'He has been taken away, carried to safety.'

Vasudeva stared at her as if wondering if she was delirious. 'Who has gone?'

'The seventh child. Our son. See. Feel for yourself.'

She took his hand and pressed it to her belly. He stared into her eyes as he groped to decipher what she wanted him to feel, then understanding shone in his eyes.

'The baby is gone,' he said in wonderment. 'I no longer feel his shape, his legs, the edge of his heel digging out of the side of your stomach.'

She nodded. 'He has been carried to safety,' she said again. 'To a place where Kamsa will not be able to seek him out.'

He stared at her. 'How do you know this?'

She shrugged. 'I was told ...' She shook her head; that was not quite right. 'It was *shown* to me. By Yogamaya.'

'Yogamaya?'

'Yes, one of the infinite forms of Devi. She came and spirited away our seventh child from my womb, transferring it to the womb of another woman.'

'Who?' he asked.

'Rohini. Your first wife. My elder sister by way of marriage. There, he will come to term and be born without incident, safe from Kamsa. For how will Kamsa kill a child when he does not be able which child to kill?'

Vasudeva stared at her, sharing her excitement, his mind racing. 'And we shall tell him that you miscarried the seventh child. He can have his women check if he wishes. There is proof too: the child is gone from your womb.'

'Yes!' she said, clapping her hands together. It was

the first time in years that both of them had exhibited such happiness so freely.

Vasudeva nodded. He pulled her closer, kissing her on the top of her head, and she sighed with joy. 'But why the seventh child?' he wondered aloud. 'If the eighth was to be the Slayer ...'

'Perhaps the seventh has some role to play that we are not yet aware of,' she said.

He thought about it, then nodded. 'Yes, that must be it. And what matters is that he will live now. We will have a son! What shall we name him?'

She thought long and hard, then said, 'We should name him Shankarshan, for he was removed from the womb. But because he is the cause of such ramana, pleasure, to us, we shall call him Rama as well. And finally, because of the greatness of his strength, his bala, we shall name him Balabhadra.'

He chuckled. 'Shankarshan, Ramana, Balabhadra. Three names for a little babe! Will they not be too much for him to carry?'

She smiled proudly, knowingly. 'He can carry Creation if he wishes. Like Sesa, the infinite serpent.'

eighteen

Kamsa prowled the corridors of his palace. He now commanded the greatest Yadava standing army ever maintained; a force great enough to challenge most other kings, perhaps even great enough to challenge Jarasandha himself. The past seven years had seen him grow from strength to strength. Today, even Jarasandha's emissaries dared not raise their eyes to look directly at him, and spoke only soft, sweet assurances and words of agreement. He still fed the occasional eunuch to the beasts in the courtyard at the back, just to ensure that they stayed humble and polite. But in *his* kingdom, none dared even speak to him unless spoken to. He ruled with an iron hand. Absolute power. He had it, he enjoyed its fruits and spoils, and he would rule forever.

Perhaps the only thing that troubled him was the change in his physical form. While at first the rakshasa elements had showed themselves only in small ways or at some times, with the human form dominating, it was the other way around now. He was almost fully a rakshasa now, and only occasionally did he lapse into human form. And even those times were not by choice; they simply happened, involuntarily, and he was never quite sure what triggered them or sustained them. The only thing he could control was his size. He had settled on a more-or-less permanent size of around one-and-a-half-times the size of a big-built human Kshatriya, which made him about ten feet in height and as thick around the chest as a bull's torso. From time to time, he would expand further, often without meaning to; but becoming smaller than his new permanent size was nigh impossible for him. He tried at times, if only because a large size often made it awkward to move through doorways and ride elephants. Even though he had had the palace redesigned to accommodate his new permanent size, if he grew several more yards in height, as he often did, even a twenty-foot-high doorway could be too low to get through comfortably. And even elephants had a limit to how much they could carry.

The more he used his rakshasa abilities, the more he became a rakshasa, and the less human he grew.

But this was not what troubled him now.

Devaki and Vasudeva had succeeded in saving their seventh child.

He knew this with perfect certainty. He had just returned from visiting his brother-in-law and sister and he had heard their account of the unfortunate mishap. They had both been visibly distraught and their performance was credible, but he had smelt through it at once. There was an odour of truth to their claims, but underlying that was a whiff of something else ... not quite a lie, but not the whole truth either. They had held something back.

He had demanded to see the remains, and had been shown a mangled mess that was convincing enough. But he knew that he had been deceived. The question was *how*. Nobody had entered or left their house, through any ingress. Anticipating treachery, he had got the house watch tripled in the past month. He had employed spasas to infiltrate the community of daimaas who assisted Devaki during pregnancy and deliveries. The verdict was unanimous: somehow, the child had miscarried. He had even bitten off the head of one spasa – a habit he had acquired over the past year or so and resorted to when one of his own people were being inefficient or obtuse; it always produced excellent results, not from the person whose head he had bitten off, of course. (The heads made for chewy snacks as well; he enjoyed the crunchy skulls and the tasty brains inside.) But while that had elicited the anticipated reactions from the other spasas – better intelligence reports – it hadn't brought forth any further intelligence on this particular matter.

He could find no way to prove that the child had been born in Mathura, or elsewhere.

Yet, he knew that, somehow, he had been deceived.

It is so, Prince Kamsa. You have indeed been deceived.

He turned to see Narada-muni standing in the corridor. The sage's image looked solid and real enough, but when Kamsa tried passing a hand – he swung a fist with enough force to fell a horse – through it, the hand passed through empty air, the image remaining undisturbed. 'You!' he said. 'It's been a long time since you showed your bearded face. And I'm king now, not prince.'

It was never my intention to become your best friend or lifelong companion. As for the title you bestow upon yourself, I may call a house built with cow-dung a palace, as many do, but that would not make it so. So long as King Ugrasena lives, you shall always be Prince Kamsa. Or simply the usurper, as you are better known amongst the people.

Kamsa snarled, expanding himself till his head touched the ceiling and his arms the walls of the four-yard-wide corridor. 'Why don't you appear before me in your real, corporeal form, Brahmin. Then let us see if you dare to insult me.'

Narada laughed shortly.

I do not come here to bandy insults or threats with you; merely to warn you. The seventh child of Vasudeva and Devaki has slipped through your grasp.

Kamsa swore and thumped the walls to either side with his fist. Plaster crumbled and great cracks appeared in the walls, running up to the curved ceiling. Narada flinched, looking up as pieces of the ceiling clattered and fell around him in a shower of dust and debris, then seemed to recall he was in no danger.

'I knew it! They deceived me somehow. But *how?*'

They have powerful allies. The devas themselves assist them. Brahma instructed Devi Yogamaya to spirit the child from Devaki's womb to another location.

'Where?' Kamsa pounded the floor with his foot, sending a giant crack running all the way up the length of the corridor – between the saptarishi's feet. Again, Narada almost jumped, but controlled himself. 'Tell me where and I can go and crush it like a grape in my fist.'

That was not made known to me.

'What do you mean, not made known? Who makes these things known to you?'

Narada hesitated, glancing over his shoulder as if concerned that someone might overhear him. Kamsa frowned. There was nobody in sight in the entire length of the corridor in both directions at this time of night. No matter what Kamsa did, or what sounds came from his chambers, none of his people would dare intrude upon his privacy until called for, unless they wanted their heads bitten off. He realized that Narada was not looking back at this corridor in Kamsa's palace. He was looking back at the place where his physical body was right now, in some distant location.

I do not have much time, son of Padmavati. I urge you; listen to my words and heed them well.

This may be your only chance of ensuring that the eighth child never takes birth in this lifetime.

Kamsa frowned. Did that mean the child could take birth in some other lifetime? There was more to the matter than Narada was revealing to him; he had always sensed this. Now he knew it was so. 'First tell me this: why do you help me?'

Narada looked at him.

What do you mean, Kamsa?

'It is a simple enough question. Why help me? I am …' He gestured at himself, not needing to describe his own appearance or nature. 'I am what I am. Usually, Brahmins like you, especially brahmarishis and saptarishis, would be training Kshatriyas to kill people like me. Instead, you appear mysteriously from time to time and offer me advice and warnings that have helped me prosper and gain power. Why are you so benevolent to me? Have I done something to merit your protection and blessing?'

Narada looked away, avoiding Kamsa's eyes.

What difference does it make? I am helping you, as you yourself admit, so take my advice and use it well. There is an old saying among cattle herders, perhaps it even originated from the Yadus: do not look a gifted cow in the mouth to check its health, for that might insult the one who gifts it to you! It is advice you would do well to heed.

Kamsa nodded. 'In that case, be gone.'

Narada blinked.

What did you say?

Kamsa waved a hand dismissively. 'Be gone. Away. Leave us be.' He looked at the saptarishi insolently, grinning wide enough to display his inner set of teeth, the ones that clamped down to crunch particularly hard items, skulls for instance, or human thigh bones. 'I do not trust intelligence provided for unknown motives by one who openly says he is not my friend.' He smiled slyly. 'And is a known associate of the devas, who are sworn enemies of all asuras, of which race, in case you were not aware, I am a member.'

Narada glared, angry now. Saptarishis and brahmarishis were not accustomed to being told to get lost.

This is an outrage!

Kamsa turned his back on the saptarishi, stretched his arms and yawned languorously. 'Now, either tell me what I wish to know, or turn into a cartwheel and roll away.'

Narada sulked for few seconds. Kamsa finished stretching and yawning and started walking away. He was amused when the sage called him back. Good. Now, he would get some real answers, and then he could figure out how to make sure that little slayer was never born.

nineteen

Vasudeva and Devaki were asleep when Kamsa's men arrived. Vasudeva leaped out of his bed, heart thudding, and thought, *this is it; he has finally broken our pact and has come to have Devaki killed.* He told his frightened wife to stay inside, went out, barred the door and stood before it. He would kill anyone who tried to harm his wife. He would rather die than stand by and watch his beloved be killed. If this was to be his last stand, so be it.

The men were led by Bana himself, clad in his resplendent robes and ornate armour proclaiming his status as saprem senapati. It offended Vasudeva's very core to see a man like Bana given charge of Mathura's armies, not merely a man without any sense of dharma or morality, but a known slaver and slave-trader even before he had allied with Kamsa. Vasudeva himself had once delegated a force to stop Bana's thriving trade in child slaves. They had crippled his operation considerably, if not quashed it altogether. He knew that Bana had always borne him a grudge for it. That showed now as the thin, tall man stood before him, slapping a free glove into the gloved palm of the other hand in a habitual rhythm as he grinned.

'Vasu,' he said, then added with heavy irony, *'deva!'*

He looked around. 'I thought devas resided in swargaloka; yet, here you are, amongst us humble mortals. What have we done to deserve your presence, lord?'

He laughed. His soldiers laughed as well. There were over a dozen of them, Vasudeva noted, all armoured and armed. Clearly, they had not come just to deliver a message. He heard the sound of heavy clinking and glimpsed a length of chain in one man's hands, attached to manacles. What was that for? Were they to be shifted to a dungeon now?

'What are your orders this time, Bana,' Vasudeva said calmly. 'Did he toss a stick and ask you to go fetch it?'

Bana's smile vanished at once. 'You would be well advised to watch your tongue, Vrishni.'

Vasudeva didn't retort. His first barb had struck home. That was enough.

'Move aside,' Bana said.

Vasudeva folded his arms comfortably. 'These are our private quarters. None may pass.'

Bana grinned. 'Why, Vrishni? Do you fear we might molest your wife?'

Several chuckles greeted that one.

Vasudeva would not let himself be provoked by such puerile taunts. He remained standing in their way.

Bana sighed irritably. 'We are here on the king's orders. It is best if you let us do what we have to and leave.'

Vasudeva shook his head. 'Not until you tell me what you are here to do.'

Bana gestured to the man at the back. He came forward, the chains dragging on the ground with a nerve-rasping sound. 'You are to be chained and manacled henceforth.' He gestured to one side of the house. 'And restricted to one half of the house.'

Bana gestured again and a pair of stonemasons came forward, their implements in hand. 'They are to raise a wall dividing the house into two halves. You will reside in one half and your wife in the other.' He added with evident pleasure: 'She is to be chained and manacled as well.'

'But why?' Vasudeva asked. Whatever he had expected, this was not it. Violence, a direct assault, an attempt on his or Devaki's life, he was prepared for these things. But what good would it do to chain Devaki and him and keep them in separate halves of the house? And why raise a brick wall between them? How would they ...? He stopped. Understanding swept through him.

Bana grinned, seeing his expression change. 'When one wishes to rest the bull, one puts the cow in another pasture, and raises a fence between them.' He took hold of the chain in his soldier's hand and shook it, making it jangle loudly. 'And to make sure the bull does not jump the fence, we chain its leg.'

He grasped Vasudeva's hand roughly and clapped the manacle on it. 'And that is how you make sure there are no calves born.'

The sound of Bana's soldiers laughing filled Vasudeva's ears.

twenty

Vasudeva sat on one side of the wall. Devaki was on the other. He could hear her but it was not possible to see her from any angle. The chains and manacles made sure of that. They were compelled to do everything within the reach of the chains, which were barely a few yards long. His heart wept at the thought of Devaki chained like a common criminal in a dungeon.

What crimes have we committed, Lord? Why do you make us suffer thus? he thought.

They talked through the wall, talked more than ever. The separation was agonizing. Only a few yards away, yet so far.

But as the days passed, he realized how brilliant Kamsa's plan had been. Without harming Vasudeva or Devaki, without breaking the pact between them, without killing his sister or brother-in-law, he had made it impossible for the eighth child to be conceived. It was a devilishly clever stratagem.

The one thing that had provided succour to them, had kept them moving forward purposefully through the terrible years and days and nights, was the knowledge that some day, the eighth child would come. Slayer of Kamsa. Now, Kamsa had ensured that the child could never be conceived, let alone be born. There would be no slayer, no end to this perpetual nightmare. And what of the future? Were they to live like this till the end of their lives? Perhaps, from time to time, Kamsa would degrade their lives further in some new way, finding new methods of harassing them, torturing them indirectly. Maybe some day he would wall them in completely, as he had done his own father and mother, neither of whom had been seen by a soul since that day seven years ago, and who were believed to be alive inside that hellish prison. A life lived thus, Vasudeva mused bleakly, was worse than a violent death. Death at least put a stop to the pain.

He turned and looked at the wall. It loomed, rising to the very ceiling, five feet thick and reinforced with rods of iron. It was as solid as a fortress wall. Even if he attempted to dig through somehow, he would be found out within a day by the guards who patrolled the house. And the attempt itself might worsen their plight.

He sat back, shoulders slumped despondently, and slept.

twenty-one

When Vasudeva awoke, the first thing he noticed was the light.

Night had fallen. The house was dark. The patch of sky visible through the open window was black as pitch. If there was a moon, he could not see it through that narrow portal, nor any stars.

But the wall glowed with light.

He blinked and looked up, certain he was dreaming.

A shape very much like a large oblong had appeared on the wall, at eye level. It seemed to be formed entirely of some kind of brilliant bluish light. He had never seen the likes of it before. It glowed rhythmically, pulsing and throbbing slowly, like ... like ... *a heartbeat?* Yes. That was exactly what that pulsing rhythm resembled, a heartbeat.

Slowly, he realized that the light was shaped like an egg. A very large egg, perhaps the size of a man's belly.

Or a woman's womb.

Yes. That was precisely it. It was not an egg, but an embryo. An unborn infant, nestled within the safety of its mother's womb, pulsating with life. And the light, this magical wondrous bluish glow he was seeing, perhaps this was how the world appeared to an embryo within the womb.

Even as he thought this, the light began to take clearer shape and form. Now, he could see the shape of the womb, the fluid-sac that acted as a vital protective shield cushioning the unborn life, and within it, the unmistakable shape of the infant child, curled in that primordial foetal pose.

He slid backwards on the ground, suddenly afraid. The chain clanked in protest. He was at its farthest limit. The manacle dug into his shin and calf, cutting open the scabs of crusted blood and making his wounds bleed again.

Do not fear me, Father, the infant exclaimed. *I will never harm you.*

Vasudeva felt himself shudder, then fought to regain control of his senses. 'Who … who are you?'

I am your son.

He did not know what to say to that. His son? Which son, he was about to ask. For he had had several, all dashed to death by their brute of an uncle. Surely, this was the restless aatma of one of those poor unfortunate dead. But the voice sensed his confusion and clarified: *Your unborn son. Your eighth child.*

Vasudeva resisted the urge to gasp aloud. With an effort, he said, 'But you have not yet been conceived!'

That momentous event shall take place tonight, in a few moments.

'But ... how?'

Through the power of your mind, I shall be transported into my mother's womb. All you have to do is will me there, and it will be done.

Vasudeva remained silent. He knew what the child was saying was true. He knew this in every fibre and cell of his being. There was no doubt at all. He felt his mind grow calmer, his pulse steady, his heartbeat return to its usual pace. 'But after that, what next? The moment Kamsa hears that his sister ... your mother ... is carrying the eighth child, he will not sit idly by and let you come to term.'

I shall tell you what you have to do. All will be well. Just do as I say, Father, and I shall take care of the rest.

Vasudeva thought a moment longer, then nodded slowly. 'Yes. I shall.'

Then let us begin. Focus your mind on me, become one with me, and the rest shall come to pass.

Vasudeva looked deep into the blue egg of light, at the being that floated there, suspended in that ethereal sac of sacred blue illumination. And slowly, by degrees, he felt his consciousness rise up out of his body. He felt his entire spirit soar ... up, up, up, high above the ether, and down, down into the blue light

... the blue light of Brahman that the sacred verses of the Upanishads referred to ... and he experienced a great sense of peace and fulfilment sweep through him. Every anxiety wiped clean. Every worry washed away. Every pore of his body alive with energy, with shakti.

He felt that energy pass from him through the wall to the other side ...

To his beloved ... Devaki.

twenty-two

A gentle breeze rose from the Yamuna and blew through the city. It stirred the senses of even the most miserable souls in Mathura, awakening them to an awareness, a tingling sense of expectation, of something about to happen. Rivers that had grown murky, sluggish or parched, began to flow in their full strength, their waters clear as crystal, sweet and fresh as if drawn directly from a glacier. Ponds that had dried up or turned to scum-covered mosquito-breeding nests, turned clear and were filled with lotuses. Trees whose branches had withered straightened their bent boughs and turned green from the roots up to the highest leaf. Bees began to buzz and make honey again, sweeter and thicker than ever before. Sacred yagna fires burned on even without fuel needing to be added, as astonished Brahmins exclaimed, each wanting to take credit for the miracle. The minds of penitents were at ease, tapasvis felt they had achieved the goal for which they had spent decades meditating. Chanteuses found themselves singing songs they had never heard before, and never knew they knew. Kinnaras and gandharva clans sang and danced for no particular reason. Siddhas and caranas offered oblations and prayers. Vidyadharas danced with danseuses and were happy as never before. Every sign, every omen, every portent, was auspicious.

In his palace, Kamsa had been gnawing on the thighbone of an uks while he listened to the tally of a new lagaan, a land tax he had imposed upon the Yadava nations. He was already enraged by the low tally, and the excuse given, that more and more Yadavas were choosing to migrate to other lands rather than continue to live under his reign. He ordered all those found leaving their homes to be killed on the spot. But it occurred to him that if he killed all those who *could* afford to pay the lagaan, who would be left to pay it? Only those who could *not* afford it.

That was when he smelt the breeze blowing into the chamber, and smelt as well the secret message it carried. He rose from his throne and, with one swift sweep of his hand, picked up the grand throne and threw it across the sabha hall, breaking the great door of the assembly chamber. He threw back his head and bellowed with rage.

Despite all his efforts, the day he had feared had come to pass. The eighth child had been born. It was impossible, with Vasudeva and Devaki kept apart all this while, and with Devaki displaying no signs of pregnancy until this very morning; but somehow, the impossible had been accomplished. And now the day was here at last.

He strode from the sabha hall, bellowing orders as he went. Bana and Canura scurried after him, trying to keep pace. Kamsa had expanded himself to thrice his normal size. As he walked, he banged his fist against walls, knocking out chunks of stone and brickwork, slammed his shoulder into pillars, cracking them in two and endangering the ceilings they helped hold up, shattered statuary as his hand brushed against them, and generally demolished his own palace without knowing or caring.

He emerged from the palace and bellowed for his elephant. A very frightened mahout bowed low and tried to find a way to tell him that he had killed Haddi-Hathi during his last ride – losing his temper and expanding himself suddenly, the elephant reduced to pulp beneath Kamsa. No elephant could seat him. Bana and Canura stood at a safe distance and attempted to pass on or execute his orders. From what they could follow, he wished to mobilize the entire army!

At that moment, the breeze gathered speed. The stench of flowers in full bloom seemed to assault Kamsa's senses. He froze, went limp, blazing-red eyes rolling up in his head, and he fell to the ground like a sack of potatoes ... or a small mountain of bricks, because the impact of his fall crushed the poor mahout who was bowing before him, as it did several soldiers standing nearby.

Bana and Canura stared at this extraordinary sight.

'The king has fainted!' Canura said, barely able to
believe the words himself, although he could clearly
see Kamsa lying prone, arms flung out, drool dribbling
from his parted lips. Something insectile – with a
thousand tiny, hairy legs – emerged from Kamsa's
mouth, then shuddered and fell back.

Bana was about to respond to Canura when,
suddenly, his eyes rolled up and he collapsed as well.
Canura followed. So did every single person in the
palace.

Across the city, the same thing was happening.
People were falling unconscious where they stood,
or sat, or rode. People, animals, birds, insects … every
living creature.

Because of the curfew, most citizens were indoors
at the time, and fell asleep in their chairs or beds and
were safe in their homes. Kamsa's soldiers, enforcing
the curfew, patrolling, or engaged in other soldierly
duties, were less fortunate. Some fell into horse
troughs, others into cess pits, hundreds fell off their
horses or elephants and broke their necks or arms or
legs. Many died in bizarre accidents, like the captain
of a company of soldiers who was about to set fire to
a house because the owner had refused to supply free
milk and butter to his soldiers. The captain had taken
the burning brand from one of his soldiers, wanting
to set fire to the house with his own hands as the
farmer and his distraught family watched and wept.
The wind changed and, as sleep overtook him, he fell

off his horse. While he slept, the brand caught a few stray strands of the hay stacked outside the house, immolating him on the spot.

Mathura slept.

twenty-three

Vasudeva held the bundle in his arms carefully and rose to his feet. As he did so, a great wind raged through the house, as if cheering his accomplishment, then passed as suddenly as it had risen. He smiled at Devaki, who beamed up at him happily, then turned and left.

As he reached the first of several doors, a loud clanging echoed and the bolt broke off the door and fell to the ground with a soft thud. The door flew open and stayed open as he passed through. The same thing happened with the other doors too. Outside each door, he found guards fallen unconscious at their posts, some in ludicrous postures and at least one with a severe fracture, or worse.

The city was quiet as he walked through the streets. Not a soul was stirring. Not so much as a bird flew across the night sky. Not a single insect chirred or cricketed. Not a dog or cat or even a mouse scurried in the shadows. He passed soldiers everywhere. They had fallen off horses, elephants and the raised towers posted at every junction … Glancing into a few houses whose doors or windows lay open, he saw the people inside sleeping as well. The entire city was asleep.

Kamsa too; for nothing else would have prevented him from being there otherwise.

As he walked, he recalled the events of the night.

Devaki and he had been awakened by the reappearance of the blue light. She saw the same thing that he saw, but from her side of the wall.

No more was the child a foetus. It appeared now within a bubble – of blue Brahman shakti – as a newborn come to full term.

The child was a boy with four arms. In his four hands he clutched a conch, a mace, a lotus and a chakra. He had a radiant jewel upon his neck. He had marks upon his chest. He was swaddled in a yellow garment which contrasted pleasantly with his fresh blue skin.

He smiled down at his father and mother and the beauty of that smile filled them both with a deep, glowing warmth and inner radiance. For the rest of their days, they had only to think of that smile to be filled with a sense of complete peace, tranquillity, and joy.

Vasudeva joined his palms in anjali and bowed. 'My son. Who are you? What are you? Pray, enlighten us. We are but simple mortals, we know nothing.'

The boy smiled.

You are Vasudeva and Devaki, my parents. Everything I know comes from you and through you. Without you, I would not have been able to set foot upon this world.

'Yes,' Devaki said, 'but it is *you* who makes this possible, Lord. We are only the instruments of your miracle. Looking at your radiance, feeling your shakti, I am convinced that you are Bhagwan, God himself, the Supreme Being.'

The boy smiled enigmatically.

He looked to one side and then looked back. His gaze brought back with it a flowing river of images, sounds and sensations. With a flick of his fingers, he diverted the flow to Devaki and Vasudeva, both of whom reeled back in amazement. Their minds were filled with palpable memories of things actually seen, experienced, heard and felt.

Vasudeva gasped. 'You are Vishnu Incarnate!'

Devaki said, 'You took an incarnation as Vaman the dwarf once. As Parshurama. As Rama Chandra. As Hamsa. As Varaha. As Narasimha. As Kurma. As Hayagriva. And as Matsya. In different ages of the world, you assume different forms for different purposes. But this alone is your Incarnate form, in this amsa.'

Not only I, you too were born before and lived other lives before these ones. Do you not recall them?

Devaki and Vasudeva shook their heads.

You, Vasudeva, were a prajapati named Sutapa. And you, my mother, were Prsni. This was during the era of Svayambhuva Manu. And I was born to you in that life as well, where I was named Prsnigarbha. Would you like to know more?

Both nodded eagerly.

Then listen. I shall show to you the entire history of our past lives together, as well as those yet to come.

Both Vasudeva and Devaki closed their eyes as a fresh flood of visions swept through them, carrying them upon the tide of time, across the oceans of eternity.

After communing with his parents for an undetermined time, the unborn child stopped and sighed.

It is now time. The hour of my birth is at hand.

Devaki reacted. The child saw her do so.

You fear your brother's wrath?

'Yes, my son.'

Have no fear. He shall not harm you tonight. Now, I shall take my place within your womb, Mother. And you shall give birth to me as any human child. Once in human form, I shall be subject to human qualities and failings as well. For though I am incarnate in this amsa and not merely a partial avatar, there are inherent limitations of the human form that cannot be overcome completely. Therefore, I shall seem to be, for all intents and purposes, a normal newborn human baby. But do not be deceived. I am here to set things right once and for all. However long it takes and no matter what I have to do, I shall see this through. You shall be freed of the yoke of the oppressor. So shall all the Yadavas. The race of Yadu shall enjoy a time of such prosperity and satisfaction as they have never seen before since the beginning of their line. This I promise you.

'Wait,' said Vasudeva, palms still pressed together. 'What shall we name you, Lord? You are no ordinary child. Surely we must grant you some special name as well?'

He smiled. And told them.

twenty-four

Now, Vasudeva stood before the Yamuna, carrying his newborn son in his arms. As he recalled the wonders that he had been shown and the knowledge and memories he had been given, he wept, and had to pause to wipe the tears of joy from his eyes.

A new challenged awaited him.

The river was in spate, flowing with a roaring rush that would sweep any and everything along. At this time of year, even elephants could not be bathed in this stretch of the river, nor bridges spanned or boats travel safely. The only way across was to go several yojanas downstream, where the river split into its tributaries, and cross using a raft anchored by an overhanging rope system.

But Vasudeva had been told by his son that he had only until dawn to deliver him to his destination and return home. The place he was to go was a fair distance away, no easy walk even without having a newborn child in one's arms. The detour downstream would make it impossible. He would not even reach his destination before daybreak, let alone return. And his son's instructions had been quite clear. The sleep would last only until dawn, at which point, Kamsa would rouse and send every soldier in Mathura in pursuit of him.

He looked around, feeling frustration – born of years of imprisonment and abuse – swell up inside him. Then he realized how foolish he was being and smiled. 'Lord,' he said quietly, 'you must surely have provided for all contingencies. Pray, allow me to cross the river.'

Certainly, Father.

The response winked in his mind like a flash of light. He thought he heard a tiny baby gurgle as well.

Thunder rumbled in the sky. Vasudeva glanced up nervously but saw only a clear night sky. Not a single cloud in sight. But he had heard the thunder distinctly.

A single bolt of lightning cracked down and struck the centre of the river.

Water rose in a geyser-like spout, rising up hundreds of yards into the air and slowly fell back. When it had settled, Vasudeva saw that a crack had appeared in the river. A thin line drawn straight across, from bank to bank. As he watched, incredulous, the line widened until it was several yards broad, revealing the very bottom of the river.

The river began to slow down. Downstream, it remained the same, gushing along at breakneck speed. But upstream of the crack, it slowed steadily, by degrees, until finally, after several moments, it ceased flowing altogether. He looked at the downstream flow – it continued unabated, though there was now a distinct gap dividing the river into two halves.

Thunder growled and grumbled overhead.

Ours not to understand everything that happens, or how or why it happens. Ours merely to do our given task.

When the gap was wide enough, he stepped down the side of the riverbank, careful not to slip, and descended to the bottom of the river.

Just as he reached, the sky cracked open and a torrential rain poured down. It was like a cloudburst, the heaviest rainfall that Vasudeva had ever seen in his life. Fat, heavy drops struck the ground, splashing mud. Within moments, the world was blanketed by rain.

Yet, not a single drop fell on Vasudeva or his newborn son.

He looked around in wonderment, raising one hand and stretching it out. At its farthest extent, he could just feel the rain. He brought back his fingers, dripping wet, and looked at them. They smelt of fresh earth and rain. Yet here, where he stood, not a drop fell. He looked around, and saw that the invisible protective canopy that shielded him from the rain took a curious shape, like a tapering ... hood? Then he remembered his son's words, explaining this very thing, from earlier: **The hood of Sesa, the eternal serpent. Sesa shall travel with you, protecting you from all dangers, big and small.**

Vasudeva nodded and started off across the bed of the river. Perfectly natural for the eternal serpent to appear out of mythology and protect him as he carried his newborn son, God Incarnate, across a divided river. Quite natural.

He reached the far side a while later, and trekked up to the other bank. He started off in the direction of Vrindavan. From there, he would make his way into one of the oldest of Yadava territories, Vrajbhoomi, the heart of the Vrishni nation. It was a long walk. And he had to complete it and return home before dawn. Otherwise, even his infinitely powerful son would not be able to save him from Kamsa's wrath.

He reached the tiny hamlet a few hours later. Bone-weary, yet filled with joy and anticipation. As he had been told, a light was burning in one of the modest huts. As he came to its doorway, he had a moment of anxiety. *What if…?*

But everything had been exactly as promised. Every single person he had passed between Mathura and this remote hamlet had been fast asleep. He had even seen a cowherd resting on his crook, dead asleep and snoring, as his cows lay asleep around him.

Inside the hut, he found a woman on a cot, with an infant lying beside her, suckling. It was evident that she had only just given birth before falling asleep as everyone else had.

A man lay prone on the floor beside the cot, as if he had been taken by the sleep as he sat or stood beside his wife. As Vasudeva entered, the infant stopped suckling and turned its head to look at him. Its arms and legs began to move in the manner of all babies, kicking out excitedly. He saw that it was a girl: as he had been told it would be.

He put his son down on the cot beside the woman and picked up the infant girl. She squealed with delight as he took her in his arms, and he felt a rush of love and tenderness. It helped make it easier for him to turn his back on his own son, whom he left beside the sleeping woman.

He returned to the house in Mathura just as the first flush of dawn was creeping across the eastern sky. He put the baby down beside Devaki, who took her in her arms and cradled her with as much welcoming love as if she were greeting her own child. He looked at Devaki for a long moment, brushed the tears from her cheeks, then kissed the baby on her head – she kicked and gurgled happily – kissed his wife on her forehead as well, then returned to his side of the wall.

He put the manacle back on his foot and waited.

Moments later, as the sky reddened and the wind changed, shouts and cries of alarm and indignation began to ring out across Mathura.

The city was awake again.

twenty-five

Kamsa was silent.

Everybody exchanged glances, their faces giving away their fear.

Never before had he been so quiet for so long. Tantrums, ranting, rages, fury, they were accustomed to all these. They did not relish them, but they expected them. They were like earthquakes and hurricanes, floods and famines – inevitable.

But not silence.

He sat there on the royal dais, head resting on one fist, the elbow resting on his thigh. The throne lay in smithereens around him. The rumour among the men was that Kamsa could no longer control his size changes and other bodily processes and had found it difficult to fit into the ornate throne that he had specially got made once he declared himself King Eternal. Nobody had any idea what his inability to fit into the throne meant or portended. But absurd and quite amusing though it was, nobody dared laugh at it or speak of it anywhere within hearing distance of him. They remained as silent as Kamsa was now, waiting with dread in their hearts.

The eighth child had been born, as prophesied.

It had been a girl.

Those who had been with Kamsa, Bana and Canura when they went to Vasudeva's house, said that they saw the newborn girl themselves. It was evident that she had been born that very night, no more than a few hours earlier.

When we were all sleeping.

How a woman could deliver a perfectly healthy baby when she had not exhibited a single sign of pregnancy just the day before was a question nobody dared to ask.

How the bolts of all the doors had been broken, the chains shattered, the manacles unclasped and the wall brought down, nobody could explain.

Kamsa had roared with rage when he saw the newborn. Bana and Canura had run away from him, no doubt fearing that he would take out his wrath on them for failing to see that Devaki was pregnant – even though she had not been pregnant; they were sure of this because even the daimaas who examined her intimately had reported no sign of pregnancy, and the daimaas were spasas who worked for Kamsa.

But Kamsa had directed his anger at the child instead.

Snatching it out of Devaki's hands – she had cried out as he did so, raising her hands in a gesture of pleading – Kamsa took the girl infant by the leg, swung her around once, twice, and then a third time as he always did when killing infants. He had been seen doing the same thing hundreds of times before. He always did it the same way, with nary a single variation. He even joked about it saying that it was the most energy-saving and efficient way to do the job!

But this time, as he swung the child around the third and final time, she flew out of his hands. She didn't fly across the house, but up, into the air, above Kamsa's head. Where she floated, gurgling happily.

Kamsa turned and stared at his empty hand, then up at the floating child. Everybody stared as well. Bana and Canura stopped their hasty flight to stare too.

The baby laughed and clapped her tiny hands together. They didn't meet perfectly, because babies do not have very good coordination. But the action was unmistakable.

Then the baby transformed into a goddess.

Resplendent with beautiful blue skin, decorated with garlands, rich robes, jewellery and accoutrements, she floated in mid-air.

'I am Yogamaya, sister of Vishnu. My brother bid me come here to give you this message.'

And then she said it, the thing that nobody dared repeat, or even speak aloud in Kamsa's presence ... though every soldier knew that across Mathura, across the Yadava nations, the same words were being repeated with laughter, with tears of joy, with cheers and applause and celebration, with festive glee.

The Slayer of Kamsa has been born. And he is safely out of your reach.

The devi then vanished, leaving only flower petals that fell in a shower to the ground in her wake. Her laughter echoed in the air, more like a baby's gurgle than a woman's laugh.

After the incident, Kamsa had returned to his palace, and sat still. Silent. He had seemed bewildered ever since the appearance of the goddess.

Finally, plucking up their courage, Bana and Canura spoke up, taking turns, as if they had decided that they should share the risk of bringing Kamsa's wrath down on themselves.

'My Lord,' Bana said, 'there is unrest in the city. The events of last night have thrown the people into a frenzy. Every hour, soldiers are bringing word that Yadavas are challenging our soldiers, defying them in small ways.'

Bana glanced at Canura who swallowed and took up the cudgels: 'We must act now to suppress them, while they are still disorganized. If we allow time to pass, there could be an uprising. What happened this morning ...'

He trailed off, looking at his associate. Bana flinched and spoke up: 'Word will surely spread soon. Once everyone knows, they may feel emboldened to rebel openly. We recommend that you act before it is too late.'

'If you wish, we could send word to Lord Jarasandha to send in a few contingents to back us up. His men will kill Yadavas more readily than our soldiers,' Canura said in a nervous rush.

Bana added hastily: 'Not that *our* men would not do as much. We are just pointing out all the possible courses of action.'

Kamsa raised his head slowly. 'There will be no need to send for Jarasandha's army. We will act ourselves. Now. Before the people have a chance to gather their wits and rise.'

He stood, towering above everyone else in the large hall. His head hit the ceiling that stood twenty feet above the floor. He seemed not to notice.

'You are right,' he said with surprising mildness to Bana and Canura. 'We must quell this petty defiance before it blossoms into outright rebellion. We must also quell the rumours that are bound to spread after this morning's events.'

'Rumour, sir?' Canura asked, hesitantly.

Kamsa looked at them. His eyes were looking in disparate directions, they noticed; and he seemed to have difficulty locating them. But he finally managed to settle at least one eye on them, while the other one roved the far wall of the sabha hall, making the soldiers on that side grow nervous for their own lives.

'This stupid rumour of a slayer being born,' he said.

He laughed. A small burst of insectile forms were thrown forth to land at the feet of several men, writhing and crawling.

'Slayer of Kamsa!' He shook with silent amusement. 'How absurd. How impossible. I cannot be slain. I am immortal.'

Then he was silent for another half hour. Just standing there, brooding, eyes rolling in separate directions, wildly.

Finally, Bana dared to speak up again. 'What shall we do, sire? Shall we do a purge, round up the most obvious troublemakers and make examples of them as usual?'

Kamsa started, as if disturbed out of deep thought. 'What? Oh yes. Of course. No, we shall dispense with the usual methods this time. This calls for something more drastic.'

'Yes, sire?'

Kamsa toyed with something growing out of the underside of his ear. Canura looked away, unable to watch.

'The people believe that my slayer has been born today. So we shall rid them of this notion. We shall kill the slayer wherever he might be.'

'But, My Lord, we do not know where he is.'

'Exactly. Therefore we shall kill them all.'

'All, sire?'

'All the newborns. Male and female. Across all the Yadava nations.'

Bana and Canura stared at him, speechless.

Kamsa's left eye peered at them. 'Assemble every soldier. Every last one. We shall need them all.'

'Even the reserves, sire?'

'Yes!'

They flinched. Kamsa was regaining his normal tone and volume now. He stalked the hall, looking like a man who had reached a decision at last after long pondering.

'They believe a slayer has been born to save them. We shall see to it that this slayer, whoever he may be, wherever he may be, will not live to see another day, let alone live long enough to slay me. We shall do this today, and quell all rebellion, all challengers, once and for all. We shall slay every newborn child in the Yadava nations today. Assemble the army, divide all the men and send them out to start work at once. Tell them to kill every newborn child …' He paused. 'No, make that every child born in the past ten days, just to be sure they don't trick us by pretending he was born last week or the week before. When in doubt, kill all the infants, even the children if you like. Cut off their heads and bring them to me. I want a full tally by tomorrow morning.'

He looked around at the hall filled with stunned faces staring up at him. 'What are you all looking at, you fools?'

Bana looked at Canura, then back at Kamsa. 'Sire, you don't mean *all* of them, do you? I mean …' he trailed off.

Canura spoke up. 'What Bana means, sire, is that he and his wife have just had twins … three days ago…' He gestured around the hall. 'There must be hundreds of our *own* soldiers whose wives have delivered babies in the past few days as well.'

Kamsa grinned a lopsided grin. 'Then we must start with *them* first. Setting an example. Bana, let us see these bonny twins of yours, hey?'

Kamsa began to expand himself, cracking open the roof of the sabha hall, growing enormous. '*AND ANY MAN WHO ATTEMPTS TO DECEIVE*

*ME OR SPARES A CHILD, I SHALL KILL HIM
AND HIS ENTIRE FAMILY MYSELF. SLAYER
OF KAMSA, IS IT? WELL, THEN LET ME BE
CALLED THE SLAYER OF MATHURA TODAY.
OR BETTER STILL, THE CHILDSLAYER!*

And then he raised his head to the sky and roared
his fury. The sound reverberated for yojanas around.

'VISHNU, I AM COMING FOR YOU!'

And as if in response, the sky replied with a burst of
thunder that shook the palace to its foundations.

acknowledgements

Deep and lasting gratitude is due to:

My wife Bithika, our daughter Yashka and our son Ayush Yoda: This book and my life are already dedicated to you. You know better than anyone else how unlikely it is for me to be the author of the Ramayana Series® and now the Krishna Coriolis, having had a mixed-race, mixed-culture, multi-national, non-religious and non-casteist upbringing. You know, too, that I tell these stories as a human being first, foremost and last. This truly secular and non-partisan outlook and world view is your legacy as much as it is mine.

R. Sabarish, my first reader, who read the first drafts of this version back in 2005 when it was still a part of my larger Mba (Mahabharata) retelling, and who shall probably be reading this published version on a different continent now – an achievement that suggests that perhaps I have managed in some way to keep the flame of our epics burning brightly across continents! Thank you, Sabs!

Tapas Sadasivan Nair, who read through the final draft of this version earlier this year and suggested many valuable corrections and amendments. He is among the first, certainly one of my best readers and I value his feedback greatly. Read on, Kanjisheikh!

The members of my erstwhile Epic India Group, forums and the 30,000+ (and counting) readers who have left their wonderful reviews, comments and feedback on my blog at ashokbanker.com over the years. Too many now to name, so I'll settle for ululating without the benefit of a vuvuzela: 'EI! EI! YO!' Proud 2b an Epicindian.

Ravi Singh of Penguin India who published my Ramayana Series® when nobody in India would even read the manuscript, and without whose support this entire genre of writing – Epic Fiction, as I like to call it – wouldn't exist today. Thank you for being an Epic Editor.

Saugata Mukherjee, who confirmed my belief that only an editor who had read and genuinely liked the Ramayana Series® could possibly understand and support what I wished to do next. It took a while, but we finally got here, and I have only him to thank for it. Everything that follows now is to his credit.

Prema Govindan, whom I didn't even know by name when she turned in the first set of edits on the manuscript of this book, but whose great love for the subject of this book, Krishna, coupled with an intense professional drive to bring out the best book possible and the rare ability to appreciate an author's individual (and very quirky) 'voice' or style – including my penchant for mixing languages, cultures, et al. in an epic khichdi – resulted in the best editing of my career. It has been a great pleasure and I hope to have her eagle eye and keen mind on every single book in this series and possibly many more as well. Thanks also to Shantanu Ray Chaudhuri who managed to complete the job with an enviable sense of perfectionism.

The entire team at HarperCollins India – many of whom I am yet to know by name, and I hope to correct that lacuna very soon – who will now take this finished book and bring it to you, aided and abetted by the distributors, stockists, retailers and other book trade professionals across the country who are helping the book publishing business defy recessions and break global records. If I may humbly offer my two-paise suggestion to you all: Fewer Books, Better Books.

And finally, you, dear reader, whether you're new to my work or a long-time familiar. If you've never read anything by me before, you should know that I approach every book as if it's my first and only book. And if you've read every single thing I've written to date, you won't be surprised when you turn the page and find that this book and series is quite unlike everything I've written before. But what really matters is that you like reading it as much as I loved writing it. Because that, and that alone, is the reason why I wrote this book and every other book I've written. Because I love writing. And love, like H1N1, is extremely contagious, though thankfully not as harmful to your health. So I really do hope you catch it and pass it on.

ASHOK KUMAR BANKER

Andheri, Mumbai
August 2010